THIS BOOK SHOULD BE RETURNED ON OR BEFORE THE LATEST
DATE SHOWN TO THE LIBRARY FROM WHICH IT WAS BORROWED

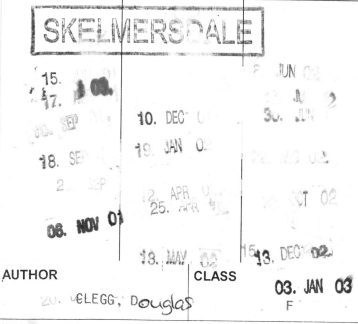

SKELMERSDALE

15.
17.
00. SEP
18. SEP
2
08. NOV 01

10. DEC
19. JAN 02
2 APR
25. APR
18. MAY 02

JUN
30. JUN 2
OCT 02
15 13. DEC 02

**AUTHOR**

20. CLEGG, Douglas

**CLASS**

03. JAN 03
F

**TITLE**

The nighmare chronicles

D0530602

# MORE RAVE REVIEWS
# FOR DOUGLAS CLEGG!

"Parts of *The Halloween Man* bring back fond memories of both Straub's *Ghost Story* and McCammon's *Boy's Life,* but Clegg adds his own unique touches in this high class horror novel. A memorable contribution to the genre."

—*Masters of Terror*

"Douglas Clegg has raised the stakes; for himself, as well as for the genre he writes in."

—*FrightNet*

"Clegg's characters are well realized and fascinating, and the story is richly steeped in history. *The Halloween Man* is a stunning horror novel, written with a degree of conviction that is rare these days."

—Fiona Webster, *Amazon.com*

"Reminded me of King and McCammon at their best. I was awestruck."

—*The Scream Factory*

"Packed with vivid imagery; a broadly scoped, but fast-paced plot; powerful, evocative writing; superb characterizations; and facile intelligence, *The Halloween Man* is more than its blurbage could ever convey. Douglas Clegg has given horror lovers the best Halloween gift possible."

—Paula Guran, *Dark Echo*

# ENTER THE NIGHTMARE

Alice wheeled her chair closer to the dirty mattress, near the boy's feet.

"I've seen so many things," said the boy who was handcuffed in front of her. "So many sights, so many people," and Alice watched as the little boy's nostrils flared, opening up.

Someone behind her pushed her wheelchair.

"Stephen? Stephen?" she cried out, her composure gone as the chair moved steadily forward.

She turned slightly in her chair, shining the flashlight at the person pushing her—but its beam hit nothing but the wall and the closed door behind her.

Then, the wheelchair jostled, and she was tossed down onto the mattress. The flashlight rolled off into a corner of the room.

"No!" she shouted. "Stephen! Help me!"

After several more shouts, she quieted. Her legs were useless, but she raised herself up on her arms, reaching for the flashlight. Not finding it.

Someone grabbed her wrist. Like a steel cuff.

The boy said, "You like treasure, don't you, Alice? Let me show you my treasures."

"What in god's name are you?" she cried out.

"I am many," the boy said. "Come closer, Alice. Let me show you the treasures of the world. All of them, here for you, all of them. Come, Alice, come into my dreams . . . ."

# THE NIGHTMARE CHRONICLES

## DOUGLAS CLEGG

LEISURE BOOKS  NEW YORK CITY

A LEISURE BOOK®

September 1999

Published by

Dorchester Publishing Co., Inc.
276 Fifth Avenue
New York, NY 10001

ISBN 0-8439-4580-X

The name "Leisure Books" and the stylized "L" with design are
trademarks of Dorchester Publishing Co., Inc.

Printed in the United States of America.

*This is dedicated completely to Raul Silva.*
*With thanks to Tim DeYoung, Brooke Borneman,*
*and Don D'Auria.*

*Note to the reader: Storytelling is a form of kidnapping.*
*Come along with me.*

Visit Doug Clegg at www.douglasclegg.com

# THE NIGHTMARE CHRONICLES

# TABLE OF CONTENTS

Alice lit her cigarette, staring straight ahead at the television set. "If we don't hear anything, the boy dies today. They must've gotten the note by now. I don't like this waiting game."

The clock on top of the television set had stopped at ten minutes to twelve. She tapped her watch—it was midnight. The first breath of smoke from the cigarette was heaven. An old mirror, part of its glass cracked and another part empty, leaned against the wall. She saw half her face in it and felt older than her age. She reached back to her hair, brushing it to the side over her ear. She was youngish for her age, even if her two boys had just grown up. She was only thirty-eight, not even middle-aged. The smoke wreathed around her face. It was as if the woman in the mirror knew something that the woman in the chair did not. She looked away.

"I was sitting there having a smoke in that room. Barely in that room. He didn't even open his mouth," Stephen said. "How could he?"

She glanced at Stephen, who stood with his back to her, watching the window. Even though the window looked upon the wall of another tenement, he watched as if waiting to see something emerge from the slim crawl space between the buildings.

"I mean, the tape held. But I stood there and had a dream. Like I blacked out standing up. I saw things . . ." Stephen wore his black leather jacket and khakis, practically advertising, in Alice's opinion, that something was not quite right in the neighborhood whenever he stepped outside. "He's evil," Stephen said.

"Stephen." Alice shook her head slowly. "You mustn't go down there. It's better to stay away except when he needs food or water."

"Tell that to Charlie. He's down there more than me. Ask him about the boy," Stephen said. He turned around to meet her gaze, leaning back against the sill. "Charlie is getting too chummy with him. It'll make it that much harder when the time comes. When Lana comes back from the store, someone should talk to her, too."

"She's been gone too long. You don't think she'd betray us, do you?" Alice sucked in the smoke and held it. She closed her eyes. Reached up, rubbing the throbbing along her forehead. Exhaled the ribbon of smoke into the pale blue room.

Stephen shrugged. "Anything's possible with her.

She's not one of us. I don't like her."

"She's fine," Alice said to reassure herself. "She's probably just looking for those shoes you wanted."

"They're just a pair of tennis shoes," he said, and she noticed the strain of the night showing in his voice and in the stiffness of his movements.

Trying to comfort him, Alice said, "If we don't get a moment with the parents in the next two hours, it's over. A loss. It won't be hard. Charlie enjoys the kill. I'm sick of thinking about that brat."

"The duct tape held. But I heard him."

Alice stubbed her cigarette out in the ashtray beside her chair. Then she wheeled her chair over nearer Stephen and tugged at his arm. "Baby, don't let him get to you."

He took her fingers in his. She could smell his cologne now—the Golden Touch, much advertised in magazines, and it reminded her of the citrus groves she'd grown up among. She leaned forward slightly, pressing her cheek against his hand, feeling the coldness of his ring. "He's only twelve, and that whole contest of wills that Charlie had with him—well, boys are like that. I raised a boy once," she said, smiling wistfully.

"Two very wonderful boys," Stephen said.

Alice nodded, turning her face into his leather sleeve, feeling its warmth. "Boys are wily creatures," and when she said this, they both laughed at how silly it sounded.

Their silence afterward was punctuated with the mindless noise of the television.

Then Stephen said, "There's something wrong with him. I could feel it when I was down there. I stood there dreaming something with my eyes open. There's something wrong—he's not okay."

"It doesn't matter," Alice said, pushing her wheelchair away from him. She went over to the small kitchenette and opened one of the lower cabinets. "He could have measles, and it won't matter. He'll be out of his misery soon enough."

"No," Stephen said. "I don't mean he's sick. I mean, there's something about him that isn't normal. He . . . changes . . . somehow."

Alice had become an expert at ignoring his flights of dark foreboding. They'd all been up too long, unable to sleep. "I feel like cooking eggs. Scrambled eggs. And coffee. None of us has eaten all night. It's nearly midnight. A good plate of eggs will help."

"Very suburban hausfrau of you," Charlie said as he entered the room, wearing his slick raincoat, taking his hat off and dropping it on the chair by the door. His grin was infectious, and it made Alice feel better just to see him. "I called twice. No answer. No word yet from the parents."

"None?" Stephen asked. Then, as if he could not utter his next thought coherently, he coughed.

Charlie glanced around from the two beds to the living-room chairs, to the open bathroom door. "No Lana yet?"

Stephen shook his head. "She's supposed to be buying me shoes and some groceries for us."

"What's open at this hour?" Charlie asked.

Alice laughed. "You boys! I can name four all-night stores within six blocks. Don't worry about Lana. She has too much at stake here."

"Yeah, sure." Charlie grinned, his cheeks rosy. "Helluva night out there. First rain, then no rain, then rain, then no rain. I wish God would make up His mind."

Charlie looked from Stephen to Alice, as if he'd walked in two seconds late on a wonderful joke. "Everything kosher here? You two look like you've been dissecting my sex life again."

Stephen wagged his hand like a vaudevillian shaking a straw hat. "That's showbiz, folks."

Alice brought out the large frying pan and set it on the stovetop. "I know everyone's starved. I know I am."

She didn't want to look at Stephen again, because he was beginning to look haunted. Finally, as she dropped a pat of butter in the pan, she could not control herself. "Stephen, if you're going to go crazy with this, then it's better you just put yourself out of it for the time being. I want you here, but I don't if you can't handle—"

"Shut up," Stephen snapped. "It's a boy. A real boy. Flesh and blood. Not a middle-aged banker who deserves to die for aiding the global corporate murder of the individual. It's a little boy."

Then, more quietly, he added, "And there's something not right about him. And about this whole thing. What about his parents? It's been forty-eight hours."

"Fifty," Charlie chimed in. "And Stevie's right.

17

The kid is a weirdo. I think he likes being hand-cuffed." He took off his raincoat, hanging it across the small bed.

Alice said, "Please, Charlie. The closet."

Charlie nodded and gathered the coat up. He opened the closet door, tossing the raincoat onto the rest of the heap of clothes.

"Two days," Stephen said. "A twelve-year-old boy from the North Shore. No history of drug use, no history of running away. A happy, healthy boy."

"He got a C minus in math last year," Charlie added. "He collects stamps and has an aquarium full of tropical fish. His little girlfriend is named Emmy. His father is a friggin' multigazillionaire."

"Really, Charlie," Alice said, shaking her head. She cracked five eggs into the pan and began stirring them with a wooden ladle. "He's a tool. Remember that, Stephen. He is our tool for changing the world. One person at a time."

Stephen shook his head. "It's weird."

Alice sighed, turning around, nearly dropping the last egg she held in her hand. "This is an unusual line of work. Unusual things happen."

"Remember that woman last year?"

Charlie glanced at Alice. Alice knew: it was starting up again with Stephen. Dear Stephen, whom she loved more than any man in the world.

"She said something before we buried her, do you remember?"

Charlie grinned as if Stephen were barmy. "I'm afraid I don't, sport."

18

"She said, 'I won't be the last for you, will I?' And I thought she was lying. But she wasn't, was she? There's always someone else, isn't there? First the banker, then the wife of the corporate thief, and now this little boy. Christ. A little boy. That woman was smart. I thought she was just saying that to play with my conscience. To buy herself four hours of breathing."

"Ha! I'll bet her conscience didn't bother her when she passed the homeless in the street and then got into her limousine," Charlie said. "And where was her conscience when she married that monster husband who raped environments and economies?"

In a sudden move, Stephen picked up a knife from the block on the kitchen counter. Jokingly, he raised it to Charlie and hacked the air in front of him. Charlie laughed, but Stephen's face tightened and shone with sweat. "Now," he muttered. He stomped toward the door.

"Stephen!" Alice shouted. "Not now. Stop."

Stephen held the knife up as if it were some alien instrument he didn't understand. He looked at it, then turned and looked at Alice. "He told me things that a boy couldn't know. Couldn't possibly know."

"How, Stephen?" Alice asked, letting the eggs burn on the stove, turning her wheelchair around. "How? His mouth is covered with tape. His hands are bound behind his back. How did he tell you?"

Charlie shook his head, and went and sat in front of the television set. "Stephen, Stephen, Stephen."

Stephen clutched the knife, then dropped it. It clattered on the parquet floor. "I should cut his throat. The piglet. But he . . . changes. He's not the same boy we took on Wednesday. . . . "

"Oh, baby," Alice said, bringing her chair over. She reached her hands up for Stephen's and held him. He collapsed to his knees in front of her, pressing his face into her lap. She stroked his soft curly hair. "Stephen, poor baby. This is too hard for you, isn't it?"

"Something about him . . . the way he stares . . . " Stephen whispered.

"It's all right," she said. "Don't worry."

From his chair Charlie said, "Christ, it's on the news, finally."

Stephen lifted his head, tears in his eyes. Alice pulled her chair back, pivoting it around and wheeling over toward the television.

A reporter stood in front of the house on Grimaldi Street.

"Turn it up," Alice said. "I can barely hear it."

The reporter said, "The discovery of the bodies of John and Paulette Early at six o'clock this evening shocked this upscale neighborhood . . . "

Charlie laughed. "This must be a scam! We didn't kill them. Christ, they weren't even awake."

Alice glanced at Stephen. Something in his eyes had changed—as if he'd woken from a dream but had not quite come out of it completely.

"They must be trying to flush us out with this, that's all," Charlie said, shaking his head. "Those feds. Christ. I mean, why would we kill the man who we want to pay us ten million dollars?"

The reporter continued, "There is still no sign of their daughter, Rosanna, eleven . . . "

A photograph of a little girl flashed on the screen. Golden hair past her shoulders, a ribbon tied about it, her eyes like an owl's eyes, not pretty exactly, but certainly pleasing to look at.

Alice turned to Stephen. "A little girl?"

Stephen grinned, a little too madly, she thought, a little too edgy. "Yes, mother. That's what the man said. And you know what? I believe him. The kid told me he's been everything, he's been girls and women and men and dogs and even flies. Even flies!"

Stephen fell silent for a moment, as if he'd opened some dam within him and had to shut it down so as not to let everything out.

Then he said, "He told me he likes the way life tastes."

Smoke billowed into the room, and Alice realized it was the eggs burning on the stove. She wheeled over and picked the pan up, dropping it into the sink. She turned on the water, and steam spat up.

"He told me," Stephen said. "He wanted us to take him because he wants to taste us, too. He made me see some things. Some awful things."

Was he weeping? Alice couldn't see his eyes, because he'd turned away from her. His shoulder shuddered.

"What could he possibly make you see?" she asked. "Stephen?"

"Where he came from. Those people in that mansion—they aren't his parents," Stephen began. "He's not even a boy, is he? He's a nightmare. He's a . . . "

21

And then Stephen told what the boy had shown him, and told it perfectly as the boy had burned it into his mind, as if it had really happened, as if Stephen had been opened up by what the boy had done to him. . . .

The first story of the night began.

# *Underworld*

They say that love never dies. Sometimes, it goes somewhere else, to a place from which it may return transformed.

We were subletting the place on Thirty-third, just down from Lexington Avenue—it was not terribly far from my job up at Matthew Bender, across from Penn Station, where I was an ink-stained drudge by day before transforming into a novelist by night. Jenny was getting day work on the soap operas—nothing much, just the walk-on nurses and cocktail waitresses that populate daytime television, never with more than a word or two to say, so it was a long way to her Screen Actors Guild card. But she made just enough to cover the rent, and I made just enough to cover everything else, plus the feeble beginnings of a savings

23

account that we affectionately named The Son'll
Come Out Tomorrow, because at about the time we
opened the account, Jenny discovered that she was
pregnant. This worried the heck out of me, not for the
usual reasons, such as the mounting bills, and the
thought that I might not be able to pursue writing full-
time, at least not in this life, but because of a habit
Jenny had of sleeping with other men.

It will be hard to understand this, and I don't completely get it myself, but I loved Jenny in a way that I
didn't think possible. It wasn't her beauty, although
she certainly had that, but it was the fact that in her
company I always felt safe and comfortable. I did not
want to ever be with another woman as long as I lived;
I suppose a good therapist would go on and on about
my self-image and self-esteem and self-whatever, but
I've got to tell you, it was simply that I loved her and
that I wanted her to be happy. I didn't worry if I was
inadequate or unsatisfying as a lover, and she never
spoke openly about it with me. I was just aware she'd
had a few indiscretions early in our marriage, and I
assumed that she would gradually, over the years, calm
down in that respect. I felt lucky to have Jenny's company when I did, and when I didn't, I did not feel
deprived. I suppose that until you have loved someone
in that way it is impossible to understand that point of
view.

So I wondered about the paternity of our child, and
this kept me up several nights to the point that I would
slip out of bed quietly (for Jenny often had to be up
and out the door by five A.M.), and go for long walks

down Third Avenue, or down a side street to Second, sometimes until the first light came up over the city. During one of these jaunts, in late January, I noticed a curious sort of building—it was on a block of Kip's Bay that began in an alley, and was enclosed on all sides by buildings. Yet there were apartments, and a street name (Pallan Row, the sign said), and two small restaurants, the kind with only eight or nine tables, one of them a Szechwan place, the other nondescript in its Americanized menu; also, a flower stand, boarded up, and what looked like a bit of a warehouse. The place carried an added layer of humidity, as if it had more of the swamp to it than the city.

I am not normally a wanderer of alleys, but I could not help myself—I had lived in this neighborhood about a year and a half, and in that time had felt I knew every block within about a mile-and-a-half radius. But it was as if I had just found the most wonderful gift in the world, a hidden grotto, a place in New York City that was as yet undiscovered except by, perhaps, the oldest residents. I looked in the windows of the warehouse but could see nothing through the filthy windows.

All day at work, I asked friends who lived in the general vicinity if they knew about Pallan Row, but only one said that she did. "It used to be where the sweatshops were—highly illegal, too, because when I was a kid, they used to raid them all the time—it was more than bad working conditions, it was white slavery and heroin, all those things. But then," she added, "so much of this city has a history like that. On the outside, carriage rides and Broadway shows, but underneath, kind of slimy."

On Saturday, I convinced Jenny to talk a walk with me, but for some reason I couldn't find the Row; we went to lunch. Afterward, I remembered where I'd led us astray, and we ended up going to have tea at the Chinese restaurant. The menu was ordinary, and the decorations vintage and tacky.

"Amazing," Jenny said, "look, honey, the ceiling," and I glanced up and beheld one of those lovely old tin ceilings with the chocolate candy designs.

The waiter, who was an older Asian woman, noticed us and came over with some almond cookies. "We usually are empty on weekends," she said, and then, also looking at the ceiling, "this was part of a speakeasy in the twenties—the café next door, too. They say that a mobster ran numbers out of the back-room. Before that, it was just an icehouse. My husband began renting it in 1954."

"That long ago?" Jenny said, taking a bite from a cookie. "It seems like most restaurants come and go around here."

"Depends on the rent." The woman nodded, still looking at the ceiling. "The owner hasn't raised it a penny in all those years." She glanced at me, then at Jenny. "You're going to have a baby, aren't you?"

Jenny grinned. "How did you know?"

The woman said, "Young couples like you, in love, eating my almond cookies. Always brings babies. You will have a strong boy, I think."

After she left the table, we laughed, finished the

tea, and just sat for a while. The owner's wife occasionally peeped through the round porthole window of the kitchen door, and we smiled at her but shook our heads to indicate that we weren't in need of service.

"When the baby comes," she said, "Mom said she'd loan us money to get a larger place."

"Ah, family loans," I warned her.

"I know, but we won't have to pay her back for a few years. Can you believe it, me, a mother?"

"And me, a father?" I leaned over and pressed my hand against her stomach. "I wonder what he's thinking?"

"Or she. Probably, 'Get me the hell out of here right now!' is what it's thinking."

"Babies aren't 'its.' "

"Well, right now it is. It has a will of its own. It probably looks like a little developing tadpole. Something like its father." She gave my hand a squeeze. I kissed her. When I drew my face back from hers, she had tears in her eyes.

"What's the matter?"

"Oh," she wiped at her eyes with her napkin, "I'm going to change."

"Into what?"

"No, you know what I mean. I've been living too recklessly."

"Oh," I said, and felt a little chill. "That's all in the past. I love you like crazy, Jen."

"I know. I am so lucky," she said. "Our baby's lucky to have two screwups like us for parents."

Now, it could be that I'm just recalling that we said these words because I want her memory to be sweeter for me than perhaps reality will allow. But we walked back up Second Avenue that Saturday feeling stronger as a couple; and I knew the baby was mine, I just knew it, regardless of the chances against it. We caught a movie, went home and made love, sat up and watched *Saturday Night Live.* Sunday we took the train out to her mother's in Stamford, and then as the week was just getting under way, I walked through the doorway of our small sublet to find blood on the faux oriental rug.

Yet the door had been locked. That was my first thought. I didn't see Jenny's body until I got to the bathroom, which is where her murderer had dragged her, apparently while she was still alive, and then had dropped her in the tub, closed the shower curtain around her. It wasn't as gruesome as I expected it to be—there was a bullet in her head, behind her left ear, but she was lying faceup, so I didn't see the damage to the back of her scalp. She didn't even look like Jenny anymore. She looked like a butcher shop meat with a human shape. She looked like some dead woman with whom I had no acquaintance. I was pretty numb, and was thinking of calling the police, when it occurred to me that the killer might still be in the apartment. So I went next door to Helen Connally's and knocked on the door. Helen, in her sweats, saw my panic, let me in, and made me some tea while we waited for the police. I hated leaving Jenny there, in the tub, for the ten minutes, but if the murderer was still lurking, I had no way of defending myself.

After the police and the neighbors and Jenny's mother had picked my brain about the crime, it hit me.

I had not only lost my partner and lover, but also my only child. I cried for days, or perhaps it was weeks— it was like living, for a time, in a dark cave where there was no hour, no minute, no day, only darkness.

When I emerged from my stupor and weeping, the police had arrested a suspect in my wife's murder, and then the mystery unraveled: we had been subletting an apartment from a man who had several such places around the city, and each one was used, occasionally, by the man's clients as a place of business on certain weekdays for drug dealing. The dealers' assumption had been that on a given day of the week, no one was home. Best the detectives could tell, Jenny had come home too early on the wrong Tuesday, a drug deal was in progress, and one of the men had killed her as soon as she'd come in the door. I was devastated to think that strangers could be in our apartment; but of course, it wasn't really ours. The renter of the apartment was arrested; he pointed the finger at a few associates; and within a year, the guilty were behind bars, and I was living in a place off Houston and Sullivan Street, over in the SoHo area. I was seeing, on a friendly basis, Helen Connally, my former neighbor—it was almost as if the tragedy of my wife's death had given us a basis on which to form a friendship. Helen was thirty-two to my twenty-eight, and, while I knew I would never love her the way I loved Jenny, she was a good friend to me through a most difficult time. We spent a year being slightly good friends, and then we became lovers.

I was taking some out-of-town friends of ours on an informal sight-seeing tour of the Big Apple, and brought them down to little Pallan Row. I thought the Szechwan place would be good for lunch, but when we entered the alley, both it and the café were closed; windows were boarded up. "Jesus," I said, "just a year ago, the woman running it told me that they'd had it since the fifties."

Helen took my elbow. "C'mon, we can go get sandwiches up at Tivoli. Or," she turned to the couple we'd brought, "there's a great deli on Third. You guys like pastrami?"

Their voices faded into the background as I looked through the section of the Chinese restaurant's window that was clear, and thought I saw my dead wife's face back along the wall, through the round glass window of the door to the kitchen.

"Oliver," Helen said, looking over my shoulder, "what's up?"

"Nothing," I said, still looking at Jenny, her dark hair grown longer, obscuring all but her nose and mouth.

"It must be something."

"It's just an old place. It was once a speakeasy, back in the twenties. Think of all that's gone on in there," I said. Jenny's face, in that round window, staring at me.

"Cool," Helen said. She was originally from California, so "cool" and "bummer" had not yet been erased from her vocabulary of irony. She stood back, and her friend Larry whispered something to her.

I watched Jenny's face, and noticed that when her hair fell more to the side of her face, there were no eyes in her eye sockets.

"Let's go," Helen whispered. "They want to take a ride on the ferry before it gets dark."

"Okay, just a sec," I said.

Jenny moved away from the round window.

My heart was beating fast.

I assumed that I was hallucinating, but the thought of spending the rest of the afternoon escorting this couple around town when I had just seen my dead wife was absurd. I made an excuse about needing to be by myself—Helen always took this well, and I caught an understanding look from Anne, who nodded. I knew they would go on to a late lunch and talk about how I still hadn't quite recovered from Jenny's death; and I knew Helen would act the martyr a bit, because it was so hard to play nurse to me over a woman who had cheated constantly behind my back. I adored Helen for her care and caution around my feelings; I wished them a good afternoon, and stood there, along the Row, watching them, until they had rounded the corner and were out of sight.

After a few minutes, I took off my shoe and broke the window glass, and tugged at one of the boards until it gave. Within half an hour, I stepped in through the broken window and walked across the dusty floor to the kitchen.

The kitchen was all long shiny metal shelves and drawers, pots and pans still piled high. But it was dark, and I saw no one. I walked across the floor, back to the walk-in freezer, and looked through its frosty pane of glass. Although I could see nothing in there, I found myself shivering, even my teeth began chattering, and I had the sudden and uncomfortable feeling that if I did not get out of that kitchen, out of that boarded-up restaurant right then, something terrible would happen.

It didn't occur to me until I was on the street again that there should've been no frost on the glass pane at the walk-in freezer, that, in fact, there was no electricity to the entire building, perhaps to the entire block.

Helen noticed, over the next few days, that I was becoming nervous. We sat across from each other in our favorite park, me with the *Times*, and her with a paperback; I looked up, and she was watching me. Another day, we went to a coffee shop, and she mentioned to me that my knees, under the table, were shaking slightly. She said this with some seriousness, as if shaking knees were an indicator of some deeper problem. But I doubted myself then, and I did not want to talk about seeing my dead wife in the Chinese restaurant kitchen on Pallan Row. Finally, my restlessness turned nocturnal, and I tossed and turned in my sleep. Helen, sleeping over, finally sat up in bed at four in the morning and flicked on the bedside lamp. Her eyes were bloodshot.

"You have not slept a full night for two days," she said. "You tell me what's going on."

I spent about an hour dodging the issue, until finally, as she pushed and pushed, I told her about seeing Jenny.

"She was blind," Helen said, speaking to me like I was a lying twelve-year-old.

"Not blind. She had no eyes. I felt she could see me, anyway. She was staring at me. She just had no eyes."

"And you went in there and no one was there . . . "

"But the freezer. Why would it be going?"

Helen shrugged. "I'm going to make a drink. You want something?"

At five-thirty A.M., she and I had vodka martinis, and went and sat out on the fire escape as all of Manhattan awoke, as the sky turned several shades of violet before becoming the blank light of day.

"I don't believe in ghosts," I said, sipping and feeling drunk very quickly. "I don't believe that the dead can rise or any of that."

"What do you believe?"

I watched a burly man lift crates out of the back of his truck down in the street. "I believe in what I see. I saw her. I really saw her."

"Assuming," she said, "that it was Jenny. Assuming that the freezer was running on its own energy. Assuming you saw what you saw. Assuming all those things as givens, what does it mean?"

"I have no idea. I thought at first maybe I was just crazy. If I hadn't seen the frost on the freezer window, I don't think I would've believed later on that it had been Jenny at all. Or anything but an hallucination."

Helen was obstinate. "But it's got to mean something."

"Why?" I asked.

I slept through the next day fairly peacefully, and when I awoke, Helen was gone. I watched television, then called a few friends to set up lunches and dinners for the following week.

Helen walked through the door at six-thirty in the evening, and said, "Well, I found that alley again. I pulled back one of the boards."

When she said this, I felt impulsively defensive—it was my alley, it was my boarded-up restaurant, I felt, it was my hallucination. "You didn't have to," I told her.

She halted my speech with her hands. "Hang on, hang on. Oliver, the windows are bricked up beneath the boards."

"No, they're not."

"Yes," she said, "they are. You couldn't have gotten in there."

We argued this point; we were both terrific arguers. It struck me that she hadn't found the right alley, or even the right Pallan Row. Perhaps there were two Pallan Rows in the city, near each other, perhaps even almost identical alleys. Perhaps there was the functional Pallan Row and the dysfunctional Pallan Row.

This idea seemed to clutch at me, as if I had known it to be true even before I thought it consciously.

The idea took hold, and that night, on the pretext of going to see a movie that Helen had already seen twice with friends, I took a cab over to Pallan Row.

\* \* \*

It was colder on Pallan Row than in the rest of the city. While autumn was well upon us, and the weather had for weeks been fairly chilly, down the alley it was positively freezing. My curiosity and even fear took hold as I peeled back one of the window boards, the very one I had pulled down on my last visit. Helen had been right: the windows were bricked up beneath the boards. But then, I had to wonder, why the boards at all?

I touched the bricks; had to draw my fingers back quickly, for they seemed like blocks of ice. I remembered the owner of the Chinese restaurant telling Jenny and me that it used to be an ice house. I touched the bricks again, and they were still bitingly cold—it hadn't been my imagination.

I walked around the alley but saw no way of getting into the buildings again, for all were bricked up.

And then I heard it.

A sound, a human sound, the sound of someone who was trapped inside that old icehouse, someone who had heard me pull the board loose and who needed help.

I am no hero, and never will be. For all I knew, there were some punks on the other side of that wall torturing one of their own, and if I walked into the middle of it, I would not see the light of day again.

And yet I could not help myself.

I found that if I kicked at the bricks, they gave a little. The noise from within had ceased, but I battered at the bricks until I managed to knock one of them out. It seemed to be an old brick job, for the cement between the blocks was cracked and powdery. After an hour, I had managed to dislodge several.

To my surprise and amazement, there was light on within the old restaurant. I looked through the sizable hole I'd made and saw the former proprietress of the Chinese restaurant standing behind the bar, dressed in a jade-colored silk gown, talking with her barman. A few people sat at the tables, eating, laughing. None of them had noticed my activity at the window.

As I put my face to the hole, I breathed in air so cold that it seemed to stop my lungs up.

I moved back and stood up. I was sure that this was a delusion; perhaps I needed some medication still, for immediately after Jenny's death, I had begun taking tranquilizers to help blot out the memory of finding her dead. Perhaps I still needed some medical help and psychological counseling.

I crouched down again to look through the opening and noticed that at one of the tables, facing the other way, was a woman who looked from the back very much like Jenny.

I noticed the ice, too. It was a shiny glaze along the walls and tables; icicles formed teatlike off the chocolate-patterned tin ceiling. I watched the people inside there as if this were a television set; I lost my fear entirely, all my shivering came from the arctic breezes that stirred up occasionally from within.

I thought I heard someone out in the alley behind me, and turned to look.

Helen stood there in a sweatshirt and pants, my old windbreaker around her shoulders; she held a sweater in her arms.

"I figured you'd be here. Look, it's getting chilly," she passed the sweater down to where I sat on the pavement. She noticed the bricks beside me, and the light from within the building. "I see you've been doing construction. Or should I say de-construction."

"Do you see the light?" I asked her.

She squatted down beside me. "What light?"

"I know you see it," I said, but when I glanced again through the hole, the place within had gone dark.

"What is it about this place for you?" she asked. "Even if you did see Jenny here, or her ghost, whatever—why here? You and she only came here once. Why would she come here?"

"I think this is hell," I said. "I think this is one of those corners of hell. I think Jenny's in hell. And she wants something from me. Maybe a favor."

"Do you really believe that?"

I nodded. "Don't ask me why. There is no why. I think this is a corner of hell that maybe shows through sometimes to some people. I don't even think maybe. I know that's what this is."

"You may be right," Helen said. She stood up, stretched, and offered me her hand to help me get up. I took it. Her hand was warm, and I felt a rush of blood in the palm of my hand as if she had managed to transfer some warmth to me.

And then, the sound again.

A human voice, indistinct, from within the walls.

Helen looked at me.

"You heard it too," I said.

"It's a cat," she said. "It's a cat inside there."

I shook my head. "You heard it. It's not just me. Maybe Jenny can only show herself to me. Maybe hell can only show itself to me, but you heard it."

"Wouldn't Jenny's ghost be in your old apartment where she died?" Something like fear trembled in Helen's voice. She was beginning to believe something that might be dreadful. It made me feel less alone.

"No. I don't think it's her ghost. A ghost is spiritual residue or something. I think she is in here, it's really her, in the flesh, and I think there are others in here. I need to go back in and find out what exactly she wants from me."

The noise again, almost sounding like a woman weeping.

"Don't go in there," Helen said. "It may not be anything. It may be something awful. It may be somebody waiting in there the way somebody waited for Jenny."

I took her face in my hands and kissed her eyelids. When I drew back from her face, I whispered, "I love you, Helen. But I have to find out if I'm crazy. I have to find out."

We went and sat in an all-night coffee shop talking about love and belief and insanity. Because I was beginning to convince myself that Pallan Row was a corner of hell, I waited until the sun came up to investigate further within its walls. Helen returned with me, and between the two of us, we managed to break enough bricks apart and away from the wall so that the hole grew to an almost-window-size entrance.

I asked her to wait outside for me, and if anything happened, to go get help. I went in through the window, scraping my head a bit. The room on the other side was empty and dark, but that unnatural ice breath was still there, and, through the kitchen portal window, there came a feeble and distant light.

Helen asked every few seconds, "You okay, Oliver? I can't see you."

"I'm fine," I reassured her as often as she asked.

I walked slowly to the kitchen door, looked through the round windowpane. The light emanated from the freezer at the other end of the long kitchen. I pushed the door open (informing Helen that this was my direction so that she wouldn't worry if I didn't respond to her queries every few minutes) and walked more swiftly to the walk-in freezer.

The freezer door was unlocked. I opened it, too, and stepped inside.

The light was blue and as cold as the air.

Through the arctic fog I could make out the shapes of human beings, hanging from meat hooks, their faces indistinct, their bodies slowly turning as if they had but little energy left within them. I did not look directly at any of these bodies, for my terror was becoming stronger—and I knew that if I were to remain sane as I walked through this icehouse of death, I would need to rein in my fear.

Finally, I found her.

Jenny.

Ice across her eyeless face, her hair, strands of thin, pearl-necklace icicles.

She hung naked from a hook, her head drooping, her arms apparently lifeless at her side.

Her belly had been ripped open as if torn at with pincers, the skin peeled back and frost-burnt.

I stopped breathing for a full minute, and was sure that I was going to die right there.

I was sure the door to that freezer, that butcher-shop of the damned, would slide shut and trap me forever.

But it did not.

Instead, I heard that human sound again, closer, more distinct.

I heard my heart beating; my breathing resumed.

The sound came from beyond the whitest cloth of fog, and I waved my hands across it to dissipate the mist.

There, lying on a metal shelf, wrapped in the clothes that Jenny had been buried in, was our baby, his small fingers reaching for me as he began to wail even louder.

I lifted him, held him in my arms, and wiped the chill from his forehead.

Someone was there, among the hanging bodies, watching me. I couldn't tell who, for the fog had not cleared, neither had the blue light increased in intensity. I could not see to *see*. I felt someone's presence, though, and thanked that someone silently. I thanked whoever or whatever had suckled my child, had warmed his blood, had met his needs. The place no longer frightened me. Whatever energy the freezer ran on, whatever power inspired it, had kept my child safe.

I took my son out into the bright and shining morning.

"This was why I was haunted," I told Helen upon emerging from the open window. "This is what Jenny wanted to give me."

I can only describe Helen's expression, through her eyes, as one approaching dread. She said, "I think you should put it back where it belongs."

"Babies aren't 'its,'" I said, and recalled saying this to Jenny once, too, at this very place. Or had Jenny said it to me? We had been so close that sometimes when she said things, I felt I'd said them too. I glanced down at my boy, so beautiful as he watched the sky and his father, breathing the vivid air.

Across his forehead, I saw a marking, a birthmark, a port-wine stain, perhaps, which spread across his skin like fire until he became something other than what might be called flesh.

Stephen stood there, his mouth hanging open after he spoke the last word.

"Stephen," Alice said. "Really. Your imagination. The meat freezer from Hell and a baby that the devil suckled? Ghost stories. Really. You're nearly twenty—get this nonsense out of your head."

Stephen's eyes were filled with tears. "He showed it all to me. I think . . . I think he's . . . "

"You aren't here to think," Alice said. "Look, I'll go down there right now if I have to and—"

"You don't want to," Stephen said.

Alice leaned forward in her chair, prodding the wheels slowly until they moved forward. "Yes, I do."

\* \* \*

Alice rode with her youngest son on the elevator down to the bowels of the building. The elevator's light flickered blue and white, and jolted at every floor. Finally, in the basement, she prodded her chair forward, moving through the narrow, dank hall with its white bulbs of flickering light. The smell of the trash they'd accumulated assaulted her, and she covered her mouth with a handkerchief. Stephen pushed her around each turn of the hallway. The hall seemed to narrow even further before they came to the room.

No lightbulb flickered above. They moved in absolute darkness.

"I want you calm, Stephen," she said. "Understand?"

Stephen flicked on a flashlight, and pointed its beam at the door.

It seemed colder here, and Alice pulled her sweater about her collar.

The trash smell was bad, mixed with the odor of the boy's waste.

"What about the light?" Alice asked. "Can't you replace the bulb?"

Stephen touched her shoulder in the darkness. "Twice in four hours. They all go out when I put them in."

"Must be some kind of short."

Stephen opened the door, and when he did, Alice felt an icy draft.

"Why is it so cold?"

Stephen whispered in her ear, "It's him."

The two work lamps they'd set up in the small room flickered blue and white, and it made Alice blink at first. Through the lightning flashes she saw the boy on the bare mattress, his arms still cuffed to the ancient radiator that stood against the far wall, his legs cuffed together. He was small for his age, and his dark hair grew long over his forehead, almost obscuring his eyes.

"Give me the flashlight," she said, and Stephen passed it over her shoulder to her. She aimed the light on the boy's face. The duct tape was in place over his mouth. When the light hit his face, his eyes opened.

"Jesus," she said. "Holy Jesus."

His eyes were still dark, dilated from the drops they'd put in. But the eyedrops should've worn off within twelve hours.

She almost felt sorry for him.

"I'm not going in there," Stephen said.

"Oh, for God's sakes, Stephen, get a grip." But even as she said this, she could not take her eyes off the little boy. The handcuffs were clanking against each other, and the dampness and chill of the room bothered her. It was only October. It wasn't yet this cold. Even this far down below the street level, it should not be this cold.

"No, I won't," Stephen said.

"Well, all right. Do you still have the knife?"

"No."

"Go back up and get it. If we have to do this now, we'll do this now," she said. Alice felt an uneasiness as she moved her chair closer in. Something had bothered her from the moment her boys had taken this child.

Something about what they'd said had happened in the house.

Or had not happened.

When they'd returned, with the boy in the back of the van, they'd told her that in the house, even though the boy cried out, no one came to check on him.

No one.

Before Stephen left the basement room, she grabbed his hand. "You're sure you didn't kill the parents?"

Stephen squeezed her hand, then let it drop. "Do you think we'd forget? Do you think Charlie wouldn't be crowing about it? Do you think . . . " He paused, as if trying to control that awful temper of his. "Mother . . . do you think we'd have a hope in hell of the money if we'd slit their throats?"

She closed her eyes, sending out a prayer. "How do you know their throats were slit?"

He ignored this comment. "I'll go get the knife. Don't let him talk to you."

Alice kept the flashlight beam on the boy's face. The duct tape held across his mouth.

She heard Stephen's heavy footfalls as he went back down toward the elevator.

Then she noticed the humming, and she pointed the flashlight over to the corner of the room where they let the boy defecate, and the area was covered with flies. In revulsion, she looked away.

"Come closer," someone said.

She pointed the flashlight back to the boy's face.

The tape still on his mouth.

The obsidian eyes.

No emotion in the boy's face at all.

The voice could not be his—for it was almost that of a little girl's.

Rosanna.

"Come," the girl said, and Alice felt an icy sweat along the back of her neck.

"What game are you playing?" Alice asked. Alice had experience with children—she'd raised two of her own, and countless others in the families that employed her. Children played games when they were naughty. That was all. Games.

Alice wheeled her chair closer to the dirty mattress, near the boy's feet.

"How are you talking?" Alice asked when she'd composed herself. No child would get the upper hand with her. No child.

"I've seen so many things," the child said, and now Alice couldn't tell—it might've been a boy or a girl, much younger than the boy who was handcuffed in front of her. "So many sights, so many people. None of you appreciate what you have inside you. The tastes. The smells," and Alice watched as the little boy's nostrils flared, opening up.

The stench of the room came at her full force, and Alice coughed into her sleeve.

Someone behind her pushed her wheelchair.

"Stephen? Stephen?" she cried out, her composure gone as the chair moved steadily forward.

She turned slightly in her chair, shining the flashlight at the person pushing her—but its beam hit nothing but the wall and closed door behind her.

Then the wheelchair jostled, and she was tossed down onto the mattress. The flashlight rolled off into a corner of the room.

"No!" she shouted. "Charlie! Stephen! Help me!"

After several more shouts, she quieted. Her legs were useless, but she raised herself up on her arms, reaching for the flashlight. Not finding it.

Someone grabbed her wrist.

Like a steel cuff going around her wrist.

Like cold stone.

The boy said, "You like treasure, don't you, Alice? You want riches. I have riches. I have wealth. Let me show you my treasures, Alice."

She jerked her hand away from his grip. The flickering blue and white work lamps became like flashes of a camera, blinding Alice for a few seconds.

"What in God's name are you?" she cried out.

"I am many," the boy said, and she watched as his lips moved beneath the duct tape—as if it were not tape at all but a smear of jelly over his lips. Flies circled around the jelly on his lips, buzzing from his lips to her face as he spoke. "Come closer, Alice. Let me show you the treasures of the world. All of them, here for you, all of them. Come, Alice, come into my dreams. . . . "

Another voice insinuated itself into her, a voice that grew into a vision of heat and smoke.

"You are a saint," the voice said, and Alice tried to fight the boy, but her body was weak. She saw the colors of a distant country explode like fireworks in the blue darkness of the room. . . .

# *White Chapel*

"You are a saint," the leper said, reaching her hand out to clutch the saffron-dyed robe of the great man of Calcutta, known from his miracle workings in America to his world fame as a holy man throughout the world. The sick woman said, in perfect English, "My name is Jane. I need a miracle. I can't hold it any longer. It is eating away at me. They are." She labored to breathe with each word she spoke.

"Who?" the man asked.

"The lovers. Oh, God, two years keeping them from escaping. Imprisoned inside me."

"You are possessed by demons?"

She smiled, and he saw a glimmer of humanity in

the torn skin. "Chose me because I was good at it. At suffering. That is whom the gods chose. I escaped but had no money, my friends were dead. Where could I go? I became a home for every manner of disease."

"My child," the saint said, leaning forward to draw the rags away from the leper's face. "May God shine His countenance upon you."

"Don't look upon me, then, my life is nearly over," the leper said, but the great man had already brought his face near hers. It was too late. Involuntarily, the leper pressed her face against the saint's, lips bursting with fire heat. An attendant of the saint's came over and pulled the leper away, swatting the beggar on the shoulder.

The great man drew back, wiping his lips with his sleeve.

The leper grinned, her teeth shiny with droplets of blood. "The taste of purity," she said, her dark hair falling to the side of her face. "Forgive me. I could not resist. The pain. Too much."

The saint continued down the narrow alley, back into the marketplace of what was called the City of Joy, as the smell of fires and dung and decay came up in dry gusts against the yellow sky.

The leper woman leaned against the stone wall and began to ease out of the cage of her flesh. The memory of this body, like a book, written upon the nerves and sinews, the pathways of blood and bone, opened for a moment, and the saint felt it, too, as the leper lay dying,

49

my name is Jane, a brief memory of identity, but had no other past to recall, her breath stopped,

the saint reached up to feel the edge of his lips, his face, and wondered what had touched him.

What could cause the arousal he felt.

*II*

"He rescued five children from the pit, only to flay them alive, slowly. They said he savored every moment, and kept them breathing for as long as he was able. He initialed them. Kept their faces." This was overheard at a party in London, five years before Jane Boone would ever go to White Chapel, but it aroused her journalist's curiosity, for it was not spoken with a sense of dread but with something approaching awe and wonder, too. The man of whom it was spoken had already become a legend.

Then, a few months before the entire idea sparked in her mind, she saw an item in the *Bangkok Post* about the woman whose face had been scraped off with what appeared to be a sort of makeshift scouring pad. Written upon her back, the name Meritt. This woman also suffered from amnesia concerning everything that had occurred to her prior to losing the outer skin of her face; she was like a blank slate.

Jane had a friend in Thailand, a professor at the university, and she called him to find out if there was anything he could add to the story of the faceless woman. "Not much, I'm afraid," he said, aware of her passion for the bizarre story. "They sold tickets to see her, you know. I assume she's a fraud, playing off the myth of the white devil who traveled to India, collecting skins as he went. Don't waste your time on this one. Poor bastards are so desperate to eat, they'll do anything to themselves to put something in their stomachs. You know the most unbelievable part of her story?"

Jane was silent.

He continued, "This woman, face scraped off, nothing human left to her features, claimed that she was thankful that it had happened. She not only forgave him, she said, she blessed him. If it had really happened as she said, who would possibly bless this man? How could one find forgiveness for such a cruel act? And the other thing, too. Not in the papers. Her vagina, mutilated, as if he'd taken a machete to open her up. She didn't hold a grudge on that count, either."

In wartime, men will often commit atrocities they would cringe at in their everyday life. Jane Boone knew about this dark side to the male animal, but she still weathered the journey to White Chapel, because she wanted the whole story from the mouth of the very man who had committed what was known, in the latter part of the century, as the most unconscionable crime, without remorse. If the man did indeed live among the Khou-dali at the farthest point along the great dark river, it was said that perhaps he sought to atone for his past—White Chapel was neither white nor a chapel, but a brutal outpost that had been conquered and destroyed from one century to the next since before recorded history. Always to self-resurrect from its own ashes, only to be destroyed again. The British had anglicized the name at some sober point in their rule, although the original name, Y-Cha-Pa when translated, was Monkey God Night, referring to the ancient temple and celebration of the divine possession on certain nights of the dry season when the god needed to inhabit the faithful. The temple had mostly been reduced to ashes and fallen stone, although the ruins of its gates still stood to the southeast.

Jane was thirty-two, and had already written a book about the camps to the north, with their starvation and torture, although she had not been well reviewed Stateside. Still, she intended to follow the trail of Nathan Meritt, the man who had deserted his men at the height of the famous massacre. He had been a war hero, who, from those court-martialed later, was said to have been the most vicious of torturers. The press had labeled him, in mocking Joseph Campbell's study, *The Hero With A Thousand Faces,* "The Hero Who Skinned A Thousand Faces." The war had been over for a good twenty years, but Nathan was said to have fled to White Chapel. There were reports that he had taken on a Khou-dali wife and fathered several children over the two decades since his disappearance. Nathan Meritt had been the most decorated hero in the war—children in America had been named for him. And then the massacre, and the stories of his love of torture, of his rituals of skin and bone . . . It was the most fascinating story she had ever come across, and she was shocked that no other writer, other than one who couched the whole tale in a wide swath of fiction, had sought out this living myth. While Jane couldn't get any of her usual magazines to send her gratis, she had convinced a major publishing house to at least foot expenses until she could gather some solid information.

To get to White Chapel, one had to travel by boat down a brown river in intolerable heat. Mosquitoes were as plentiful as air, and the river stank of human waste. Jane kept the netting around her face at all times, and her boatman took to calling her Nettie. There were three other travelers with her: Rex, her photographer, and a British man and wife named Greer and Lucy. Rex was not faring well—he'd left Kathmandu in August, and had lost twenty pounds in just a few weeks. He looked like a balding scarecrow, with skin as pale as the moon, and eyes wise and weary like those of some old man. He was always complaining about how little money he had, which apparently compounded for him his physical miseries. She had known him for seven years, and had only recently come to understand his mood swings and fevers. Greer was fashionably unkempt, always in a tie and jacket, but mottled with sweat stains, and wrinkled; Lucy kept her hair up in a straw hat, and disliked all women. She also expressed a fear of water, which amazed one and all since every trip she took began with a journey across an ocean or down a river. Jane enjoyed talking with Greer, as long as she didn't have to second-guess his inordinate interest in children. She found Lucy to be about as interesting as a toothache.

The boatman wanted to be called Jim because of a movie he had once seen, and so, after morning coffee (bought at a dock), Jane said, "Well, Jim, we're beyond help now, aren't we?"

Jim grinned, his small dark eyes sharp, his face wrinkled from too much sun. "We make White Chapel by night, Nettie. Very nice place to sleep, too. In town."

Greer brought out his book of quotes, and read, "'Of the things that are man's achievements, the greatest is suffering.' " He glanced to his wife and then to Jane, skipping Rex altogether, who lay against his pillows, moaning softly.

"I know," Lucy said, sipping from the bowl, "it's Churchill."

"No, dear, it's not. Jane, any idea?"

Jane thought a moment. The coffee tasted quite good, which was a constant surprise to her, as she had been told by those who had been through this region before that it was bitter. "I don't know. Maybe— Rousseau?"

Greer shook his head. "It's Hadriman the Third. The Scourge of Y-Cha."

"Who's Y-Cha?" Rex asked.

Jane said, "The Monkey God. The temple is in the jungles ahead. Hadriman the Third skinned every monkey he could get his hand on, and left them hang-

ing around the original city to show his power over
the great god. This subdued the locals, who believed
their only guardian had been vanquished. The legend
is that he took the skin of the god, too, so that it might
not interfere in the affairs of men ever again. White
Chapel has been the site of many scourges throughout
history, but Hadriman was the only one to profane the
temple."

Lucy put her hand to her mouth in a feigned deli-
cacy. "Is it . . . a decent place?" Greer and Lucy spent
their lives mainly traveling, and Jane assumed it was
because they had internal problems all their own that
kept them seeking out the exotic, the foreign, rather
than staying with anything too familiar. They were
rich, too, the way that only an upperclass Brit of the
Old School could be and not have that guilt about it: to
have inherited lots of money and to be perfectly content to spend it as it pleased themselves without a care
for the rest of mankind. Greer had a particular problem
that Jane recognized without being able to understand:
he had a fascination with children, which she knew
must be of the sexual variety, although she could've
been wrong—it was just something about him, about
the way he referred to children in his speech, even the
way he looked at her sometimes, that made her
uncomfortable. She didn't fathom his marriage to
Lucy at all, but she fathomed very few marriages.
While Greer had witnessed the Bokai Ritual of Cir-
cumcision and the Resurrection Hut Fire in Calcutta,
Lucy had been reading Joan Didion novels and paint-

ing portraits of women weaving baskets. They had money to burn, however, inherited on both sides, and when Greer had spoken, by chance to Jane at the hotel, he had found her story of going to White Chapel fascinating; and he, in turn, was paying for the boat and boatman for the two-day trip.

Jane said, in response to Lucy, "White Chapel's decent enough. Remember, British rule, and then a little bit of France. Most of them can speak English, and there'll be a hotel that should meet your standards."

"I didn't tell you this," Greer said to both Jane and Lucy, "but my grandfather was stationed in White Chapel for half a year. Taxes. Very unpopular job, as you can imagine."

"I'm starved," Lucy said, suddenly, as if there were nothing else to think of, "do we still have some of those nice sandwiches. Jim?" She turned to the boatman, smiling. She had a way of looking about the boat, eyes partly downcast, which kept her from having to see the water—like a child pretending to be self-contained in her bed, not recognizing anything beyond her own small imagined world.

He nodded, and pointed toward the palm leaf basket.

While Lucy crawled across the boat—she was too unbalanced, Greer often said, to stand without tipping the whole thing and this was, coincidentally, her great terror—Greer leaned over to Jane and whispered, "Lucy doesn't know why you're going. She thinks it's for some kind of *National Geographic* article," but he had to stop himself for fear that his wife would hear.

Jane was thinking about the woman in Thailand who claimed to have forgiven the man who tore her face off. And the children from the massacre, not just murdered, but obliterated. She had seen the pictures in *Life*. Faceless children. Skinned from ear to ear.

She closed her eyes and tried to think of less unpleasant images.

All she remembered was her father looking down at her as she slept.

She opened her eyes, glancing about. The heat and smells revived her from dark memories. She said, "Rex, look, don't you think that would be a good one for a photo?" She pointed to one of the characteristic barges that floated about the river, selling mostly rotting meat and stuffed lizards, although the twentieth century had intruded, for there were televisions, on some of the rafts, and a hibachi barbecue.

Rex lifted his Nikon up in response, but was overcome by a fit of coughing.

"Rex," Lucy said, leaning over to feel his forehead, "my God, you're burning up," then, turning to her husband, "He's very sick."

"He's seen a doctor, dear," Greer said, but looked concerned.

"When we get there," Jane said, "we'll find another doctor. Rex? Should we turn around?"

"No, I'm feeling better. I have my pills." He laid his

head back down on his pillow and fanned mosquitoes back from his face with a palm frond.

"He survived malaria and dengue fever, Lucy, he'll survive the flu. He's not one to suffer greatly."

"So many viruses," Lucy shook her head, looking about the river, "isn't this where AIDS began?"

"I think that may have been Africa," Greer said in such a way that it shut his wife up completely, and she ate her sandwich and watched the barges and the other boatmen as though she were watching a National Geographic Special.

"Are you dying on me?" Jane asked, flashing a smile through the mosquito net veil.

"I'm not gonna die," Rex said adamantly. His face took on an aspect of boyishness, and he managed the kind of grin she hadn't seen since they'd first started working together several years back—before he had discovered needles. "Jesus, I'm just down for a couple of days. Don't talk about me like that."

Jim, his scrawny arms turning the rudder as the river ran, said, "This is the River of Gods, no one die here. All live forever. The Great Pig God, he live in Kanaput, and the Snake God live in Jurukat. Protect people. No one die in paradise of Gods." Jim nodded toward points that lay ahead along the river.

"And what about the Monkey God?" Jane asked.

Jim smiled, showing surprisingly perfect teeth, which he popped out for just a moment because he was so proud of the newly made dentures. When he had secured them into his upper gum again, he said,

"Monkey God trick all. Monkey God live where river goes white. Have necklace of heads of childs. You die only once with Monkey God, and no come back. Jealous god, Monkey God. She not like other gods."

"Monkey God is female," Jane said. "I assumed she was a he. Well, good for her. I wonder what's she's jealous of?"

Greer tried for a joke. "Oh, probably because we have skins, and hers got taken away. You know women."

Jane didn't even attempt to acknowledge this comment.

Jim shook his head. "Monkey God give blood at rainy times, then white river goes red. But she in chains, no longer so bad, I think. She buried alive in White Chapel by mortal lover. Hear her screams, sometime, when monsoon come, when flood come. See her blood when mating season come."

"You know," Greer looked at the boatman quizzically, "you speak with a bit of an accent. Who did you learn English from?"

Jim said, "Dale Carnegie tapes, Mr. Greer. *How to Win Friends and Influence People*."

Jane was more exhilirated than exhausted by the time the boat docked in the little bay at White Chapel. There was the Colonial British influence to the port, with guard booths, now mainly taken over by beggars, and an empty customshouse. The place had fallen into beloved disrepair, for the great elephant statues, given for the god Ganesh, were overcome with vines, and cracked in places; and the lilies had all but taken over the dock. Old petrol storage cans floated along the pylons, strung together, with a net knotted between the cans: Someone was out to catch eels or some shade-dwelling scavenger. A nervous man with a straw hat and a bright red cloth tied around his loins ran to the edge of the dock to greet them; he carried a long fat plank, which he swept over the water's edge to the boat, pulling it closer in. A ladder was lowered to them.

The company disembarked carefully. Rex, the weakest, had to be pulled up by Jim and Jane both. Lucy proved the most difficult, however, because of her terror of water—Jim the boatman pushed her from behind to get her up to the dock, which was only four rungs up on the ladder. Then, Jane didn't feel like haggling with anyone, and so, after she tipped Jim, she left the others to find their ways to the King George Hotel by the one taxicab in White Chapel. She chose instead to walk off her excitement and perhaps get a feel for the place.

She knew from her previous explorations that there was a serendipity to experience—she might, by pure chance, find what she was looking for. But the walk proved futile, for the village—it was not properly a town—was dark and silent, and except for the lights from the King George, about a mile up the road, the place looked like no one lived there. Occasionally, she passed the open door to a hut through which she saw the red embers of the fire, and the accompanying stench of the manure that was used to stoke the flame.

Birds, too, she imagined them to be crows, gathered around huts, kicking up dirt and waste.

She saw the headlights of a car and stepped back against a stone wall. It was the taxi taking the others to the hotel, and she didn't want them to see her.

The light was on inside the taxi, and she saw Rex up front with the driver, half asleep. In back, Lucy, too, had her eyes closed; but Greer, however, was staring out into the night, as if searching for something, perhaps even expecting something. His eyes were wide, not with fear but with a kind of feverish excitement.

He's here for a reason. He wants what White Chapel has to offer, she thought, like he's a hunter. And what did it have to offer? Darkness, superstition, jungle, disease, and a man who could tear the faces off children. A man who had become a legend because of his monstrosity.

After the car passed and was just two sets of red lights going up the narrow street, she continued her journey up the hill.


When she got to the hotel, she went to the bar. Greer sat at one end; he had changed into a lounging jacket that seemed to be right out of the First World War. "The concierge gave it to me," Greer said, pulling at the sleeves, which were just short of his wrists, "I imagine they've had it since my grandfather's day." Then, looking at Jane, "You look dead to the world. Have a gin and tonic."

Jane signaled to the barman. "Coca-Cola?" When she had her glass, she took a sip and sighed. "I never thought I would cherish a Coke so much. Lucy's asleep?"

Greer nodded. "Like a baby. And I helped with Rex, too. His fever's come down."

"Good. It wasn't flu."

"I know. I can detect the D.T.'s at twenty paces. Was it morphine?"

Jane nodded. "That and other things. I brought him with me mainly because he needed someone to take him away from it. It's too easy to buy where he's from. As skinny as he is, he's actually gained some weight in the past few days. So, what about you?" She didn't mean for the question to be so fraught with unspoken meaning, but there it was: out there.

"You mean, why am I here?"

She could not hold her smile. There was something cold, almost reptilian about him now, as if, in the boat, he had worn a mask and now had removed it to reveal rough skin and scales.

"Well, there aren't that many places in the world . . . quite so . . . "

"Open? Permissive?"

Greer looked at her, and she knew he understood. "It's been a few months. We all have habits that need to be overcome. You're very intuitive. Most women I know aren't. Lucy spends her hours denying that reality exists."

"If I had known when we started this trip . . . "

"I know. You wouldn't have let me join you, or even fund this expedition. You think I'm sick. I suppose I am—I've never been a man to delude himself. You're very—shall I say—liberal to allow me to come even now."

"It's just very hard for me to understand," she said. "I guess this continent caters to men like you more than Europe does. I understand for two pounds sterling you can buy a child at this end of the river. Maybe a few."

"You'd be surprised. Jane. I'm not proud of my interest. It just exists. Men are often entertained by perversity. I'm not saying it's right. It's one of the great mysteries—" He stopped midsentence, reached over, touching the side of her face.

She drew back from his fingers.

In his eyes, a fatherly kindness. "Yes," he said, "I knew. When we met. It's always in the eyes, my dear. I can find them in the streets, pick them out of a group, out of a schoolyard. Just like yours, those eyes."

Jane felt her face go red, and wished she had never met this man who had seemed so civil earlier.

"Was it a relative?" he asked. "Your father? An uncle?"

She didn't answer, but took another sip of Coke.

"It doesn't matter, though, does it? It's always the same pain," he said, reaching in the pockets of the jacket and coming up with a gold cigarette case. He opened it, offered her one, and then drew one out for himself. Before he lit it, with the match burning near his lips, he said, "I always see it in their faces, that pain, that hurt. And it's what attracts me to them, Jane. As difficult as it must be to understand, for I don't pretend to, myself, it's that caged animal in the eyes that—how shall I say—excites me?"

She said, with regret, "You're very sick. I don't think this is a good place for you."

"Oh," he replied, the light flaring in his eyes, "but this is just the place for me. And for you, too. Two halves of the same coin, Jane. Without one, the other could not exist. I'm capable of inflicting pain, and you, you're capable of bearing a great deal of suffering, aren't you?"

"I don't want to stay here," she told Rex in the morning. They had just finished a breakfast of a spicy tea and shuvai, with poached duck eggs on the side, and were walking in the direction of the village center.

"We have to go back?" Rex asked, combing his hands through what was left of his hair. "I—I don't think I'm ready, Janey, not yet. I'm starting to feel a little stronger. If I go back . . . and what about the book?"

"I mean, I don't want to stay at the hotel. Not with those people. He's a child molester. No, make that child rapist. He as much admitted it to me last night."

"Holy shit," Rex screwed his face up, "you sure?"

Jane looked at him, and he turned away. There was so much boy in Rex that still wasn't used to dealing with the complexities of the adult world—she almost hated to burst his bubble about people. They stopped at a market, and she went to the first stall, which offered up some sort of eely thing. Speaking a pidgin version of Khou-dali, or at least the northern dialect that she had learned, Jane asked the vendor, "Is there another hotel? Not the English one, but maybe one run by Khou-dali?"

He directed her to the west and said a few words. She grabbed Rex's hand and whispered, "It may be some kind of whorehouse, but I can avoid Greer for at least one night. And that stupid wife of his."

Rex took photos of just about everyone and everything they passed, including the monkey stalls. He was feeling much better, and Jane was thrilled that he was standing tall, with color in his cheeks, no longer dependent on a drug to energize him. He took one of her with a dead monkey. "I thought these people worshiped monkeys."

Jane said, "I think it's the image of the monkey, not the animal itself." She set the dead animal back on the platform with several other carcasses. Without meaning to, she blurted, "Human beings are horrible."

"Smile when you say that." Rex snapped another picture.

"We kill, kill, kill. Flesh, spirit, whatever gets in our way. It's like our whole purpose is to extinguish life. And for those who live, there's memory, like a curse. We're such a mixture of frailty and cruelty."

The stoop-backed woman who stood at the stall said, in perfect English, "Who is to say, miss, that our entire purpose here on Earth is perhaps to perform such tasks? Frailty and cruelty are our gifts to the world. Who is to say that suffering is not the greatest of all gifts from the gods?"

Her Khou-dali name was long and unpronounceable, but her English name was Mary-Rose. Her grandmother had been British; her brothers had gone to London and married, while she, the only daughter, had remained behind to care for an ailing mother until the old woman's death. And then, she told them, she did not have any ambition for leaving her ancestral home. She had the roughened features of a young woman turned old by poverty and excessive labor and no vanity whatsoever about her. Probably from some embarrassment at hygiene, she kept her mouth fairly closed when she spoke. Her skin, rough as it was, possessed a kind of glow that was similar to the women Jane had seen who had face-lifts—although, clearly, this was from living in White Chapel with its humidity. Something in her eyes approached real beauty, like sacred jewels pressed there. She had a vigor in her glance and speech; her face was otherwise expressionless, as if set in stone. She was wrapped in several cloths, each dyed clay red, and wrapped from her shoulders down to her ankles; a purple cloth was wrapped about her head like a nun's wimple. It was so hot and steamy that Jane was surprised she didn't go as some of the local women did—with a certain discreet amount of nakedness. "If you are looking for a place, I can give you a room. Very cheap. Clean. Breakfast included." She named a low price, and Jane immediately took her up on it. "You help me with English, and I make coffee, too. None of this tea. We are all dizzy with tea. Good coffee. All the way from America, too. From Maxwell's house."

Mary-Rose lived beyond the village, just off the place where the river forked. She had a stream running beside her house, which was a two-room shack. It had been patched together from ancient stones from the ruined Y-Cha temple, and tar paper coupled with hardened clay and straw had been used to fill in the gaps. Rex didn't need to be told to get his camera ready: the temple stones had hieroglyphic-like images scrawled into them. He began snapping pictures as soon as he saw them.

"It's a story," Jane said, following stone to stone. "Some of it's missing."

"Yes," Mary-Rose said, "it tells of Y-Cha and her conquests, of her consorts. She fucked many mortals." Jane almost laughed when Rose said "fucked," because her speech seemed so refined up until that point. No doubt, whoever had taught Rose to speak had not bothered to separate out vulgarities. "When she fucks them, very painful, very hurting, but also very much pleasure. No one believes in her much no more. She is in exile. Skin stolen away. They say she could mount a believer and ride him for hours, but in the end, he dies, and she must withdraw. The White Devil, he keeps her locked up. All silly stories, of course, because Y-Cha is just so much lah-dee-dah."

Jane looked at Rex. She said nothing.

Rex turned the camera to take a picture of Mary-Rose, but she quickly hid her features with her shawl. "Please, no," she said.

He lowered the camera.

"Mary-Rose," Jane said, measuring her words, "do you know where the White Devil lives?"

Seeing that she was safe from being photographed, she lowered the cloth. Her hair spilled out from under it—pure white, almost dazzlingly so. Only the very old women in the village had hair even approaching gray. She smiled broadly, and her teeth were rotted and yellow. Tiny holes had been drilled into the front teeth. "White Devil, he cannot be found, I am afraid."

"He's dead, then. Or gone," Rex said.

"No, not that," she said, looking directly into Jane's eyes, "you can't find him. He finds you. And when he finds you, you are no longer who you are. You are no longer who you were. You become."

Jane spent the afternoon writing in her notebooks.

Nathan Meritt may be dead. He would be, what, fifty? Could he have really survived here all this time? Wouldn't he self-destruct, given his proclivities? I want him to exist. I want to believe he is what the locals say he is. The White Devil. Destruction and Creation in mortal form. Supplanted the local goddess. Legend beyond what a human is capable of. The woman with the scoured face. The children without skins. The trail of stories that followed him through this wilderness. Settling in White Chapel, his spiritual home. White Chapel—where Jack the Ripper killed the prostitutes in London. The name of a church. Y-Cha, the Monkey God, with her fury and fertility and her absolute weakness. White—they say the river runs white at times, like milk, it is part of Y-Cha. Whiteness. The white of bones strung along in her necklace.

68

The white of the scoured woman—her featureless face white with infection.

Can any man exist who matches the implications of this?

The Hero Who Skinned A Thousand Faces.

And why?

What does he intend with this madness, if he does still exist, if the stories are true?

And why am I searching for him?

And then she wrote:

> *Greer's eyes looking into me. Knowing about my father. Knowing because of a memory of hurt somehow etched into my own eyes.*
>
> *The excitement when he was looking out from the taxi.*
>
> *Like a bogeyman on holiday, a bag of sweeties in one hand, and the other, out to grab a child's hand.*
>
> *Frailty and cruelty. Suffering as a gift.*
>
> *What he said, two halves of the same coin. Without one, the other could not exist. Capable of great suffering.*

White Chapel, and its surrounding wilderness, came to life just after midnight. The extremes of its climate: chilly at dawn, steamy from ten in the morning till eight or nine at night, and then hot, but less humid, as darkness fell, led to a brain-fever siesta between noon and ten o'clock at night. Then families awoke and made the night meal, baths were taken, love was made—all in preparation for the more sociable and bearable hours of one A.M. to about six or seven, when most physical labor, lit by torch and flare, was done, or when hunting the precious monkey and other creatures more easily caught just before dawn. Jane was not surprised at this. Most of the nearby cultures followed a similar pattern based on climate and not daylight. What did impress her was the silence of the place while work and play began.

Mary-Rose had a small fire going just outside the doorway; the dull orange light of the slow-burning manure cast spinning shadows as Mary-Rose knelt beside it and stirred a pan. "Fried bread," she said as Jane sat up from her mat. "Are you hungry?"

"How long did I sleep?"

"Five, six hours, maybe."

The frying dough smelled delicious. Mary-Rose had a jar of honey in one hand, which tipped, carefully, across the pan.

Jane glanced through the shadows, trying to see if Rex was in the corner on his mat.

"Your friend," Mary-Rose said, "he left. He said he wanted to catch some local color. That is precisely what he said."

"He left his equipment," Jane said.

"Yes, I can't tell you why. But," the other woman said, flipping the puffed-up circle of bread and then dropping it onto a thin cloth, "I can tell you something about the village. There are certain entertainments

70

which are forbidden to women which many men who come here desire. Men are like monkeys, do you not think so? They frolic, and fight, and even destroy, but if you can entertain them with pleasure, they will put other thoughts aside. A woman is different. A woman cannot be entertained by the forbidden."

"I don't believe that. I don't believe that things are forbidden to women, anyway."

Mary-Rose shrugged. "What I meant, Miss Boone, is that a woman is the forbidden. Man is monkey, but woman is Monkey God." She apparently didn't care what Jane thought one way or another. Jane had to suppress an urge to smile, because Mary-Rose seemed so set in her knowledge of life, and had only seen the jungles of Y-Cha. She brought the bread into the shack and set it down in front of Jane. "Your friend, Rex, he is sick from some fever. But it is fever that drives a man. He went to find what would cool the fever. There is a man skilled with needles and medicines in the jungle. It is to this man that your friend has traveled tonight."

Jane said, "I don't believe you."

Mary-Rose grinned. The small holes in her teeth had been filled with tiny jewels. "What fever drives you, Miss Jane Boone?"

"I want to find him. Meritt. The White Devil."

"What intrigues you about him?"

Jane wasn't sure whether or not she should answer truthfully. "I want to do a book about him. If he really exists. I find the legend fascinating."

71

"Many legends are fascinating. Would someone travel as far as you have for fascination? I wonder."

"All right. There's more. I believe, if he exists, if he is the legend, that he is either some master sociopath or something else. What I have found in my research of his travels is that the victims, the ones who have lived, are thankful of their torture and mutilation. It is as if they've been—I'm not sure—baptized or consecrated by the pain. Even the parents of those children—the ones who were skinned—even they forgave him. Why? Why would you forgive a man of such unconscionable acts?" Jane tasted the fried bread; it was like a doughnut. The honey that dripped across its surface stung her lips—it wasn't honey at all, but had a bitter taste to it. Some kind of herb mixed with sap?

It felt as if fire ants were biting her lips, along her chin where the thick liquid dripped; her tongue felt large, clumsy, as if she'd been shot up with Novocain. She didn't immediately think that she had been drugged, only that she was, perhaps, allergic to this food. She managed to say, "I just want to meet him. Talk with him," before her mouth seemed inoperable, and she felt a stiffness to her throat.

Mary-Rose's eyes squinted, as if assessing this demand. She whispered, "Are you not sure that you do not seek him in order to know what he has known?" She leaned across to where the image of the household god sat on its wooden haunches—not a monkey, but some misshapen imp. Sunken into the head of this imp, something akin to a votive candle. Mary-Rose lit this with a match. The yellow-blue flame came up

72

small, and she cupped the idol in her hand as if it were a delicate bird.

And then she reached up with her free hand and touched the edges of her lips—it looked as if she were about to laugh.

"Miss Jane Boone. You look for what does not look for you. This is the essence of truth. And so you have found what you should run from, the hunter is become the hunted," she said, and began tearing at the curve of her lip, peeling back the reddened skin, unrolling the flesh that covered her chin like parchment.

Beneath this, another face. Unraveling like skeins of thread through some imperfect tapesty, the sallow cheeks, the aquiline nose, the shriveled bags beneath the eyes, even the white hair came out strand by strand. The air around her grew acrid with the smoke from the candle, as bits of ashen skin fluttered across its flame.

A young man of nineteen or twenty emerged from beneath the last of the skin of Mary-Rose. His lips and cheeks were slick with dark blood, as if he'd just pressed his face into wine. "I am the man," he said.

The burning yellow-blue flame wavered, and hissed with snowflake-fine motes of flesh.

Jane Boone watched it, unmoving.

Paralyzed.

Her eyes grew heavy. As she closed them, she heard Nathan Meritt clap his hands and say to someone, "She is ready. Take her to Sedri-Y-Cha-Sampon. It is time for Y-Cha-Pa."

The last part she could translate: Monkey God Night.

She was passing out, but slowly. She could just feel someone's hands reaching beneath her armpits to lift her. I am Jane Boone, an American citizen, a journalist, I am Jane Boone, you can't do this to me, her feeble mind shouted while her lips remained silent.

*III*

Two years later, the saint lay down in the evening and tried to put the leper he had met that day out of his mind. The lips, so warm, drawing blood from his own without puncturing the skin.

Or had it been her blood that he had drunk?

Beside his simple cot was a basin and a ewer of water. He reached over, dipping his fingers into it, and brought the lukewarm droplets up to his face.

He was, perhaps, developing a fever.

The city was always hot in this season, though, so he could not be certain. He wondered if his fear of the leper woman was creating an illness within his flesh. But the saint did not believe that he could contract anything from these people. He was only in Calcutta to do good. Even Mother Teresa had recognized his purity of heart and soul; the Buddhist and Hindu monks, likewise, saw in him a great teacher.

The saint's forehead broke a sweat.

He reached for the ever, but it slipped from his sweaty hands and shattered against the floor.

He sat up, and bent down to collect the pieces.

The darkness was growing around him.

He cut his finger on a porcelain shard.

He squeezed the blood and wiped it across the over-sized cotton blouse he wore to bed.

He held the shard in his hand.

There were times when even a saint held too much remembered pain within him.

Desires, once acted upon in days of innocence and childhood, which now seemed dark and animal and howling.

He brought the shard up to his lips, his cheek, pressing.

In the reflecting glass of the window, a face he did not recognize, a hand he had not seen, scraping a broken piece of a pitcher up and down and up and down the way he had seen his father shaving himself when the saint was a little boy in Biloxi, the way he himself shaved, the way men could touch themselves with steel, leaning into mirrors to admire how close one could get to skin such as this. Had any ever gone so far beneath his skin?

The saint tasted his blood.

Tasted his skin.

Began slicing clumsily at flesh.

## IV

Jane Boone sensed movement.

She even felt the coolness of something upon her head—a damp towel?

She was looking up at a thin, interrupted line of slate-gray sky emerging between the leaning trees and vines; she heard the cries of exotic birds; a creaking, as of wood on water.

I'm in a boat, she thought.

Someone came over to her, leaning forward. She saw his face. It was Jim, the boatman who had brought her from upriver. "Hello, Nettie," he said, calling her by the nickname they'd laughed about before, "you are seeing now, yes? Good. It is nearly the morning. Very warm. But very cool in temple. Very cool."

She tried to say something, but her mouth wasn't working; it hurt to even try to move her lips.

Jim said, apparently noticing the distress on her face, "No try to talk now. Later. We on sacred water. Y-Cha carry us in." Then he moved away. She watched the sky above her grow darker; the farther the boat went on this river, the deeper the jungle.

She closed her eyes, feeling weak.

Ice-cold water splashed across her face.

"You go back to sleep, no," Jim said, standing above her again, "trip is over." He poled the boat up against the muddy bank. When he had secured it, he returned to her, lifting her from beneath her armpits. She felt as if every bone had been removed from her body. She barely felt her feet touch the ground as he dragged her up a narrow path. All she had the energy to do was watch the immense green darkness enfold about her, even while day burst with searing heat and light beyond them.

When she felt the pins-and-needles feeling coming

into her legs and arms, she had been set down upon a round stone wheel, laid flat upon a smooth floor. Several candles were lit about the large room, all set upon the yellowed skulls of monkeys, somehow attached to the walls. Alongside the skulls, small bits of leaf and paper taped or nailed or glued to the wall; scrawled across these, she knew from her experience in other similar temples, were petitions and prayers to the local god.

On one of the walls, written in a dark ink that could only have been blood, were words in the local dialect. Jane was not good at deciphering the language.

A man's voice, strong and pleasant, said, " 'Flesh of my flesh, blood of my blood, I delight in your offering.' It's an incantation to the great one, the Y-Cha."

He emerged from the flickering darkness. Just as he had seemed beneath the skin of Mary-Rose, Nathan Meritt was young, but she recognized his face from his college photographs. He was not merely handsome, but he had a radiance that came from beneath his skin, as if something fiery lit him, and his eyes, blue and almost transparent, inflamed. "She is not native to this land, you know. She was an import from Asia. Did battle in her own way with Kali, and won this small acre before the village came to be. Gods are not as we think in the West, Jane, they are creatures with desires and loves and weaknesses like you or I. They do not come to us, or reveal themselves to us. No, it is we who approach them, we who must entertain them with our lives. You are a woman, as is the Y-Cha. Feelings that you have, natural rhythms, all of these, she is prey to, also."

Jane opened her mouth, but barely a sound emerged.

Meritt put his finger to his lips. "In a little while. They used to use it to stun the monkeys—what the bread was dipped in. It's called *hanu,* and does little harm, although you may experience a hangover. The reason for the secrecy? I needed to meet you, Miss Boone, before you met me. You are not the first person to come looking for me. But you are different from the others who have come."

He stepped farther into the light, and she saw that he was naked. His skin glistened with grease, and his body was clean-shaven except for his scalp, from which grew long dark hair.

Jane managed a whisper. "What about me? I don't understand. Different? Others?"

"Oh," he said, a smile growing on his face, "you are capable of much suffering, Miss Boone. That is a rare talent in human beings. Some are weak, and murder their souls and bodies, and some die too soon in pain. Your friend Rex—he suffers much, but of the garden variety. I have already played with him—don't be upset. He had his needles and his drugs, and in return, he gave me that rare gift, that," Meritt's nostrils flared, inhaling, as if recalling some wonderful perfume, "moment of mastery. It's like nothing else, believe me. I used to skin children, you know, but they die too soon, they whine and cry, and they don't understand, and the pleasure they offer . . . "

"Please," Jane said. She felt strength seeping back into her muscles and joints. She knew she could run, but would not know to what exit, or where it would take her. She had heard about the temple having an underground labyrinth, and she didn't wish to lose herself within it.

But more than that, she didn't feel any physical threat from Nathan Meritt.

"You're so young," she said.

"Not really."

"You look like you're twenty. I never would've believed in magic, but . . . "

He laughed, and when he spoke, spoke in the measured cadences of Mary-Rose. "Skin? Flesh? It is our clothing, Miss Jane Boone, it is the tent that shelters us from the reality of life. This is not my skin, see." He reached up and drew back a section of his face from the left side of his nose to his left ear, and it came up like damp leaves, and beneath it, the chalk white of bone. "It may conform to my bones, but it is another's. It's what I learned from her, from the Y-Cha. Neither do I have blood, Miss Boone. When you prick me, I don't spill."

He seemed almost friendly; he came and sat beside her.

She shivered in spite of the familiarity.

"You mustn't be scared of me," he said in a rigid British accent, "we're two halves of the same coin."

Jane Boone looked in his eyes and saw Greer there, a smiling, gentle Greer. The Greer who had funded her trip to White Chapel, the Greer who had politely revealed his interest in children.

79

"I met them in Tibet, Greer and Lucy," Meritt said, resuming his American accent. "He wanted children, we had that in common, although his interests, oddly enough, had more to do with mechanics than with intimacy. I got him his children, and the price he paid. Well, a pound or more of flesh. Two days of exquisite suffering, Jane, along the banks of a lovely river. I had some children with me—bought in Bangkok at one hundred dollars each—and I had them do the honors. Layers of skin, peeled back, like some exotic rind. The fruit within was for me. Then the children, for they had already suffered much at Greer's own hands. I can't bear to watch children suffer more than a few hours. It's not yet an art for them; they're too natural."

"Lucy?"

He grinned. "She's still Lucy. I could crawl into his skin, but I was enjoying the game. She could not tell the difference because she didn't give a fuck, both literally and figuratively. Our whole trip down the river, only Jim knew, but he's a believer. Sweet Lucy, the most dreadful woman from Manchester, and that's saying a lot. I'll dispose of her soon, though. But she won't be much fun. Her life is her torture—anything else is redundant."

Jane wasn't sure how much of this monologue to believe. She said, "And me? What do you intend to do?"

Unexpectedly, he leaned into her, brushing his lips against hers but not kissing. His breath was like jasmine flowers floating on cool water. He looked into her eyes as if he needed something that only she could give him. He said softly, "That will be up to you. You have come to me. I am your servant."

He pulled away, stood, turned his back to her. He went to the wall and lifted a monkey skull candle up. He held the light along the yellow wall. "You think from what I've done that I'm a monster, Miss Boone. You think I thrive on cruelty, but it's not that way. Even Greer, in his last moments, thanked me for what I did. Even the children, their life force wavering, and the stains along their scalps spreading darker juices over their eyes, whispered praise with their final breaths that I had led them to that place."

He held a light up to the papers stuck to the wall. His shadow seemed enormous and twisted as he moved the light in circles; he didn't look back at her, but moved from petition to petition. "Blessings and praises and prayers, all from the locals, the believers in Y-Cha. And I, Miss Boone, I am her sworn consort, and her keeper, too, for it was Nathan Meritt and no other, the Man Who Skinned A Thousand Faces, who is her most beloved, and to whom she has submitted herself, my prisoner. Come, I will take you to the throne of Y-Cha."

A pool of water, a perfect circle, filled with koi and turtles, was at the center of the chamber. Jane had followed Nathan down winding corridors, whose walls seemed to be covered with dried animal skins and smelled of animal dung. The chamber itself was poorly lit; but there was a fire, in a hearth at its far end; she thought she heard the sound of rushing water just beyond the walls.

"The river," Nathan said, "we're beneath it. She needs the moisture, always. She has not been well for hundreds of years." He went ahead of her, toward a small cot.

Jane followed, stepping around the thin bones that lay scattered across the stones.

There, on the bed, head resting on straw, was Lucy. Fruit had been stuffed into her mouth, and flowers in the empty sockets of her eyes. She was naked, and her skin had been brutally tattooed until the blood had caked around the lines: drawings of monkeys.

Jane opened her mouth to scream, and knew that she had, but could not even hear it. When she stopped, she managed, "You bastard, you said you hadn't hurt her. You said she was still alive."

He touched her arm, almost lovingly. "That's not what I told you. I didn't hurt her, Jane. She did this to herself. Even the flowers. She's not even dead, not yet. She's no longer Lucy." He squatted beside the cot, and combed his fingers through her hair. "She's the prison of Y-Cha, at least as long as she breathes. Monkey God is a weak god, in the flesh, and she needs it, she needs skin, because she's not much different than you or me, Jane, she wants to experience life, feel blood, feel skin and bones and travel and love and kill, all the things animals take for granted, but the gods know, Jane. Oh, my baby," he pressed his face against the flowers, "the beauty, the sanctity of life, Jane, it's not in joy or happiness, it's in suffering in flesh."

He kissed the berry-stained lips, slipping his tongue into Lucy's mouth. With his left hand, he reached back and grasped Jane's hand before she could step away. His grip was tight, and he pulled her toward the cot, to her knees. He kissed from Lucy to her, and back, and she tasted the berries and sweet pear. She could not resist—it was as if her flesh required her to do this, and she began to know what the others had known, the woman with the scraped face, the children, Greer, even Rex, all the worshipers of Y-Cha. Nathan's penis was erect and dripping, and she touched it with her hand, instinctively. The petals on the flower quivered; Nathan pressed his lips to Lucy's left nipple, and licked it like he was a pup suckling and playing; he turned to Jane, his face smeared with Lucy's blood, and kissed her, slipping a soaked tongue, copper taste, into the back of her throat; she felt the light pressure of his fingers exploring between her legs, then watched as he brought her juices up to his mouth; he spread Lucy's legs apart, and applied a light pressure to the back of Jane's head.

For an instant, she tried to resist.

But the tattoos of monkeys played there, along the thatch of hair, like some unexplored patch of jungle, and she found herself wanting to lap at the small withered lips that Nathan parted with his fingers.

Beneath her mouth, the body began to move.

Slowly at first.

83

Then more swiftly, bucking against her lips, against her teeth, the monkey drawings chattered and spun.

She felt Nathan's teeth come down on her shoulder as she licked the woman.

He began shredding her skin, and the pain would've been unbearable, except she felt herself opening up below, for him, for the trembling woman beneath her, and the pain slowed as she heard her flesh rip beneath Nathan's teeth, she was part of it, too, eating the dying woman who shook with orgasm, and the blood like a river.

A glimpse of her, not Lucy.

Not Lucy.

But Monkey God.

Y-Cha.

You suffer greatly. You suffer and do not die. Y-Cha may leave her prison.

She could not tell where Nathan left off and where she began, or whether it was her mouth or the dying woman's vagina that opened in a moan that was not pleasure, but was beyond the threshold of any pain she had ever imagined in the whole of creation.

She ripped flesh, devouring, blood coursing across her chin, down her breasts, Nathan inside her now, more than inside her, rocking within her, complete love through the flesh, through the blood, through the wilderness of frenzy, through the small hole between her legs, into the cavern of her body, and Y-Cha, united with her lover through the suffering of a woman whose identity as Jane Boone was quickly dissolving.

Her consciousness: taste, hurt, feel, spit, bite, love.

V

In the morning, the saint slept.

His attendant, Sunil, came through the entrance to the chamber with a plate of steamed vegetables. He set them down on the table and went to get a broom to sweep up the broken ewer. When he returned, the saint awoke, and saw that he stared at his face as if he were seeing the most horrifying image ever in existence.

The saint took his hand to calm him, and placed his palm against the fresh wounds and newly formed scars.

Sunil gasped, because he was trying to fight how good it felt, as all men did when they encountered Y-Cha.

His mouth opened in a small O of pleasure.

Already, his body moved, he thrust, gently, at first, he wanted to be consort to Y-Cha.

He would beg for what he feared most, he would cry out for pain beyond his imagining, just to spill his more personal pain, the pain of life in the flesh.

It was the greatest gift of humans, their flesh, their blood, their memories. Their suffering. It was all they had, in the end, to give, for them all else was mere vanity.

Words scrawled in human suffering on a yellow wall:

*Flesh of my flesh, blood of my blood*
*I delight in your offering*
*Make of your heart a lotus of burning*

# Douglas Clegg

*Make of your loins a pleasure dome*
*I will consecrate the bread of your bones*
*And make of you a living temple to Monkey*
  *God.*

The servant opened himself to the god, and the god enjoyed the flesh as she hadn't for many days, the flesh and the blood and the beauty—for it was known among the gods that a man was most beautiful as he lay dying.

The gift of suffering was offered slowly, with equal parts delight and torment, and as she watched his pain, she could not contain her jealousy for what the man possessed.

Alice moaned, feeling his breath inside her—the boy's breath, and his fingers, digging in her scalp, in her mind, pushing through the fragments of skull and gray matter, rearranging her mind—

But he was not a boy, nor was he a girl, but something else—

Something trapped in flesh, something bound in the cage of flesh that way that she had thought they'd trapped a small boy in the basement of an old tenement building

"Let me show you my garden, Alice," he whispered. "You like gardens, don't you? I know a place where the gardens are lovely, quite lovely. The flowers . . . "

She felt his small hand as it touched the edge of her cheek, curling slightly.

"The most beautiful flower that ever was."

And then she felt his hand press into the flesh of her face and grow inside her.

"Do you know," he asked, "what human love is, Alice? Do you?"

"No," Alice moaned, trying to push him away, but his fingers seemed to be inside her face, behind her eyes, moving something within her, forcing it to see what he wanted her to see, to experience the world he carried like a virus in his touch—

# O, Rare and Most Exquisite

"What is human love?" I have heard my mother ask when she was sick, or when she was weary from the rotted wood dams of marriage and children. It's a question that haunts my every waking hour. I, myself, never experienced love, not the kind between a man and a woman. I once learned about it secondhand. When I was seventeen, I worked in a retirement home, in the cafeteria, and on my afternoons off I went up to the third floor. This was the nursing facility, and I suppose I went there to feel needed; all the elderly patients needed attention, often someone to just sit with them, hold their hands, watch the sun as it stretched down across the far-off trees heavy with summer green. I don't know why I was so taken with the older people, but I felt more comfortable around them than I often did around my peers. One day, an old man was shouting from his bed, "O, rare and most exquisite! O, God, O God, O, rare and most exquisite creation! Why hast thou forsaken me?" His voice was strong and echoed down the slick corridor; his neighbors, in adjacent beds, cried out for relief from his moans and groans. Since the orderlies ignored all this, routinely, I went to his room to find out what the trouble was about.

He was a ruffian. Bastards always lived the longest, it was a rule of thumb on the nursing floor, and this man was a prince among bastards. Something about the lizard leather of his skin, and the grease of his hair, and the way his forehead dug into his eyebrows as if he were trying to close his translucent blue eyes by forcing the thick skin down over them. He had no kindness in him; but I sat down on the edge of his bed, patted his hand, which shook, and asked him what the matter was.

"Love," he said. "All my life, I pursued nothing but love. And look where it's gotten me." He was a rasping old crow, the kind my brother used to shoot at in trees.

"Did you have lunch yet?" I asked, because I knew that the patients would become irritable if they hadn't eaten.

"I will not eat this raw sewage you call food."

"You can have roast beef, if you want. And pie."

"I will not eat." He closed his eyes, and I thought he was about to go to sleep, so I began to get up off the bed. He whispered, coughing a bit, "Bring me the box under the bed."

90

I did as he asked. It was a cheap strongbox, the kind that could be bought in a dimestore. When I set it beside him, he reached under the blankets and brought out a small key. "Open it for me," he said. I put the tiny key in the hole, turned, and brought the lid up. The box was filled with what appeared to be sand. "Reach in it," he said, and I stuck my hands in, and felt what seemed to be a stick, or perhaps it was a quill. I took it out.

It was a dried flower, with only a few petals remaining.

"Do you know about love?" he asked me.

I grinned. "Sure."

"You're too young," he said, shaking his head. He took the dried flower from my hand and brought it up to his nose. Dust from the petals fell across his upper lip. "You think love is about kindness and dedication and caring. But it is not. It is about tearing flesh with hot pincers."

I smiled, because I didn't know what else to do. I wondered if he was sane; many of the patients were not.

He said, "This is the most rare flower that has ever existed. It is more than sixty years old. It is the most valuable thing I own. I am going to die soon, boy. Smell it. Smell it." He pressed the withered blossom into the palm of my hand, and cupped his shaking fingers under mine. "Smell it."

I lifted it up to my nose. For just a second, I thought I smelled a distant sea, and island breezes of blossoming fruit trees and perfumes. Then nothing but the rubbing alcohol and urine of the nursing floor.

"I will give this to you," he said, "to keep, if you promise to take care of it."

Without thinking, I said, "It's dead."

He shook his head, a rage flaring behind his eyes, a life in him I wouldn't have expected. "You don't know about love," he grabbed my arm, and his grip was hard as stone, "and you'll live just like I did, boy, unless you listen good, and life will give you its own whipping so that one day you'll end up in this bed smelling like this and crying out to the god of death just for escape from this idiot skin so that the pain of memory will stop."

To calm him, because now I knew he was crazy, I said, "Okay. Tell me."

"Love," he said, "is the darkest gift. It takes all that you are, and it destroys you."

And he told me about the flower of his youth.

His name was Gus, and he was a gardener at a house that overlooked the Hudson River. The year was 1925, and his employer was an invalid in his fifties, with a young wife. The wife's name was Jo, and she was from a poor family, but she had made a good marriage, for the house and grounds occupied a hundred acres. As head gardener, Gus had a staff of six beneath him. Jo would come out in the mornings, bringing coffee to the workers. She was from a family of laborers, so she understood their needs, and she encouraged their familiarity. Her husband barely noticed her, and if he did, he wouldn't approve of her mixing with the staff.

One morning she came down to Gus where he stood in the maze of roses, with the dew barely settled upon them, and she kissed him lightly on the cheek. He wasn't sure how to take this. She was wearing her robe, as she always did when she brought the coffee out to the men, although it revealed nothing of her figure. She was the most beautiful woman he had ever seen, with thick dark hair, worn long and out of fashion, a throwback to the long Victorian tresses of his mother's generation. She had almond-shaped eyes, and skin like olives soaked in brandy—he had never seen a woman this exotic in Wappingers Falls, which was his hometown. She smelled of oil and rosewater, and she did not greet him, ever, without something sweet on her lips, so that her breath was a pleasure to feel against his skin. She drew back from him, and with her heavy accent, said, "Gus, my handsome boy of flowers, what will you find for me today?"

Gus had had girls before, since he was fourteen, but they had been lust pursuits, for none of the girls of the Falls, or of Poughkeepsie, or even the college girl he had touched in Connecticut, stirred in him what he felt with Jo. He called her, to his men, "my Jo," for he felt that, if things were different, she would not be with this wealthy man with his palsied body, but with him. Gus and Jo—he wrote it on the oak tree down near the river, he carved it into a stone he had placed in the center of the rose garden.

When she kissed him on the cheek, he waited a minute, then grabbed her in his arms, for he could no longer contain himself, and they made love there, in the morning, before the sun was far up in the sky.

He knew that she loved him, so he went that day to find her the most beautiful flower that could be had. It was a passion of hers, to have the most beautiful things, for she had lived most of her life with only the ugly and the dull. He wished he were wealthy so that he might fly to China, or to the south of France, or to the stars, to bring back the rarest of blooms. But, having four bits on him, he took the train into New York City, and eventually came to a neighborhood that sold nothing but flowers, stall upon stall. But it was midsummer, and all the flowers available were the same that he could grow along the river. As he was about to leave, not knowing how he could return to his Jo without something very special, a woman near one of the stalls said, "You don't like these, do you?"

Gus turned, and there was a woman of about twenty-two. Very plain, although pretty in the way that he thought all women basically pretty. She was small and pale, and she wore no makeup, but her eyes were large and lovely. "I've been watching you," she said.

"You have?"

"Yes. Do you think that's rude? To watch someone?"

"It depends."

"I think it's rude. But then," she said, smiling like a mischievous child, "I've never been ashamed of my own behavior, only the behavior of others. I'm ashamed of yours. Here I've watched you for fifteen minutes, and you barely took your eyes off the flowers. How rude do you think that is? Very. You like flowers, don't you?"

"I'm a gardener. I take care of them."

"Lovely," she said wistfully, "imagine a life of caring for beautiful things. Imagine when you're very old, and look back on it. What lovely memories you'll have." Although she seemed forthright, the way he knew city people were, there was something fitful in the way she spoke, almost hesitant somewhere in the flow of words, as if all this snappy talk was a cover for extreme shyness. And yet, he knew, city women were rarely shy.

He had not come all the way to the city to flirt with shop girls. "I'm looking for something out of the ordinary."

She gave a curious smile, tilting her head back. She was a shade beautiful in the thin shaft of daylight that pressed between the stalls. She was no Jo, but she would make some young man fall in love with her, he knew that. Some city boy who worked in the local grocer's, or ran a bakery. Or, perhaps, even a junior bondsman. She would eventually live in one of the boxcar apartments in Brooklyn, and be the most wonderful and ordinary bride. She would have four children, and grow old without fear. Not like Jo, who was destined for romance and passion and tragedy and great redemption, not Italian Jo of olive skin and rose water. The woman said, "I know a place where you can find very unusual flowers."

"I want a beauty," he said.

"For a lady?"

Because Gus knew how women could be, and because he detected that he might get further along with this girl if he feigned interest in her, he lied. "No. Just for me. I appreciate beautiful flowers." He felt bad then, a little, because now he knew that he was leading her on, but she seemed to know where the interesting flowers were, and all he could think of was Jo and how she loved flowers. Gus was considered handsome in his day, and women often showed him special attention, so he was used to handling them, charming them. "I need a beauty," he repeated.

"I'm not saying beautiful," she cautioned him, and began walking between the stalls, through an alley, leading him, "but unusual. Sometimes unusual is better than beautiful." She wore a kind of apron, he noticed, the long kind that covered her dress, and he wondered if she was the local butcher's daughter, or if she was a cook. The alley was steamy; there was some sort of kitchen down one end of it, a Chinese laundry, too, for he smelled the soap and the meat and heard someone shouting in a foreign language, but nothing European, for Gus knew how those languages sounded, and this must've been Oriental. The woman came to an open pit, with a thin metal staircase leading down to a room, and she hiked her apron up a bit, and held her hand out for him to steady her as she descended. "My balance isn't too good," she told him. "I have a heart problem—nothing serious—but it makes me light-headed sometimes on stairs."

"There're flowers down there?" he asked as he went

down the steps slowly.

"It's one of my father's storage rooms. He has a flower shop on Seventh Avenue, but there's an icehouse above us, and we get shavings for free. They stay colder down here," she said, and turned a light up just as he had reached the last step. "There's another room three doors down, beneath the laundry. We keep some there, too."

The room was all of redbrick, and it was chilly, like winter. "We're right underneath the storage part of the icehouse." As the feeble light grew strong, he saw that they were surrounded by flowers, some of them brilliant vermillion sprays, others deep purples and blacks, still more of pile upon pile of dappled yellows on reds on greens. "These are all fresh cut," she said, "you can have any you want. My father grows them underneath the laundry, and when he cuts them, we keep them on ice until we ship them. Here," she said, reaching into a bowl that seemed to be carved out of ice. She brought up tiny red and blue blossoms, like snowballs, but in miniature. She brought them up to his face, and the aroma was incredible; it reminded him of Jo's skin when he pressed his face against her breasts and tasted the brightness of morning.

The woman kissed him, and he responded, but it was not like his kiss with Jo. This woman seemed colder, and he knew he was kissing her just because he wanted the blossoms. He remembered the cold kiss all the way to the big house, as he carried his gift to his beloved.

\* \* \*

Jo was shocked by the tiny, perfect flowers. He had left them for her in a crystal bowl of water on the dining-room table so that she would see them first when she came to have breakfast. He heard her cry out, sweetly, and then she came to the kitchen window to search the back garden for him. She tried to open it, but it had rained the night before and all that morning, so it was stuck. She rushed around to the back door, ran bare-foot into the garden and grabbed his hand. "Sweet-est—precious—blessed," she gasped, "where did you find them? Their smell—so lovely."

He had saved one small blossom in his hand. He crushed it against her neck, softly. He kissed her as if he owned her, and he told her how much he loved her.

She drew back from him then, and he saw some-thing change in her eyes. "No," she said.

When the flowers had died, he ventured back into the city, down the alley, but the entrance to the pit was closed. He rapped on the metal doors several times, but there was no response. He went around to the entrance to the icehouse and asked the manager there about the flowers, but he seemed to not know much about it other than the fact that the storage room was closed for the day. Gus was desperate, had brought his month's pay in order to buy armloads of the flowers, but instead, ended up in an Irish bar on Horace Street drinking away most of it. Jo didn't love him, he knew that now. How could he be such a fool, anyway? Jo could never leave her husband, never in a thousand years. Oh, but for another moment in her arms, another moment of that sweet mystery of her breath against his neck!

He stayed in the city overnight, sleeping in a flophouse, and was up early, and this time went to the Chinese laundry. The man who ran it took him to the back room, where the steam thickened. Gus heard the sounds of machines being pushed and pressed and clanked and rapped, as a dozen or more people worked in the hot fog of the shop. The owner took him farther back, until they came to a stairway.

"Down." The man said nodding, then disappeared into the fog.

Gus went down the stairs, never sure when he would touch bottom, for the steam was still heavy. When he finally got to the floor, it dissipated a bit, and there was a sickly yellow light a ways off. He went toward it, brushing against what he assumed were flowers growing in their pots.

Then someone touched his arm.

"Gus." It was the woman from the week before. "It's me. Moira."

"I didn't know your name," he told her. "I didn't know how to find you."

"How long did the flower last?"

"Six days."

"How sad," she said, and leaned against him. He kissed her, but the way he would kiss his sister, because he didn't really want to lead her on.

The mist from the laundry enveloped the outline of her face, causing her skin to shine a yellow-white like candles in luminaria, revealing years that he had not anticipated—he had thought she might be a girl in her early twenties, but in this steam she appeared older, ashes shining under her skin.

"I loved the flowers."

"What else do you love, Gus?"

He didn't answer. He pulled away from her, and felt the edges of thick-lipped petals.

She said, "We keep the exotics here. There's an orchid from the Fiji Islands—it's not properly an orchid, but it has the look of one. It's tiny, but very rare. In its natural state, it's a parasite on fruit trees, but here, it's the most beautiful thing in the world."

"I never paid you for the last flower."

"Gus," she said, and reached up to cup the side of his face in the palm of her hand, "whatever is mine, is yours."

She retreated into the mist, and in a few moments laid in the palm of his hand a flower so small that he could barely see it. She set another of its kind into a jewelry box and said, "This is more precious than any jewel I know of. But if I give it to you, I want you to tell me one thing."

He waited to hear her request.

"I want you to tell me—no, promise me—you will take care of this better than those last ones. This should live, if cared for, for over a month. You do love flowers, don't you?"

"Yes," he said, and, because he wanted this tiny flower so much for his Jo, he brought Moira close to him and pressed his lips against hers, and kissed around her glowing face, tasting the steam from the laundry. He wanted it so badly, he knew this flower would somehow win his Jo. Somehow, she would manage to leave her husband, and they would run away together, maybe even to the Fiji Islands to live off mango and to braid beautiful Jo's hair with the island parasite flowers.

Yet there was something about Moira that he liked, too. She wasn't Jo, but she was different from any woman he knew. When he drew his face back from hers, her face was radiant and shining, and not the middle-aged woman he had thought just a minute before. She was a young girl, after all, barely out of her teens, with all the enthusiasm of fresh, new life. He wondered what his life would be like with a girl like this, what living in the city with her would feel like, what it would be like to live surrounded by the frozen and burning flowers.

There were tears in Moira's eyes when she left him, and he sensed that she knew why he wanted the beautiful flowers.

And still, she gave him the rare and exquisite ruby blossom.

The tiny flower died in fourteen days. Gus could not return to the city for more than six weeks, because a drought had come down the valley, and he had to take special pains to make sure that the gardens didn't die. Jo did not come and see him, and he knew that it was for the best. She was married, he was merely the gardener, and no matter how many gorgeous flowers he brought to her, she would never be his. He thought of

Moira, and her sweetness and mystery; her generosity was something he had never experienced before in a woman, for the ones he had known were often selfish and arrogant in their beauty. He also knew that the old man must suspect his overfamiliarity with Jo, and so his days would be numbered in the Hudson River house.

One afternoon he took off again for the city, but it took several hours, as there was an automobile stuck on the tracks just before coming into Grand Central Station. He got there in the evening, and went to the Chinese laundry, but both it and the icehouse were closed for the day. He remembered that Moira had mentioned her father's shop, and so he went into the flower district and scoured each one, asking after her. Finally, he came to the shop on Seventh Avenue and there she was, sitting behind a counter arranging iris into a spraylike arrangement. She turned to see him, and in the light of early evening she was the simple girl he had seen the first day they had met. How the mist and the ice could change her features, but in the daylight world, she was who she was!

"Gus," she said, "I thought you weren't coming back. Ever."

"I had to," he said, not able to help his grin, or the sweat of fear that evaporated along his forehead, fear that he would not find her. It was like in the moving pictures, when the lover and his beloved were reunited at the end. He ran around the counter and grabbed her up in his arms, "Oh, Moira, Moira," he buried his face in her neck, and she was laughing freely, happily.

She closed the shop and pulled down the shade. "Gus, I want you to know, I love you. I know you might not love me, but I love you."

Gus sighed and looked at her. Here he was, a gardener, and she, a flower shop girl. How could a more perfect pair be created, one for the other?

"There's something I want to give you," she said.

"You've given me—" he began, but she didn't let him finish.

"Something I want to give you," she began unbuttoning the top of her blouse.

When she was completely naked, he saw what was different about her. "I could never give my heart freely . . . knowing I was . . . different . . . like this . . . "

He stepped back, away from her.

"Who did this to you?" he asked, his voice trembling.

She looked at him with those wide, perfect eyes, and said, "I was born this way."

The threads.

There, in the whiteness of her thighs.

He was horrified, and fascinated, for he had never seen this before.

Her genitals had been sewn together, you see, with some thread that was strong, yet silken and impossibly slender, like a spider's web. She brought his hand there, to the center of her being, and she asked him to be careful with her. "As careful as you are with the flowers."

"It's monstrous," he said, trying to hide the revulsion in his voice, trying to draw back his fingers.

"Break the threads," she said, "and I will show you the most beautiful flower that has ever been created in the universe."

"I can't." He shivered.

Tears welled in her eyes. "I love you with all my being," she said, "and I want to give you this . . . this . . . even if it means . . . " Her voice trailed off.

He found himself plucking at the threads, then pulling at them, until finally he got down on his hands and knees and placed his mouth there, and bit into the threads to open her.

There must have been some pain, but she only cried out once, then was silent.

Her labia parted, curling back, blossoming, and there was a smell, no, a scent, like a spice wind across a tropical shore, and the labia were petals, until her pelvis opened, prolapsed like a flower blooming suddenly, in one night, and her skin folded backward on itself, with streaks of red and yellow and white bursting forth from the wound, from the pollen that spread golden, and the wonderful colors that radiated from between her thighs, until there was nothing but flower.

He cupped his hands around it. It was the most exotic flower he had ever seen, in his hands, it was the beauty that had been inside her, and she had allowed him to open her, to hold this rare flower in his hands.

Gus wondered if he had gone insane, or if this indeed was the most precious of all flowers, this gift of love, this sacrifice that she had made for him.

\* \* \*

He concealed the bloom in a hatbox and carried it back to the estate with him. In the morning, he entered the great house without knocking, and his heart pounded as loud as his footsteps as he crossed the grand foyer. He called to the mistress of the house boldly: "Jo!" he shouted, "Jo! Look what I have brought you!" He didn't care if the old man heard him, he didn't care if he would be without a job, none of it mattered, for he had found the greatest gift for his Jo, the woman who would not now deny him. He knew he loved her now, his Jo, he knew what love was now, what the sacrifice of love meant.

She was already dressed for riding, and she blushed when she saw him. "You shouldn't come in like this. You have no right."

He opened the hatbox and retrieved the flower.

"This is for you," he said, and she ran to him, taking it up in her hands, smelling it, wiping its petals across her lips.

"It's beautiful," she said, smiling, clasping his hand, and just as quickly letting go. "Darling," she called out, turning to the staircase, "darling, look at the lovely flower our Gus has brought us, look," and like a young girl in love, she ran up the stairs, with the flower, to the bedroom where the old man coughed and wheezed.

Gus stood there, in the hall, feeling as if his heart had stopped.

"It was three days later," he told me as I sat on the edge of the nursing room bed, "that the flower died, and Jo put it out with the garbage. But I retrieved it, what was left of it, so that I would always remember that love. What love was. What terror it is."

The old man finally let go of my arm, and I stood. He was crying, like a baby, as if there were not enough tears in a human body to let go of, and he was squeezing his eyes to make more.

"It's all right," I said, "it's just a bad dream. Just like a bad dream."

"But it happened, boy," he said, and he passed me the flower. "I want you to keep this. I'm going to die someday soon. Maybe within a month, who knows?"

"I couldn't," I said, shaking my head. "It's yours."

"No," he said, grinning madly, "it never was mine. Have you ever been with a woman, boy?"

I shook my head. "Not yet."

"How old are you?"

"Seventeen. Just last month."

"Ah, seventeen. A special time. What do you think human love is, boy?"

I shrugged. "Caring. Between people. I guess."

"Oh, no," his smile blossomed across his face, "it's not caring, boy, it's not caring. What it is, is opening your skin up to someone else, and opening theirs, too. Everything I told you is true, boy. I want you to take this dried flower—"

I held it in my hand. For a moment I believed his story, and I found myself feeling sad, too. I thought of her, of Moira, giving herself up like that. "She loved you."

"Her? She never loved me," he said. "Never."

"How can you say that? You just told me—"

His voice deepened, and he sounded as evil as I have ever heard a man sound. "Jo never loved me."

I looked again at the dried flower. He plucked it from my fingers and held the last of its petals in his open palm.

He said, "You thought that was Moira? Oh, no, boy, I buried her beneath the garden. This is Jo. She finally left her husband for me. And then, when I had her . . . O, Lord, when I had her, boy, I tore her apart, I made her bloom, and I left her to dry in sand the way she had dried my heart." He laughed, clinging more tightly to my arm so that I could not get away. "Her flower was not as pretty as Moira's. Moira. Lovely Moira." He sniffed the air, as if he could still smell the fragrance of the opening flower. "I made Jo bloom, boy, and then I stepped on her flower, and I kept it in darkness and dust. Now, boy, that's what love is." He laughed even while he crushed the dried blossom with his free hand.

"O, rare and most exquisite!" He shouted after me as I pulled away from him and backed out of that madman's room.

"O, why," he laughed, "why hast thou forsaken me?"

"We'll let you go." Alice moaned, the pain within her like being hooked up to machines in a hospital and forced to breathe air, to see things, to feel the touch of so many. "We won't hurt you. You can go home."

"I don't wish to be free," the boy said as he caressed her neck, rubbing his hand beneath it, feeling for the place where her blood pumped. "If I wish to be free, I would not have been waiting there in that child's bedroom. Waiting for your two sons to take me and hit me on the head and wrap me in a blanket. Do you know what they called you when they threw my body in the back of their van? They called you a bitch. They called you a fucked-up bitch. Did you know that's how your children felt about you?"

"Stop it, you're lying," Alice said, reaching up to push herself away from him.

Her hands met air.

The boy was not lying next to her at all.

She sat up in the room, the lights still flickering blue and white.

The little boy was no longer on the mattress—the handcuffs were empty.

She glanced about the room. The wheelchair, overturned, a few feet away from her.

But she sensed something, and could smell that stench—his stench.

Its stench.

She glanced up.

Hovering midair in a corner, a little girl glared at her. No—not glared at her, for the girl's eyes were shut. The girl looked like an old print Alice had once owned—a print of a famous painting by Renoir—of a girl with golden hair playing with a hoop. The girl looked like that girl in the painting, only her eyes were sewn shut with some black thread.

"You like magic tricks?" the girl asked.

"No," Alice said, sitting up. The wheelchair was not far. If she crawled . . .

"I could make you walk again, if you wanted to. If you wanted to badly enough," the girl said.

Alice kept watch on the girl and slowly pulled herself down across the mattress, toward her wheelchair.

"I could make those legs work, and then you wouldn't need that chair," the girl said.

Alice stopped. "Are you the devil?" she asked, and began weeping. "Of course I want to walk again! What kind of monster are you?" She shuddered, the tears pouring forth as if all of her had become liquid.

The girl shook her head. "There is no devil. Don't you know that? There is no devil."

After she'd wiped away the tears, Alice looked up at her again. "Then what are you?"

The girl raised her hand to her forehead. "I know what you're thinking right now, Alice. I know what you want to do." She began giggling, and covered her mouth with both hands. "You can't run from me, Alice. We've bonded, you and I. We are in each other's minds now."

Then the girl evaporated slowly from the wall, and in her place, a dark mound of flies. Alice watched them, frozen by the fear that she had lost her mind in all this—that the little boy was still chained to the mattress, but that Alice had finally stepped off the path of sanity as she'd feared. As her father had one bright spring day, gibbering about visions he saw, about devils who tormented him.

This is all, Alice thought. I'm losing my mind. But the world is still as it should be.

Then the flies swooped down upon her, covering her, crawling inside the openings they could pry with their small bodies.

I'm somewhere else, Alice thought as she felt them crawl inside her. I'm not here, I'm far away. I'm in another place. . . .

110

# *Only Connect*

## I

Watch the scenery awhile. It'll take your mind off the pain. I'll tell you all about him, if you'll just listen. You must never breathe a word of this to anyone, but I can tell you're simpatico—you won't betray me.

His name was Jim, and he worked at the train station taking tickets. He grew up in Hartford, but moved to Deerwich-On-Sparrow, called Deerwich by most, on the Connecticut coast—in his early twenties, the job had seemed good. He'd begun his career riding the rails taking tickets and cleaning the cars, but he'd moved up so that at twenty-nine he could sit behind the glass and say, "Round-trip to Boston leaves at 9:15. That'll be 49.50." His head often pounded when it rained, and he was prone to popping aspirin as if it were hard candy and just sucking on it until the headache went away. The sound of the train as it arrived in the station aggravated his condition, but Jim had begun to think of the headaches as normal. He'd long before forgotten that they had never existed before he began working with the railroad.

It was the train wreck that had begun his journey toward discovery. One night, fairly late for the train—which had been due in before midnight—there was an awful screeching, from some great distance along the track. The old-timers knew what this meant, and they all ran out to see the spectacle. All except for Jim, who stayed back.

He went to grab another bottle of aspirin from beneath his perch. He felt around, but all his fingers found was a completely empty bottle. He stood from his stool, stretching, yawning. Outside, he heard the scraping of metal—the train, he would later learn, went over an embankment, into the river, and some child some-where would be blamed for playing quarters on the tracks—the shouts of onlookers as the train tossed like a restless sleeper from its bed—but Jim took the opportunity to walk across the street to the drugstore for aspirin.

Inside the store, the fluorescent lights flickered. The old man who worked the pharmacy stood up on his platform behind the white counter, measuring his nos-trums and philters. Jim walked the aisles, glancing briefly at the magazine covers and the greeting card displays. Finally, he turned the last aisle and saw the large bottles of aspirin.

The fluorescent light above his head flickered in a dark way, as if it were just about to go out. As Jim reached for the aspirin bottle, he watched as his hand seemed to go through water and touch—not a bottle of aspirin, but a green tile on a bathroom wall. As the light flickered again, he sensed that he was no longer in a drugstore down near the train station in Old Deerwich, but in a small bathroom with lime-green tiles and a large mirror above the toilet. He glanced in the mirror and for a moment thought he saw the aisles of the drugstore behind his reflection, but this faded, and all was green tile.

He almost said something, as if someone stood near him, but he was most definitely alone.

He turned about, facing a door. He pushed at the door, and it opened out onto a room that was all green and white and smelled of rubbing alcohol with an undersmell of urine. Flowers on the windowsill. The window looked out on a courtyard and garden, and there, as he went to look out it, were a half a dozen or more patients. He knew they were patients by their bathrobes and by the nurses that pushed some of the wheelchairs, or stood beside a patient who used a walker or cane to get around. Across the courtyard, a silver-metal building, probably precisely like the one he occupied at the moment.

"Mrs. Earnshaw," someone said at the door. British accent. He knew he was in a British hospital.

Jim turned, sensing others' presence in the room.

The fluorescent lamp flickered a liquid green.

Jim glanced up at the light overhead—a large brown water blotch spread like the profile of a face next to the ice-tray lamps.

"It's terrible," someone said as he glanced down again.

He was in the drugstore, holding a bottle of aspirin in his hand. A woman looked up at him queerly.

"I can't imagine anyone survived."

Jim had to squint a moment to focus on his new environment. His head throbbed now. He calmed himself with the thought that the pain in his head had caused the brief and vivid hallucination of the hospital room.

The little old woman, half bent over, reached for a box of arthritis pain reliever. "Did you see it?"

"No," Jim said. Then, "See what?"

"The crash. I was in my car and driving down Water Street, and I heard it. It was terrible. It's so unsafe."

"Yes." Jim nodded.

"Travel is always dangerous. To get there from here, one must risk one's life these days," she said, nodding as if they'd understood each other.

Jim stood there a moment. Then, feverishly, he opened the jar of pills and grabbed three, tossing them down his throat.

When he paid for the bottle, the pharmacist said, "Finally found what you wanted."

"Excuse me?"

"The aspirin. I saw you standing there reading labels for nearly half an hour."

"Half an hour?"

"Bad headache, huh? You probably drink too much caffeine."

Jim walked out into the rain, feeling as if he still vibrated with his hallucination. He remembered his brief romance with peyote in college, and began to worry that this might be the flashback from that. He forgot about it for days—the hospital—and buried himself in work.

The photograph in the local papers showed all angles of the train crash. It had fallen on its side, plunging seventy-nine people into the river, all of whom died. Another two hundred and fifteen people were injured.

What struck Jim most about the pictures of the fallen train was that it looked—if you squinted at the photos—like a sleeping person made entirely of metal, lying on a gray blanket.

The flashes began a week or two later.

The first time, when he tried to unlock his car, a small Honda Civic, and found that the lock was jammed. He twisted the key so hard that it broke off in his hand. Again, the headache kicked in, and he saw the aspirin bottle on the passenger seat inside the car. He felt angry suddenly—angry at the car for not opening, angry at his job for its dullness, angry at his parents for not really preparing him for the world in the way he'd wished.

Then the flash—he thought it was heat lightning. In the same moment, he was in the hospital again. This time, he sat in a wheelchair in the courtyard as a light rain fell.

"You all right, now?"

"Yes," he said, adapting quickly to his new environment. "It's only a little rain."

"A little rain." The pretty nurse beside him smiled. "Yes, that's all it is. But all the others have gone inside."

He looked about the path through the garden with its iris and hibiscus, and saw that they were indeed alone. The silver of the buildings dulled in the gray rain, but he liked the fresh smell of it.

"What's your name?" he asked her.

"Nora," she said, glancing up from her magazine.

"Your reading's going to get soaked," he said, nodding.

"I don't mind. It's only a little rain, after all." She had a warm smile, and her eyes were a toasty brown. "Been feeling good today, then, have we?"

"Very," Jim said. "The pains are gone."

"A few days is what they said."

"Yes, and they were right," Jim said.

Then he bit his tongue slightly. "Where am I?"

"Holyrood," she said.

"What town?"

"Oh, you." Nora laughed. "More tricks. Is this like that dream you told me about? The one where you're a railroad man taking tickets in some little town in—Where was it?"

"Connecticut."

"That's right. Connecticut. The effects should've worn off by now," Nora said, glancing at her watch. "You were only on the IV for two hours before ten. It's nearly three." Then she reached over, patting Jim's hand. "All of this for just a little information. It does seem daft, doesn't it? You holding up? No more weeping at midnight?"

"No," Jim said, feeling more lost and yet extremely comfortable. "Was it the aspirin?"

"Or lack thereof," Nora said. "Do you ever read these?" She held the magazine up. It was the *London TellTale* magazine. "All these royals and celebs knocking each other up. You'd think they'd have other things to occupy them, don't you?"

"What town are we in?" he asked.

"Why," Nora shook her head, glancing at the magazine, "just look at what the Prince is up to today." Then, "What, dear? Town? Does it matter?"

"Yes."

"I'm sorry, I'm not supposed to tell too much. You know that more than anyone, Mrs. Earnshaw."

Jim felt a warm salty taste in the back of his throat. He glanced down at the hand that she had just finished patting. It was the hand of a middle-aged woman, and the hospital bracelet he wore read, "Catherine Earnshaw."

When the lightning flashed overhead and the rain began coming down in earnest, Nora said, "Oh, dear, let's get the two of us in out of this nasty weather, shall we?" But then there was no Nora, and she faded, and all that was there was the Honda and the rain and his headache and a man who was not sure why he was going mad at the age of twenty-nine.

## II

You didn't think he was married? Well, of course Jim was married—they'd tied the knot at twenty-four, almost got divorced at twenty-seven, but managed for a couple of more years because their jobs put them at opposite shifts so that every weekend was a honeymoon. Her name was Alice, and she worked at the sandwich shop on Bank Street. When she got off work at five, she went first to the library, since she was an avid reader, and then to the video shop. Her evenings, while Jim worked late, were mainly spent with the cat and a good book and a mediocre movie nine times out of ten. She'd slip into bed around midnight, fall asleep with a glass of wine, and then feel him next to her just before she got fully awake at seven in the morning. She'd cuddle with him, unbeknownst to Jim, and then get up to make a pot of coffee and begin the day again.

The movie that night was to be an old musical, and the novel, a light romance to take her mind off her worries. She slipped into the tub at about seven-fifteen, and while she dried herself off, the bathroom door opened. At first Alice was frightened, but she saw quickly it was her husband.

"Jim? What are you doing home?"

"Called in sick," he said. "I've been napping since six."

"Migraine? Poor baby."

"It's not that." But he nodded anyway.

"Come here," Alice said, reaching her hand out. Jim approached her, his head down. She touched the back of his neck, squeezing lightly. "You're tense."

"Baby, I think I'm going nuts," he said.

"You've been nuts a long time."

"I mean it," he said, and his tone was so serious it almost shocked her.

Later, by the fire, she held him and told him it would be all right, and he wept.

Then he told her.

At first she had a hard time not laughing.

But when he told her the woman's name, she cackled.

He looked hurt.

"Oh, honey, that's a name from a book. Catherine Earnshaw. It's from *Wuthering Heights*. You must have seen the movie."

He shook his head. "Was she in a hospital?"

Alice grinned. Her grin was not as warm as Nora's, but it was familiar. "No, no. It must be some kind of dream brought on by those headaches. Let's get you into the doctor's for a checkup."

"A head exam?"

"So you're an invalid woman in a British hospital with silver buildings and your name is Catherine Earnshaw. What an imagination," Alice said, kissing his forehead. "My big baby. It's your job. It's getting to you. I told you you needed to finish your degree and maybe get into computers or something."

Jim smelled her hair—like petals on a wet bough—and glanced at the fire as the flames spat and curled and flickered. He closed his eyes, his head beginning to pound, but he was going to fight it off, the pain, the throbbing, the near blindness that the headaches brought with them when at their worst.

When he opened his eyes, he was sitting in a large white room with no windows. In an uncomfortably hard chair. In a circle, with others. Some men, a few women—nine in all. The nurses stood toward the back, sitting on chairs, crossing and uncrossing their legs, looking at their watches now and then, seeming to reach into their breast pockets for cigarettes or mints or something they needed desperately but were unwilling to give themselves.

A man sitting across from Jim was talking, and gradually Jim began to understand what he was saying.

"It's not as if we all aren't going through the same thing. What did they call it? Adjustment?"

A woman laughed. "Mine told me to get used to it."

Someone else chuckled at this. "I was told it was a period of containment."

"Well, it's been working for me to some small extent," the man continued, his voice slight and nervous as if he were afraid of being overheard or of making a mistake in what he said. "At least in the mornings. The mornings are good. It's only about now."

"Yes," another man said, just to the left of Jim. "At about three every day. Sometimes as late as four. These flashes."

"Flashes of insight," a woman said.

"Hot flashes," another woman said, and they all had a good laugh. "Not that you can't have those, Norman."

Norman, the man who had originally been talking, blushed. He was handsome, mid-forties, and reminded Jim a bit of his father. Actually, the more he spoke, the more Jim was becoming convinced that Norman was related to him in some way. The thin tall frame, the thick black hair, the nose a bit beaky and the chin a bit strong and the teeth a bit much. "Well," Norman said, "since we're all in this together, and since they," and he nodded backward, to the row of nurses behind him, "seem to want us to get it all out in these groups, I think we should tell everything we know."

"Not everything," a man said. "I couldn't. It'd be too much."

"All right, then," Norman said. "Whatever we feel comfortable with."

"You'll have to begin, then, Norman. Mine is rather embarrassing," the laughing woman said. "It involves me and another man, and I can't tell you what we seem to do all day long."

More laughter.

"Mine is not that . . . invigorating." Norman smiled. "I'm just a little boy of ten, perhaps eleven. I live in a small village in Morocco."

"Good Lord, not Morocco," the woman said. "Are you a Berber bed-warmer?"

Norman lost his smile. "No, I just help bring water to the house and do a bit of feeding of animals and cleaning and running errands. I'm constantly hungry, and I can't seem to talk with others there, but I can understand them."

"Oh!" the woman gasped. "So interesting compared to mine. I'm the wife to a man who hallucinates."

Jim almost laughed; something in him told him to laugh a bit. He glanced down at his hands and saw the wedding ring on the left hand. He drew it carefully off his finger as the woman told her story. He looked inside the ring. "Cathy and Cliff Forever."

"Yes, and while he's at work in his dull job, I go have mad affairs up and down Main Street," the woman continued, "only . . . it's not called Main Street. I find this entertaining, if disconcerting. My husband really is a fool. He surprised me a bit today, however."

Jim reached up and felt his neck. It was slender. He drew his fingers across his throat and up around his chin—a small slightly round chin—up to his fullish lips, his small nose, around his eyelashes, which seemed long and feathery.

"Dear," someone whispered behind him, "you'll smudge your makeup."

He recognized the voice; it was Nora.

He put his hands down.

"You should listen to the stories," Nora whispered. "It might help your condition?"

Jim nodded, glancing over to the woman who was just finishing up hers.

"He hasn't a clue," she said. "He lies constantly himself. It's easy to fool a liar." She looked over at

Jim. "Mrs. Earnshaw, you haven't told yours, have you?"

The woman seemed to look at Jim with a special knowledge. He began to feel his skin crawl a bit. A coldness seeped into his voice as he spoke.

"There's not much to tell, really. To be honest, I think I'm more there than here." Laughter across the room. "This feels less me than the other. I know so much about him."

"Him?" The woman laughed. "Oh, Lord, you got to change sex. Do you play with it much?"

"Juliet!" the man named Norman exclaimed. "What a filthy mind you have."

Jim felt slightly offended, particularly for Mrs. Earnshaw, whom he imagined to be a very circumspect and polite woman of fifty-two. "Really," he said. He reached down, smoothing the lines of the bathrobe. "Even now, sitting among you, I feel more him than me."

"Tell us about him," Norman said.

"Yes," another chimed in.

"Perhaps I will." Jim paused a moment, wondering where to begin. "He's a nice young man in his late twenties who works for the rails in a little New England town. He is happily married, drives some kind of Japanese car, an older model, and likes rock and roll music from the 1950s. He has terrible headaches . . ."

After a moment, Jim continued. "Actually, I am more sure I'm him than I am sure that I am me."

Norman's eyes lit up as he nodded. "That's how it's

supposed to be, isn't it? They said you get a gleam at first."

"A glimmer," the woman named Juliet said. The smile on her face grew impossibly wide. "They called it a glimmer. It feels like . . . like . . . "

"A warm rain," another said.

"Yes, and then," Norman nodded as if feeling a religious transformation, "the warmth spreads over you."

"Like you've been rewired," another said.

The woman next to him said, "Well, Mrs. Earnshaw's certainly been rewired if she's a man now."

"He's not just a man," Jim said, and for the first time noticed that he spoke with Mrs. Earnshaw's voice. "He's a special young man. He doesn't know it yet, but he's very special."

Behind him, Nora touched his shoulder. She whispered, "I knew you'd be the first, Mrs. Earnshaw."

Jim leaned his head back slightly. "The first to what, dear?"

"The first to cross the bridge," the nurse said.

*III*

When Jim next recollected anything, he was in bed with Alice, his wife, in their small apartment on Hop Street, the peppermint smell of the nearby toothpaste factory assaulting his senses. Alice was snoring lightly, and as Jim glanced around in the scrim darkness, moonlight and the summer steam pouring in through the open window, he saw evidence of sexual abandon—the packet of condoms, open, on the dressing table, the clothes strewn about the floor in a trail, the half-empty glasses of red wine, one spilled on the carpet. Had they been animals? He wished he could remember. Because of their schedules, they didn't make love all that often, and now he had been in some kind of dream support group in a British hospital rather than in his Alice.

Then a disturbing thought occurred to him: was someone else occupying his own body while he occupied Mrs. Earnshaw's? Did Mrs. Earnshaw herself enter his skin and make love to Alice, drink his wine?

He sat up most of the night, just watching Alice as she slept. Sweet Alice, lost in some dreamworld . . . She stirred, her fingers curled, once, her hand went to her throat, once, she seemed to weep but it was like a puppy sound—a puppy at the door to a room that she wanted to be set free from.

She awoke in the early morning, her eyes opening wide. "What are you doing?"

"Nothing," he said. "Just watching you."

"Why?" She wiped her face with her hands as if washing off a mask of sleep. "You scared me for a moment."

"What was it like?"

"What?"

"What we did last night."

"Weren't you there?" She grinned, giggling.

"I'm not sure."

"Oh stop it. It's too early for jokes." She looked

across the bed to the clock. "It's only five-thirty. I can sleep some more. That is," she arched an eyebrow, "if you'd quit staring."

She turned over, facing the window. The sunlight had crept up. "Can you close the curtains," she said. "I need some dark."

*IV*

Jim wandered downtown, walked along the river, along the railroad tracks, alongside the boatslips and the chemical factory—miles of walking at dawn, when the town seemed to wake like a baby, from a gasp to a full cry. When the sun was fully up, he got a cup of coffee from the doughnut shop and walked out to the pier, watching the ferry as it crossed to New-buryport.

The 7:15 blew its whistle, coming into the station, and he turned to watch it—remembering the train crash of a few weeks earlier, and the first time he remembered being in the silver British hospital as Mrs. Earnshaw.

Then it came to him. That had not been the first time. That had been the first time he'd remembered it so vividly. Closing his eyes, he recalled an incident when he'd been four or five, and he'd been in a hospi-tal—was it the same one? Only, it was not in England. It had been in Massachusetts, when he'd been taken to visit Grammy Evans, her drinking out of control—the white and green rooms, the silver flask she hid even there to take a nip now and then when the nurses weren't looking. "Hold this," she'd said, passing him the silver flask. "Don't let them see it." So he'd hidden it in his shorts, feeling the cold metal against his thighs. Then he'd wandered the halls of the hospital while the grown-ups talked and did not notice him missing. He began playing "Spy" and decided that the doctors were Secret Agents. When he came across one, he'd run up some stairs and down some others, and through double doors and hallways with words written in bright red and yellow along them. And then he'd come to a room where four men in green masks stood about a table. On the table, a naked old woman who was probably dead. Jim had kept himself hidden away, and he watched as the four doctors injected something terrible into the old woman so that she sat up screaming.

It had made Jim scream, too, and one of the four men turned and saw him, and before he could get out the door, someone else grabbed him.

"What in God's name is this kid doing in here? Where the hell is security?" a man said.

The woman screamed again, and then began coughing.

Jim, sitting on the pier, sipped his coffee, trying to remember more, but that had been all.

What he knew without a doubt was that the woman on the table had been Mrs. Earnshaw, and that she was dead when he was a little boy and that somehow this was all a hallucination caused by a traumatic incident.

The coffee grew cold as he closed his eyes, and he determined to go into Mrs. Earnshaw in the hospital.

He willed a headache to come on, he tried to simulate the pain that arrived, and the flickering lights.

After an hour, he gave up.

Several days later, while he was sitting on the toilet, he arrived into Mrs. Earnshaw again, who was sitting in the garden with Nora. Nora was reading one of her magazines, and Jim was doing a little needlepoint.

"Nora. Tell me about myself," he said.

The nurse glanced up. "All right. I suppose this is good."

"It seems I'm losing bits of me," Jim said, nodding as if to the will of the universe. "I'm not sure where I fit in with all this."

"Well, that was the issue, after all," Nora said. She set her magazine aside and crossed her leg. "Mind if I light up?"

"Go right ahead, dear."

Nora drew a cigarette from her breast pocket and struck a match along the edge of the low brick wall she leaned against. After the first puff, she said, "You're a psychiatrist from Bristol who worked with NASA and spent a good deal of time in Belize working on the Arc Project."

"Whatever is that?"

Nora shrugged. "I wish I knew." She said this warmly and without a trace of deception. "All I know is my end of this."

"The Arc Project doesn't even sound familiar to me."

"All of you were involved with it. That's all any of us knows." Another long drag on the cigarette. "You have the mind link to this man named Jim, as do the others to various people. And you're dying."

"I had no idea," Jim said, setting his needlepoint on his lap. "Why am I called Catherine Earnshaw? That's obviously not my real name."

"You picked it. All of you picked names from books and movies. You liked the name Cathy."

"Do you know who I am, really?"

Nora closed her eyes for a minute. Smoked. Scratched a place just above her eyebrows. Opened her eyes. "Not really."

"Doesn't all of this seem inhuman?"

Nora sighed. "We have to trust that this is saving something important for us."

"Saving from what?"

Nora dropped her cigarette to the ground, stubbing it out with the toe of her white shoe. "From loss. The information has to be retained, and it's not like you're a computer that can just be downloaded."

"I wish I could remember the information you're talking about, but really, I can't. There seem to be great gaps in my memory."

"It's just the connection," Nora said. She stepped over to the wheelchair and crouched down before it. She placed her hands over Jim's and looked up into his eyes. "I know that Mrs. Earnshaw is leaving us. I know that you're this other person, this Jim. I can see you when you come into her."

Jim trembled, and felt sweat break out along his neck. "Really?"

Nora nodded. She glanced about, slightly nervous. "I have to tell you something, Jim. There's someone here who is an Intruder from the Arc Project. I'm not sure who, but Mrs. Earnshaw is in danger."

Jim shivered. "What is this all about? Am I crazy?"

Nora grinned. Then she grew serious again. "Maybe. I never would've thought I'd be involved in this too. None of us really thought it would work. But someone is after you, Jim, not here, in this hospital. But the Intruder is already trying to track you down."

"Who is the Intruder?"

"Someone who is inside one of you. Someone who wants to sabotage the entire operation. A very bad person," Nora said.

"Do you have any idea who it might be?" Jim leaned forward.

But Nora grew silent. An old man in a white jacket walked up beside them.

"Dr. Morgan."

"Here, the rain's coming again," the doctor said. "Let's get Mrs. Earnshaw inside for another series of shots, shall we?"

As Nora wheeled Jim across the path toward the door, as the first drops of rain fell, Jim whispered, "She's already dead, isn't she? Mrs. Earnshaw?"

Nora put her hand on his shoulder, squeezing slightly. She waited until they were in the corridor before she said yes.

V

And that was the last of it for Jim. He returned to work the following day, sitting behind the glass, selling tickets for the train. He tried to induce the headaches, but they seemed to be gone for good. His aspirin bottle stayed full, and he had a feeling of well-being that he almost despised. Occasionally, when he didn't even realize he was doing it, he glanced at his hands, half expecting to see Mrs. Earnshaw's in their place, her wedding ring on her slightly wrinkled left finger.

A woman said, "Two plus a child for Penn Station."

"One hundred and fifty-two," he said, typing the information into the computer.

She passed him the money, he counted it out. As he passed her the three tickets, he said, "Boarding on the river side, the train's delayed by ten minutes. Arrive Penn Station at 7:30."

She said, "I wanted to get there by seven."

He looked at her. She was forty, trim, brown hair cut short and left to fly like a halo around her face. "It won't happen."

The woman looked slightly tense. "It has to happen."

"You could try the airport."

She shook her head. "Damn it," she muttered. She reached for the tickets, grabbing them. Her husband and little girl stood back, near the benches. She turned away, then turned back. "Is this the same Deerwich where the train crashed once?"

131

Jim chuckled. "Everyone asks that. Yep, it is. Just to the north, when it crossed the bridge over the river."

The woman frowned. "It's dangerous to cross bridges. I hope there aren't too many bridges between here and Manhattan. I never fly, and I don't like to cross a bridge that's already had a crash on it. Bad luck."

She and her family went to wait for the train, but Jim sat there with his mouth open. She'd said it, and it felt like a secret code. It's dangerous to cross bridges. I don't like to cross a bridge that's already had a crash on it. Bad luck.

On his break at 9:30, he took a walk out along the tracks, trying to remember the night of the train crash when he'd first had the experience. He followed the track up to the bridge over the Sparrow River. He saw the place where it had been repaired, where the train had cut loose and gone off.

They'd blamed it on kids playing quarters, or on a faulty switch. The investigation was ongoing. Maybe they'd never know what had malfunctioned about the train on the tracks.

He stood there, staring at the tracks, and thinking about the woman complaining about the danger of travel, and remembering Nora's words: the first to cross the bridge.

And then he knew, even before he found the list of names in the newspaper of several weeks earlier.

It read like a joke list of names from books and movies, the names of the dead:

Juliet Capulet, Norman Bates, Paul Bunyan, Zazu

Pitts, Ramon Navarro, Silas Marner, Gregor Roche . . . The list of the dead included, he believed, every one he met in that group in the hospital room. Every single one.

In that list, too, was the name Catherine Earnshaw.

All just happened to be in the one car of the train in which all were killed.

Another name, too, that he recognized: Nora Fitch.

He sat down in the library with the newspaper and wept. He drank too much that night, and went wandering along the docks and backstreets, as if somehow the answer would be revealed to him if he searched hard enough. Finally, after two A.M., he ambled home.

As he lay down next to his sleeping wife, he wrapped his arms around her, wanting to feel safe from a world he did not understand, another world he'd somehow been thrust into, whether through madness or design.

Alice's skin was almost hot to the touch, and he realized she was burning with fever. She moaned slightly in her dream, and he let go of her, for her fever seemed to spread.

She woke with a start, and said, "What are you doing?"

"Sorry," he said, his breath a blast of whiskey. "I just needed to touch you."

She rolled onto her back, staring up at the ceiling. "You're drunk."

"Sure am," Jim said, wanting to touch his wife so badly, wanting to wrap himself around her and be part of her so he would not feel so alone in his madness, in his fears.

"Go to sleep," she commanded. "In the morning you'll be sober and we can talk about things."

"What things?" he asked, ready to fall into the coma of drunken sleep.

"Things about us. Things we should talk about. Things we need to talk about," Alice said. She sat up. Switched on the bedside lamp. He looked at her naked back, wishing it could be pressed against his chest and stomach.

"I love you," he whispered hoarsely, unsure whether or not he had really said it aloud or had only wanted to say it.

"I'm not who you think I am," Alice said, still not facing him. "Not anymore."

"Yes you are," he said. "Of course you are. You're my wife. You're Alice."

But he hadn't said Alice, had he? As he lay there, the fear washing over him like a warm bath, he knew he had said "You're Juliet," because something within him knew it was Juliet, the Mrs. Earnshaw part of him knew, had known, and had been trying to tell him in her own way, had been trying to tell him that this was no longer the woman he loved but a woman who called herself Juliet Capulet and might not even be a woman at all or even a human being as far as he knew.

The Mrs. Earnshaw part of him let him know that this was the Intruder in his bed.

He lay there, feeling his heartbeat accelerate as Alice slowly turned in the lamplight, a half-grin on her face. As her smile curled up and her eyes glimmered with a dark onyx that might have been shadow, might have been stone, she said, "We have to have a long talk, you and I, about what really is going on inside that mind of yours."

"Juliet?" he asked.

She smiled. "I'm Alice. Alice. Remember? Your Alice."

She sat there, watching him, and he could not sleep. In the morning, she rose and went to shower.

Jim lay there, frozen, waiting for what was to come, remembering the woman on the table surrounded by doctors. He realized that in some respects he was still there in that room watching Mrs. Earnshaw—or whoever the body had been—being brought back to life, or some form of life, some kind of intelligence within the skin that had so recently been shed.

How he had felt a presence in that room when he was only four, a presence that was not entirely human, not entirely like a middle-aged woman whose heart had given out and who now was going to have another being within her.

Just as he had felt that being, briefly, within him.

When the water stopped, he heard Alice sing as she toweled off, and then she opened the bathroom door and something that was not entirely Alice moved like silver liquid toward him.

But even as he felt something warm and metallic inject itself into his throat, he had the sense that he was not Jim at all, but something that lived within the skin of a nice lady sitting on a moving train as it headed down the New England coast.

135

*VI*

You mustn't pass this on, because I know who you are on the inside, but you haven't crossed the bridge fully, have you, dear? You're still only halfway across, feeling the warm rain, the glimmer as it warms you, but it has not burst within you yet.

Mustn't make this worse than it is. It's only a train after all, and travel by rail is so safe these days.

Look at that little town we're coming to now.

Isn't it lovely.

Across that river.

Across that bridge.

Get ready, dear. Our connection's coming up shortly

Alice opened her eyes to see the blue and white flickering lights. Just let me die, she thought. Just let me die.

"No," the little boy's voice said, tickling her ear. "Not until you beg."

# *The Fruit of Her Womb*

## I

I woke up one morning, after a nightmare, and turned to my wife. "I feel like there's no hope left in the world," I said. I felt all my sixty years seeping through in that one sentence.

Her voice was calm, and she held me. "Old man," she said, her sweet mocking, "you need to get your joy back. That's what you need."

After several such mornings, she and I had to make some decisions. We had some savings, and the left-overs of my inheritance, and I felt it was time to retire to the country. When my first pension cheek came, I told Jackie it was time for the move while we were still fairly young and able, and she went along with it because she always adapted herself to whatever was available. The truth was, I had lost my love for life, and I needed a plot of earth; I just didn't know where or when I would need to be buried in it. I wanted a small town, with woods, with groves, with jays bickering at the window and the sound of locusts in the summer evening—and then, when I turned seventy or so, I wanted to die. These were my projections, and having been an actuarist, I knew that given my height, weight, and predilection for tobacco, that death by stroke might come in the next decade.

And we found all the birds and gardens and quiet in Groveton, not two hours out of Los Angeles, and more, we found a house and I found a reason to wake up in the morning.

The house was beautiful on the outside, a mess within. It had a name: Tierraroja, because one of the owners (there had been nine) was named Redlander, and decided to Spanish it up a bit in keeping with the looks of the place. An adobe, built in the forties, it had been a featured spread in *Sunset,* The Magazine of Western Living, in 1947, as "typifying the California blend of Spanish and Midwestern influences." Its rooms were few, considering its length: three bedrooms, living room, kitchen, but enormous boxcar corridors connecting each chamber around a courtyard full of bird of paradise, trumpet-flower vine, and bougainvillea. Beyond the adobe wall to the north, crisscrossed thatches of blackberry vines, dried and mangled by incompetent gardeners, providing natural nests for foxes and opossums. Beyond this, a vast field, empty except for a few rows of orange trees, the last of its grove—ownership unknown, the field separated the property from a neighbor who lived a good four acres away.

We loved it, and the price was reasonable, as we'd just moved out of a house in the city that was smaller and more expensive. Jackie had a carpenter in to redo the kitchen cabinets the same day escrow closed. I asked the realtor about the empty field, and he reassured me that the owner, who was a very private person, had no wish to sell the vacant lot. We would have the kind of house we had dreamed of, where I could relax in my relatively early retirement (at sixty), and where Jackie could put in the art studio she'd dreamed of since she'd been twenty.

It was on the third day of our occupation of the place that we found the urn. It was ugly, misshapen from too much tossing about, a bit of faux Victoriana, dull green nymphs against a dark green background. Jackie found it at the back of the linen closet, behind some old Christmas wrapping papers that had been left behind, presumably by a previous resident. The urn was topped with a lid that looked as if it were an ashtray put to a new use, and sealed with wax.

My wife shook it. "Something inside."

"Here," I said, and she passed it to me. I gave it a couple of good shakes. "Rocks," I said. I sniff everything before I let it get too close to me; this is an odd habit at best, annoying at worst, and applies to clothes, my wife, the dog, and especially socks—a habit acquired in childhood from observing my father doing the same, and feeling a certain pride in a heightened nasal sense as if it were an inherited trait. So I put the urn to my nose. "Stinks. Like cat vomit." I looked at the pictures. Not just nymphs, but three nymphs dancing with ribbons between them. On closer inspection, I saw that the nymphs had rather nasty expressions on their faces. In one's hand was a spindle of thread, another held the thread out, and the last held a pair of scissors. "It's the Fates in some young aspect," I told my wife, remembering from my sketchy education in the Mediterranean myth pool. "See, this one spins the thread of life, this one measures it out, and this one cuts it. Or something like that."

Jackie didn't bother looking. She smiled and said, sarcastically, "You're such a classicist."

"It's pretty ugly," I said. I was ready to take it out to the trash barrel, but Jackie signaled for me to pass it to her.

"I want to keep it," she said, "I can use it for holding paintbrushes or something." Jackie was one of those people who hated to waste things; she would turn every old coffee can into something like a pencil holder or a planter, and once even tried to make broken glasses into some unusual sculpture.

My wife turned the garage into her studio. The garage door opened on both sides, so that while she painted, she could have an open-air environment; the fumes would come up at me, in the bedroom, where I stayed up nights reading, waiting for her to come to bed. But she loved her studio, loved the painting, the fumes, the oils, the ability to look out into the night and find her inspiration. I played with my computer some nights, called some buddies now and again from the old job, and read every book I could on the history of the small California town to which we had come to enjoy the good life. I was even going to have a servant, of sorts: a gardener, named Stu, highly recommended by our realtor, to tend the courtyard and to keep the blackberry bushes, ever encroaching, in check, and to bring in ripe plums in August from the two small trees in the back. I was happy about this arrangement, because I knew nothing about dirt and digging and weeding, beyond the basics. And I didn't intend to spend my retirement doing something that I seemed incapable of. Stu and I got on, barely—he was not a man of many words, and, although only ten years or so younger than I, we seemed to have no common ground to even begin a conversation. He liked his plants and bushes, and I liked my books and solitude.

Within weeks of being settled, I knew I had nothing to do with my time. I found myself going into town on small, useless errands, to get paper clips, or to see if I could find *The New York Times* at some newsstand within a fifteen-mile radius. The town, while not worth describing, was less planned than it was spontaneous; it had been a citrus-boom town before the Second World War, and after, it was a town for people to find cute places in, but to not do much else. From the freeway, it looked like stucco and smog, but from within, it was pretty, quaint, quiet, and even charming on a cool October afternoon. The library captivated my interests, since I had been a history teacher and was an avid reader. It was full of documents about the town and its architecture, fairly unique to southern California, because most of its buildings were a hundred years old rather than built since 1966.

I found our house, Tierraroja, had at least one story about it. This I learned, briefly, at first, from a local newspaper account from 1952. It seemed the Redlander family had left suddenly, and the house was empty; no one could discover the mystery of their whereabouts. When I went to the librarian, a man named Ed Laughlin, he asked me why I was so interested in the house.

"I live there," I said.

He smiled. "Yeah, right."

"No, really. My wife and I moved in the middle of September."

He chuckled. "Who's your realtor?"

I told him the name.

Again he laughed. "Should've known. She's been trying to unload that place for two years."

"Are there ghosts?" I asked, hoping that there might be just for something different.

He shook his head. "Nothing that unbelievable. Just that old Joe Redlander chopped up his wife and kids one night. Nobody knew it until about a year after they were gone. The new owners found body parts all over the place, hidden in secret places. They found Joe eventually up in Mojave, but he claimed he didn't do it. He'd found them like that, he said, but the police weren't buying because first off he ran and second off his prints were all over the ax. Heard he blew his brains out up in Atascadero or someplace like it."

*II*

I parked in front of my wife's studio; the doors were open, letting in the last of October sun, almost a light blue sunlight, through her canvases and jars, making her brown-gray hair seem almost cool and icy. I went up to her, kissed her, and looked at the painting she was doing. It was from memory, of the pond that had been behind her mother's house back in Connecticut. She had just put the light on the water; and it wasn't New England light, but sprays of California light. I waved to Stu, our gardener, who was trimming back what had in midsummer been a blossoming trumpet vine, but which was becoming, as winter approached, a tangle of gray sticks.

"He's so dedicated," Jackie said, "I think I'm going to ask him to sit for a portrait. His face—it has those wonderful crags in it. He's just about our age, but he looks younger, and then, those lines. And the way he holds the flowers sometimes." She shook her head in subtle awe, and I wondered if my wife was in the throes of a schoolgirl crush on our gardener.

"We had some murders in our house," I told her, figuring it was the best way to make her think of something other than Stu.

She grinned, shaking her head at me as if I'd been a bad boy. "Good God, you'd think you'd have better things to do than make up stories just to frighten me."

143

"No, really. I was down at the library. The guy who named our house killed his family. You're not afraid, are you?"

She gave me what I had come, through the years, to call her Look Of False Brain Damage. Then she set the large flat board she used as a palette down on the cement floor, and began dipping her brushes in turpentine. "Well, I'm finished for the day," she said. "You making dinner, or me?"

I shrugged. "I guess I can. Spaghetti or chicken?"

"Spaghetti's fine," she said, and then, bending over, picked something up. It was the urn. "I still can't get this lid off. I've been prying and prying. Think my Mister Strong-Man can do it?" She passed it to me.

I tried, but could not get the old ashtray off the urn. "You tried melting the wax?"

She shook her head. "Not yet. You're so smart and strong," mocking me, "I'm sure you can get it open for me."

I gave the urn a good shake, and heard that thing inside it again. Hard. Like a large rock. "You know," I said, "this guy Redlander chopped his wife and kids up—there were three—and then put their body parts in weird places in the house. Maybe they didn't find all of them. Maybe one of them's in here. Maybe it's the missing hand of little Katy Redlander."

Jackie made a face. "Don't you dare try and scare me."

"Maybe," I said, "it's Mrs. Redlander's left breast, all hardened around the mummified nipple."

I didn't bother trying to open the urn until after dinner. Jackie went into the living room to watch TV, and I stayed in the kitchen. I turned on the gas stove and put the edge of the urn's top near it. Wax began dripping down into the flame, making blue hisses. When the wax seemed to be loosening enough, I pulled on the ashtray, and it made a sucking sound. Then I twisted it, and it came off. I wondered if, in fact, little Katy Redlander's missing hand might not be inside the urn. I sniffed at it, and it smelled of tobacco. I held the urn up and tipped it, and out dropped a smoking pipe.

I picked it up off the floor, setting the urn on the edge of the counter. I sniffed the pipe. Smelled like cherry tobacco. A very uninteresting find, although the pipe was quite beautifully carved in rich red wood, a satyr's face. A satyr, I thought, to chase the nymphs of fate on the outside of the urn. Carved clumsily, as if by a child, into the base of the satyr's bearded chin, were the initials "J. R."

Joe Redlander.

"So that's why it's covered with an ashtray," my wife said when I showed her. "Somebody was trying to quit smoking."

"So he seals his pipe up and hides it."

"Or has someone else hide it for him."

"Joe Redlander," I said.

"Who?"

"The guy—you know, the guy I told you about."

"Oh, right. The Lizzie Borden of Groveton, California."

I paced about the room, holding the pipe in one hand, the urn in the other. Jackie kept shooing me around so she could watch TV in peace, but I kept crossing in front of her. "His wife wants him to quit smoking the pipe. But he wants it. So she seals it up and hides it. He begs her for it. He begs the kids, maybe even bribes them, to show him where Mommy put it. But the kids know better, or else they don't have a clue. And then, when it gets to be too much, he gets the ax he's chopped up all the wood with that afternoon, and he says, 'Dolores.' "

Jackie interrupted. "Dolores?"

"Whatever," I said. "Joe says, 'Nancy, if you don't tell me where my pipe is, I'm taking you and the kids out.' And she thinks he's joking, so she laughs, and he," and here I mimed whacking my invisible wife with the pipe.

As if she had a moment of supreme victory, Jackie said, "Ah, just like you and your Baskin-Robbins pistachio ice cream?"

"I never chopped you up for that, did I?"

"You would've liked to. You were going to become a blimp the way you ate it, it was a kindness to throw it out. The way you whined for days after that, you'd think I took away your soul."

I made a Three Stooges eye-poking gesture at her and an appropriate noise. "Okay, anyway, so then he goes to the kids, and they're screaming, so he does them, too. And to think, if he'd only looked behind the old wrapping paper . . . "

"The paper was old," Jackie said, "but I don't think it was from the fifties. And that pipe could've belonged to anybody. Jesus, Jim, you need a hobby."

"Look at the initials," I said to further prove my case, passing the pipe to her.

She looked at the pipe, its carved face, and then squinted at the satyr's beard.

"J. R.," I said, "Joe Redlander. The man who killed his family."

"Your initials, too, Mister Smartypants. Could be James Richter," she reminded me, "maybe the pipe's meant for you."

Later, I put some tobacco in the pipe (for I was an inveterate smoker) and lit it, as if this would give me some inspiration.

## III

I found the old crime, and the pipe and urn, occupying my thoughts after that. The wrapping paper wasn't from the fifties, I discovered, but a kind that was sold by Girl Rangers in the mid-seventies. So, I figured, someone else had found the urn, too, and had hidden it. Maybe someone else knew of its secret. I went to the linen closet and looked back at the cubbyhole where the urn had been secreted; I reached back to it and found that by pushing one of the shelves aside, there was another hiding area. I moved the towels around and brought the shelf out. I leaned forward and reached back into this newfound hole, and came up with only a wadded scrap of notebook paper. It was wrapped in a spiderweb, which I dusted off, and then unfolded the paper. It was yellowed, and the kind that had large gaps between the thin red lines—the kind of paper elementary-school-age children use before they've become adept at rocker curves and the like. In scraggly block letters in ink, it had several figures written across it. It actually looked like a pictographic language, until I realized that it was not some ancient tongue recorded, but the doodlings of perhaps a six-year-old. At the bottom, an initial: "K." I folded it neatly and put it in my pocket. I would ignore it, perhaps throw it out. I didn't even tell Jackie about finding it, because I didn't want her to know the extent to which I was fascinated by the story of the Redlander family.

I went back and read the obituaries of the old local newspaper, *The Groveton Daily*. For 1952, March 17, it listed Virginia Redlander and her children, Eric, eleven, May Lynne, nine, and Katherine, seven. So there was a Katy Redlander after all, I thought, how clairvoyant of me to have guessed it, considering I couldn't predict weather or my own wife's mood with anything greater than five percent accuracy. So little Katy had written what looked like a highly stylized hieroglyphics and had put it back in her secret place, not far from the urn.

"Or maybe you're just bored to death," Jackie said when I finally showed her the wrinkled piece of paper that had occupied my mind for three nights in a row.

We were in bed, and she was feeling amorous, while I was being indifferent to sex. "These diagrams," I said, pointing to the one that looked as if it had an eye in the middle of it, with some kind of strange animal (a unicorn?) in its iris, "you think a second-grader really did this?"

"My exact question to you," my wife said, turning over finally. "I think, Jim, maybe you need to go back into teaching at least part-time or as a substitute, because you're driving yourself and me crazy with all this weirdness."

I hadn't even noticed how weird I had become in the past few nights. I looked around my side of the king-size bed, and there were books on Egyptology, and runes, and Greek mythology. I had checked out half the local library's classical section, because those diagrams of Katy's resembled a mix of mythic images, and I wondered if there were some key to it all.

But I was being weird. So I leaned into my wife, kissing her neck. "I love you," I said.

"I was sure you were enamored of Katy Redlander's ghost."

"I'll throw those things out tomorrow," I whispered, and she turned her face so I could kiss her, and we made love that night, but it was not like it had been when I'd felt more vital. I knew, at my age, I was still fairly young, but I did not believe it, and as my wife and I held each other, afterward, I wondered why it was not as interesting as when I was twenty, or thirty, or even forty, why sex and even food were pleasures that were losing their taste for me; and I wondered why life had to slip like that, why, I thought, looking out the window at the few deciduous trees in the yard, their leaves having turned the pale yellow of California autumn, why can't we be like leaves, more beautiful when we are closer to the ends of our lives?

I thought I saw something there, as I looked at the trees, something dark against the floodlights, not quite human, trotting away from the window as if it had just watched us.

## IV

In the morning I went to check the window, as if I would see footprints, but there were none. Jackie skipped her painting that day, and was going to drive into Los Angeles to visit with a friend, so I took to wandering. The empty field that bordered us beckoned me with its orange trees, for they held small but juicy yellow-green fruit, and I decided it was high time to pick an orange right from the tree. The grass in the field was just turning green again because of a recent rain, and I waded through it, mindful of snakes and fire ants. When I approached the fat orange trees, I glanced back at my house: It seemed tiny, like a house on the edge of a toy train track. The trees were powerfully aromatic, for some tiny white blossoms still clung to the branches; most of the oranges were wrinkled and inedible, but there were a few, at the highest branches, that were plump and only just mature. I got a stick and knocked on the uppermost branches until I managed to bat one down. It rolled into the rich earth that was dark and grassless between the several trees, and I went to retrieve it.

There, on the ground, someone had drawn, with a stick, one of the same diagrams I had seen on Katy's paper.

The eye with the unicorn.

I looked around the other trees, and by each of them, another drawing or diagram. A sketch of a dog? Or a pig? And then several lines with forked endings—snakes?

But something else, too, there, in the dirt, beneath one of the orange trees: an animal, torn up beyond recognition, the size of a small dog.

Dressed as if for a celebration with dozens of tiny orange blossoms stitched with a gay red thread through its mouth and arounds its eyes, and sutured along its guts.

V

It was a pig, as best I could determine, because in spite of its mutilations, its corkscrew tail was intact, and rather than stink of slaughter, it smelled fragrant with orange and just the scent of mint and sweet pepper—both of which grew wild in any direction across the field.

Children, I thought, and then: Katy Redlander.

The conflicting thought: but she's dead.

Then: a playmate.

Some friend of hers from 1952, who giggled over arcane rituals they'd found in—a book? *The Golden Bough?* Or Jaspar's *The Birth of Mythology?*

Some friend who grew up—would be, what? Forty-nine or so now? And still believed in ritual sacrifice in a sacred grove?

I had read reports of Satanic cults in surrounding towns, and of fringe fundamentalist groups that held snakes and drank poison—how far from that was this?

I left the animal there and went to spend the rest of the day in the library. I looked up pigs in both the Frazer and Jaspar texts. In Frazer, pigs were associated with the Eleusinian Mysteries, the rites of Demeter, and the loss of Persephone for half the year—a resurrection cult. But it was in Jaspar's *Birth of Mythology* that I struck gold. In the fifth chapter, on mystery cults, Jaspar writes:

"What 20th century man fails to realize about these so-called 'cults' is that these rites brought the god or goddess closer to man, so that man, in his ignorance, would be inducted into the mystery of creation. The virgin would be buried with the other offerings for a moon, during which time the participants would dance and sing themselves into a frenzy, and fast, and often commit heinous acts as a way of unleashing the chaos of the human and divine soul, intermingled—all in the name of keeping the world spinning the correct way, of keeping it all in balance. Thus, when the virgin was buried alive, it was not an act of cruelty, but of unbound love for the child and for the very breath of life, for the virgin represented the eternal daughter, who died, was buried, and then resurrected into the arms of the Great Mother after a time in Hell. This is not so different from the rites of crucifixion, and burial of Christ, after all? And in this act, the young woman who was sacrificed mated with the God, and returned to impart wisdom to the other participants in the Mysteries . . . "

Beneath this were the diagrams I had found in the wadded paper.

On the following page, a color plate showing the urn, of which mine was an obvious replica, of what I had thought were the Three Fates, dancing.

The caption beneath it read: "The furies in disguise, dancing to lure youths into their circle, so that they might torment them into eternity."

I remembered a quote from somewhere: "Those whom the gods would punish, they first make mad."

And the story of Orestes, who had brought tragedy and dishonor down upon his House, tormented by the Furies in their most horrible aspect.

Joe Redlander with an ax in his hand, holding down little Katy's neck while he went chop-chop-chop.

I could picture the house in disarray, the walls splattered with red, the boy trying to crawl away even while his father slammed the ax into his skull; and the mother, dead, cradling her other daughter, as if both were sleeping on the small rug in the hallway.

I closed my eyes, almost weeping; when I opened them, I was still in the armchair of the reference room of the library. Ed Laughlin, the librarian I'd spoken with before, stood near me. He wore a pale suit that hid most of his paunch; his hair was slick and white, drawn back from the bald spot on top of his head. He squinted to read the cover of the book I had in my hands.

"You feeling okay?" he asked, then, before I could answer, he said, "Ah, the ancient world. Fascinating. Coincidentally, I hope you noticed who donated most of our reference works on mythology, particularly fertility cults."

He gestured for the book, and I handed it to him. He flipped it closed, then opened it to the inside cover. He passed it back to me.

I was not surprised.

The bookplate read: "From the Library of Joseph and Virginia Redlander."

"He kills his family and then donates books?" I asked.

Ed didn't smile. "Believe it or not, Joe was a smart man, well-read, quiet, but strong. Admired, here in town, too. When a man cracks, you never know where the light's gonna show through. I guess with Joe it just showed through a bit strong."

"Did you know them well?"

He shook his head. "Barely, I was involved in the library here, but also the County museum over in Berdoo. Joe was always nice, and careful with books. That's about how well I knew him. A hello–good-bye–nice weather kind of thing. It bothers you too, though, huh?"

I assumed he meant living in the house, knowing about the murders. "Not too much. I find it more fascinating than frightening."

"Well, always got to be some mystery in life, anyway, stirs the blood up a little, but it seems strange to me she never showed."

I asked, "Who?"

"The oldest one. Kim. She was sweet and pretty. Fifteen. Some say she ran about a year before the killings—she may have had a boyfriend here, met on the sly because her folks were real strict about that kind of thing. Maybe she ran off with him. Maybe she did the killings, gossip was. But I don't think so—she was fifteen and sweet and small, like a little bird. Me, I think she got killed, too, only Joe, he did it somewhere else. I hope I'm wrong. I hope that pretty little girl is all grown up and living across the world and putting it all behind her best she can."

## VI

My wife was sitting at her canvas, painting, and I arrived swearing, as I went through the area packed with art supplies that surrounded her. "Damn it all," I said, "this is the only garage in creation without garage things."

"Damn right," she responded, "now take your damn language and get the hell out of here." All of this in a calm, carefully modulated voice.

I gave a false laugh and slapped the inside wall with my hand. "Now, where in hell would a shovel be when I need one?"

Jackie pointed with her paintbrush to the courtyard. "He'd know, Mister Brainiac." She looked more beautiful now, with the late-afternoon light on her hair, her face seeming unlined, like she always had, to me, and it amazed me, that moment, how love did that between two people: how it takes you out of time, and makes you virtually untouchable.

I turned in the direction of her pointing—it was to Stu, our gardener, kneeling beside the bird of paradise, trimming back the dying stems that thrust from between the enormous, stiff leaves. I went out into the yard. "You have a shovel I can borrow?"

He didn't hear me at first.

He was humming; then he saw my shadow. He turned.

He was only a few years younger than I, but he actually looked older. Not on the surface of his skin (except in laugh and smile lines), but in something I'd seen mainly in cities: a hard life. Not difficult, for all lives are difficult to varying degrees, and some people suffer with more relish than others, but hard, as if the lessons learned were not pleasant ones. I had always thought the gardening life would be a fairly serene one: the planting, growing, flowering, seasonal, balanced kind of thing.

"I need a shovel," I repeated.

"No problem," he said, and stood. He led me out to his truck and reached in the back of it, withdrawing a hoe and a shovel. "I assume," he said, "You've planting."

"Just digging," I said.

He nodded, handed me the shovel, and set the hoe back down.

"You've done a good job around here," I said.

He almost smiled with pride, but another kind of pride seemed to hold him back. "It's my life," he said simply, then returned to work.

I watched him go, his overalls muddy, the muscles in his back and shoulders so pronounced that he seemed to ripple like something dropped into still water. Then I turned. I didn't know if I was going to bury a dead animal, or to dig something up, something that had been in the ground for four decades. I used the shovel to press my way through the blackberry bush fence that had become thin with autumn, and headed into the field.

The stink of the dead pig came back to me, along with the scent of its orange blossom garlands. There was a wind from downfield, and it brought with it these, and other smells: of car exhaust, of pies baking, of rotting oranges and other fruit ripening. It almost made bearable the task I was about. When I got to the brief clutch of orange trees, I saw the flies had devoured much of the dead animal, but, oddly, the local coyotes had left it alone.

Behind me, a man's voice: "You planning on burying it?"

I turned; it was Stu, the gardener. He shrugged. "Decided to follow you out here. Figured you could use some help."

He reached up to a branch of one of the trees and plucked off a small blossom. He brought it to his nose, inhaled, and then to his lips. It seemed to me that he kissed the blossom before letting it fall.

"Do you know anything about this?" I asked, indicating the pig. "Local kids?"

Stu shook his head. He had kind but weary eyes, as if he'd been on the longest journey and had seen much, but now wanted only sleep. "You won't be burying the pig, will you, Mr. Richter?"

"No," I said.

"What the hell," he said. "I know you know about it."

"What's that?"

"I hear her sometimes," he said, "when I touch the leaves."

"Who?"

He looked dead at me, almost angrily. "I don't have nothing to hide. I didn't put her there." He pointed to the ground beneath the dead pig.

"The dead girl."

He whispered, "Not dead." His eyes seemed to grow smaller, lids pressing down hard, like pressing grapes for wine, tears. "I don't believe it."

"You were her friend," I said.

"I love her. I always will love her." Stu wiped at his eyes. "Look around. This field used to be nothing. Dirt. Nothing would grow. No orange trees. And your house, dead all around, a desert. But she's done this." He spread his arms out wide, as if measuring the distance of the earth.

"Did you do it?" I asked, even though I didn't want to.

"I killed the pig, if that's what you're asking. It's an offering."

"To whom? To Kim Redlander?" I glanced at the ground, wondering how deep she had been buried; buried alive for a mystery more ancient than what was written down in a book.

"To the goddess," he said.

We went out into the field, as two farmers might after a long day of work, and spoke of the past.

He said, "I have faith in this. I have faith. It wasn't strong at first. He told me he and her mother went all crazy and it was their festival time or something, and what he did . . . to the other kids . . . and to Kim . . . was 'cause she didn't come up that spring. He went wild, Joe did. I read all the books, later, and I came to a kind of understanding. I spoke to Joe before he killed himself. He lost his faith, you know? He didn't believe anymore. But I had nothing but faith. I know she's there. Look." He showed me the palm of his dirt-smeared hand. "She's in the earth, I can see her, there."

Joe Redlander and his family buried their daughter alive, I thought.

For the Mother of Creation, buried her in the earth, Persephone going to the underworld to be with her sworn consort, and they must have expected her to return in the spring. A family of religious nuts, and one teenage boy, hopelessly in love with a girl.

In love forever.

"It never happened," Stu said, "that's what her dad told me. They waited in the spring, and she didn't return. But I knew she was still here. I know she'll come back, one fine spring day. Till then, gardening seems to bring me closer to her."

"She's dead, Stu. I know you weren't responsible. But she's dead. It's been over forty years." I was shivering a little, because I sensed the truth in his story.

He looked across the land, back to the orange trees. "She's in everything here, everything. You may not believe, but I do. I've known things. I've seen things. She's down there, fifteen, beautiful, her hands touching the roots of the trees. She's going to come up one day. I absolutely know it."

As we both stood there, I knew that I was going to have to fire Stu, because there was something unbalanced in his story, in his fervor. I didn't think I could bear to look out the windows and see him gardening, thinking of love and loss as he tended flowers.

I knew I would lose sleep for many nights to come, looking out at that field, wondering.

*VII*

Then, one night the following April, someone set fire to the field, and in spite of the best efforts of the local firemen, my wife and I awoke the next morning and found we were living next door to a blackened wasteland. I got my morning coffee and went to the edge of the field, near the road. The orange trees were standing, but had been turned to crouching embers. I walked across dirt, stepping around the bits of twig that continued to give off breaths of fugitive smoke.

Where the girl had been buried: a deep gouge in the earth.

I watched the field after that but saw nothing special. In a month new grass was growing, and by summer, only through the dark bald patches could anyone tell that there'd been a fire at all.

And today, while my wife painted a picture of the courtyard, I went into the garage and found an old tool, a scythe. I took it up and went out into the field to mow. This action was not taken because of some fear or knowledge, for the Mystery remained—I didn't know if some animal had been digging at the hole where Kim Redlander was offered to the world, or if Stu himself had dug her up days before, moving rotting bones to another resting place. I didn't go to the field with any knowledge. I went singing into the field, cutting the hair of the earth, propelled by an urge that seemed older than any other.

Some have called this instinct the Mystery, but the simpler term is Stu's:

Faith.

I swiped the scythe across the fruit of her womb, then gave thanks and praise to the Mother all that day, for I could feel Her now, walking among her children; I spilled my own blood in the moistened dirt for Her.

My wife called to me, waving from the yard, and I turned, holding fast to the bloodied scythe, while I heard a young girl whisper in my ear that faith demands sacrifice.

Life was precious, for that moment, full of meaning, and wonder.

I walked wearily but gladly across the field, and when I reached my wife, her face brightened. "You've found it," she said.

"What's that?"

"Your joy," and she seemed truly happy for me.

"I have." I thought of Joe Redlander, and Stu, and Kim, the believers who brought me to this place.

The scythe seemed to shine like a crescent moon in my hand as I brought it across my wife's neck.

Alice opened her eyes, for the lights flared up, briefly, fantastically—

The nightmare was like a drug now, and her addiction, extreme.

She opened her mouth, and the flies hummed along, into her, filling her . . .

# The Rendering Man

## I

"We're gonna die someday," Thalia said, "all of us. Mama and Daddy, and then you and then me. I wonder if anyone's gonna care enough to think about Thalia Inez Canty, or if I'll just be dust under their feet." She stood in the doorway, still holding the ladle that dripped with potato chowder.

Her brother was raking dried grass over the manure in the yard. "What the heck kind of thing's that supposed to mean?"

"Something died last night." Thalia sniffed the air. "I can smell it. Out in the sty. Smelt it all night long, whatever it is. Always me that's first to smell the dead. 'Member the cat, the one by the thresher? I know when

163

things's dead. I can smell something new that's dead, just like that. Made me think of how everything ends."

"We'll check your stink out later. All you need to think about right now is getting your little bottom back inside that house to stir the soup so's we'll have something decent come suppertime." Her brother returned to his work, and she to hers. She hoped that one day she would have a real job and be able to get away from this corner of low sky and deadland.

The year was 1934, and there weren't too many jobs in Moncure County, when Thalia Canty was eleven, so her father went off to Dowery, eighty miles to the northeast, to work in an accountant's office, and her mother kept the books at the Bowand Motel on Fourth Street, night shift. Daddy was home on weekends, and Mama slept through the day, got up at noon, was out the door by four, and back in bed come three A.M. It was up to Thalia's brother, Lucius, to run the house, and make sure the two of them fed the pigs and chickens, and kept the doors bolted so the winds—they'd come up suddenly in March—didn't pull them off their hinges. There was school, too, but it seemed a tiny part of the day, at least to Thalia, for the work of the house seemed to slow the hours down until the gray Oklahoma sky was like an hourglass that never emptied of sand. Lucius was a hard worker, and since he was fifteen, he did most of the heavy moving, but she was always with him, cleaning, tossing feed to the chickens, picking persimmons from the neighbor's yard (out back by the stable where no one could see) to bake in a pie. And it was on the occasion of going to check on the old sow that Thalia and her brother eventually came face-to-face with the Rendering Man.

The pig was dead, and already drawing flies. Evening was coming on strong and windy, a southern wind which meant the smell of the animal would come right in through the cracks in the walls. Lucius said, "She been dead a good long time. Look at her snout."

"Toldja I smelled her last night." Thalia peeked around him, scrunched back, wanting to hide in his lengthening shadow. The snout had been torn at—blood caked around the mouth. "Musta been them yaller dogs," she said, imitating her father's strong southern accent, "cain't even leave her alone when she's dead."

The pig was enormous, and although Lucius thrust planks beneath her to try and move her a ways, she wouldn't budge. "Won't be taking her to the butcher, I reckon," he said.

Thalia smirked. "Worthless yaller dogs."

"Didn't like bacon, anyways."

"Me, too. Or ham."

"Or sausage with biscuits and grease."

"Chitlins. Hated chitlins. Hated knuckles. Couldn't chaw a knuckle to save my life."

"Ribs. Made me sick, thought a ribs all drownin' in molasses and chili, drippin' over the barbecue pit," Lucius said, and then drew his hat down, practically making the sign of the cross on his chest. "Oh, Lord, what I wouldn't give for some of her."

Thalia whispered, "Just a piece of skin fried up in the skillet."

"All hairy and crisp, greasy and smelly."

"Yes." Thalia sighed. "Praise the Lord, yes. Like to melt in my mouth right now. I'd even eat her all rotten like that. Maybe not."

The old sow lay there, flies making halos around her face.

Thalia felt the familiar hunger come on; it wasn't that they didn't have food regularly, it was that they rarely ate the meat they raised—they'd sold the cows off, and the pigs were always for the butcher and the local price so that they could afford other things. Usually they had beans and rice or eggs and griddle cakes. The only meat they ever seemed to eat was chicken, and Thalia could smell chicken in her dreams sometimes, and didn't think she'd ever get the sour taste out of her throat.

She wanted to eat that pig. Cut it up, hocks, head, ribs, all of it. She would've liked to take a chaw on the knuckle.

"She ain't worth a nickel now," Thalia said, then, brightening, "You sure we can't eat her?"

Lucius shook his head. "For all we know, she's been out here six, seven hours. Look at those flies. Already laid eggs in her ears. Even the dogs didn't go much into her—look, see? They left off. Somethin' was wrong." He shuffled over to his sister and dropped his arm around her shoulder. She pressed her head into the warmth of his side. Sometimes he was like a mama and daddy, both, to her.

"She was old. I guess. Even pigs die when they get old." Thalia didn't want to believe that Death, which had come for Granny three years before, could possibly want a pig unless it had been properly slaughtered and divvied up.

"Maybe it died natural. Or maybe," and her brother looked down the road to the Leavon place. There was a wind that came down from the sloping hillside sometimes, and coughed dust across the road between their place and the old widow's. "Could be she was poisoned."

Thalia glanced down to the old gray house with its flag in front, still out from Armistice Day, year before last. A witch lived in that house, they called her the Grass Widow because she entertained men like she was running a roadhouse; she lived alone, though, with her eighteen cats as company. Thalia knew that the Grass Widow had wanted to buy the old sow for the past two years, but her parents had refused because she wasn't offering enough money and the Cantys were raising her to be the biggest, most expensive hog in the county. And now, what was the purpose? The sow was fly-ridden and rotting. Worthless. Didn't matter if the Grass Widow killed it or not. It recalled for her a saying her daddy often said in moments like this:

"How the mighty are fallen." Even among the kingdom of pigs.

Lucius pulled her closer to him and leaned down a bit to whisper in her ear. "I ain't sayin' anything, Thay, but the Widow wanted that sow and she knew Daddy wasn't never gonna sell it to her. I heard she hexed the Horleichs' cows so they dried up."

"Ain't no witches," Thalia said, disturbed by her

brother's suspicions. "Just fairy tales, that's what Mama says."

"And the Bible says there is. And since the Bible's the only book ever written with truth in it, you better believe there's witches, and they're just like her, mean and vengeful and working hexes on anything they covet." Lucius put his hand across his sister's shoulder and hugged her in close to him again. He kissed her gently on her forehead, right above her small red birthmark. "Don't you be scared of her, though, Thay, we're God-fearin' people, and she can't hurt us 'less we shut out our lights under bushels."

Thalia knew her brother well enough to know he never lied. So the old Grass Widow was a witch. She looked at her brother, then back to the pig. "We gonna bury her?"

"The sow? Naw, too much work. Let's get it in the wheelbarrow and take it around near the coops. Stinks so bad, nobody's gonna notice a dead pig, and then when Mama gets home in the mornin', I'll take the truck. We can drive the sow out to the Renderin' Man." This seemed a good plan, because Thalia knew that the Rendering Man could give them something in exchange for the carcass—if not money, then some other service or work. The Rendering Man had come by some time back for the old horse, Dinah, sick on her feet and worthless. He took Dinah into his factory, and gave Thalia's father three dollars and two smoked hams. She was aware that the Rendering Man had a great love for animals, both dead and alive, for he paid money for them regardless. He was a tall, thin man with a potbelly, and a grin like walrus's, two teeth thrusting down on either side of his lip. He always had red cheeks, like Santa Claus, and told her he knew magic. She had asked him (when she was younger), "What kind of magic?"

He had said, "The kind where you give me something, and I turn it into something else." Then he showed her his wallet. She felt it. He'd said, "It used to be a snake." She drew her hand back; looked at the wallet; at the Rendering Man; at the wallet; at her hand. She'd been only six or seven then, but she knew that the Rendering Man was someone powerful.

If anyone could help with the dead sow, he could.


The next morning was cool and the sky was fretted with strips of clouds. Thalia had to tear off her apron as she raced from the house to climb up beside Lucius in the truck. "I didn't know you's gonna take off so quick," she panted, slamming the truck door shut beside her, "I barely got the dishes done."

"Got to get the old sow to the Rendering Man, or we may as well just open a bottleneck fly circus out back."

Thalia glanced in the back; the sow lay there peacefully, so different from its brutal, nasty dumb animal life when it would attack anything that came in its pen. It was much nicer dead. "What's it, anyways?" she asked.

"Thay, honey?"

"Renderin'."

"Oh," Lucius laughed, turning down the Post Road, "it's taking animals and things and turning them into something else."

"Witchcraft's like that."

"Naw, not like that. This is natural. You take the pig, say, and you put it in a big pot of boiling water, and the bones, see, they go over here, and the skin goes over there, and then, over there's the fat. Why you think they call a football a pigskin?"

Thalia's eyes widened. "Oh my goodness."

"And hog bristle brushes—they get those from renderin'. And what else? Maybe the fat can be used for greasing something, maybe . . . "

"Goodness' sakes," Thalia said, imitating her mother's voice. "I had no idea. And he pays good money for this, does he?"

"Any money on a dead sow's been eaten by maggots's good money, Thay."

It struck her, what happened to the old horse. "He kill Dinah, too? Dinah got turned into fat and bones and skin and guts even whilst she was alive? Somebody use her fat to grease up their wheels?"

Lucius said nothing; he whistled faintly.

She felt tears threatening to bust out of her eyes. She held them back. She had loved that old horse, had seen it as a friend. Her father had lied to her about what happened to Dinah; he had said that she just went to retire in greener pastures out behind the Rendering Man's place.

She took a swallow of air. "I wished somebody'd told me, so I coulda said a proper goodbye."

"My strong, brave little sister," Lucius said, and brought the truck to an abrupt stop. "Here we are." Then he turned to her, cupping her chin in his hand the way her father did whenever she needed talking to. "Death ain't bad for those that die, remember, it's only bad for the rest of us. We got to suffer and carry on. The Dead, they get to be at peace in the arms of the Lord. Don't ever cry for the Dead, Thay, better let them cry for us." He brought his hand back down to his side. "See, the Rendering Man's just sort of a part of Nature. He takes all God's creatures and makes sure their suffering is over, but makes them useful, even so."

"I don't care about the sow," she said. "Rendering Man can do what he likes with it. I just wish we coulda et it." She tried to hide her tears, sniffed them back; it wasn't just her horse Dinah, or the sow, but something about her own flesh that bothered her, as if she and the sow could be in the same spot one day, rendered, and she didn't like that idea.

The Rendering Man's place was made of stone, and was like a fruit crate turned upside down—flat on top, with slits for windows. There were two big smokestacks rising up from behind it like insect feelers; yellow-black smoke rose up from one of them, discoloring the sky and making a stink in the general vicinity. Somebody's old mule was tied to a skinny tree in the front yard. Soon to be rendered, Thalia thought. Poor thing. She got out of the truck and walked around to pet it. The mule was old; its face was

171

almost white, and made her think of her granny, all white of hair and skin at the end of her life.

The Rendering Man had a wife with yellow hair like summer wheat; she stood in the front doorway with a large apron that had once been white, now filthy, covering her enormous German thighs tight as skin across a drum. *"Guten Tag,"* the lady said, and she came out and scooped Thalia into her arms like she was a tin angel, smothered her scalp with kisses. *"Ach, mein Liebchen.* You are grown so tall. Last I saw you, you was barely over with the cradle."

Just guessing as to what might be smeared on the woman's apron made Thalia slip through her arms again so that no dead animal bits would touch her. "Hello, ma'am," she said in her most formal voice.

The lady looked at her brother. "Herr Lucius, you are very grown. How is your *Mutter*?"

"Just fine, ma'am," Lucius said, "we got the old sow in the back." He rapped on the side of the truck. "Just went last night. No good eating. Thought you might be interested."

*"Ach, da,* yes, of naturally we are," she said, "come in, come in, children, Father is still at the table *mit* breakfast. You will have some ham? Fresh milk and butter, too. Little Thalia, you are so thin, we must put some fat on those bones," and the Rendering Man's wife led them down the narrow hall to the kitchen. The kitchen table was small, which made its crowded plates seem all the more enormous: fried eggs on one, on another long fat sausages tied with ribbon at the

end, then there were dishes of bread and jam and butter. Thalia's eyes were about to burst just taking it all in—slices of fat-laced ham, jewels of sweets in a brightly painted plate, and two pitchers, one full of thick milk, and the other, orange juice.

The Rendering Man sat in a chair, a napkin tucked into his collar. He had a scar on the left side of his face, as if an animal had scratched him deeply there. Grease had dripped down his chin and along his neck. He had his usual grin and sparkle to his eyes. "Well, my young friends. You've brought me something, have you?"

His wife put her hand over her left breast as if she was about to faint, her eyes rolling to the back of her head. "*Ach*, a great pig, *Schatze*. They will want more than just the usual payment for that one."

Thalia asked, "Can I have a piece of ham, please?"

The Rendering Man patted the place beside him. "Sit with me, both of you, yes, Eva, bring another chair. We will talk business over a good meal, won't we, Lucius? And you, sweet little bird, you must try my wife's elegant pastries. She learned how to make them in her home country, they are so light and delicate, like the sundried skin of a dove, but I scare you, my little bird, it is not a dove, it is bread and sugar and butter!"

After she'd eaten her fill, ignoring the conversation between her brother and the Rendering Man, Thalia asked, "How come you pay good money for dead animals, Mister?"

He drank from a large mug of coffee, wiped his lips,

glanced at her brother, then at her. "Even dead, we are worth something, little bird."

"I know that. Lucius told me about the fat and bones and whiskers. But folks'd dump those animals for free. Why you pay money for them?"

The Rendering Man looked at his wife, and they both laughed. "Maybe I'm a terrible businessman," he said, shaking his head. "But," he calmed, "you see, my pet, I can sell these things for more money than I pay. I am not the only man capable of rendering. There is competition in this world. If I pay you two dollars today for your dead pig, and send you home with sweets, you will bring me more business later on, am I right?"

"I s'pose."

"So, by paying you, I keep you coming to me. And I get more skins and fat and bones to sell to places that make soap and dog food and other things. I would be lying if I didn't tell you that I make more money off your pig than you do. But it is a service, little bird."

"I see." Thalia nodded, finishing off the last of the bacon. "It seems like a terrible thing to do."

"Thay, now, apologize for that." Lucius reached over and pinched her shoulder.

She shrugged him off.

The Rendering Man said, "It is most terrible. But it is part of how we all must live life. Someone must do the rendering. If not, everything would go to waste and we would have dead pigs rotting with flies on the side of the road, and the smell."

"But you're like a buzzard or something."

The man held his index finger up and shook it like a teacher about to give a lesson. "If I saw myself as a buzzard or jackal I could not look in the mirror. But others have said this to my face, little bird, and it never hurts to hear it. I see myself as a man who takes the weak and weary and useless empty shells of our animal brethren and breathes new life into them, makes them go on in some other fashion. I see it as a noble profession. It is only a pity that we do not render ourselves, for what a tragedy it is to be buried and left for useless, for worm fodder, when we could be brushing a beautiful woman's hair, or adorning her purse, or even, perhaps, providing shade from the glare of a lamp so that she might read her book and not harm her eyes. It is a way to soften the blow of death, you see, for it brings forth new life. And one other thing, sweet," he brought his face closer to hers until she could smell his breath of sausage and ham, "we each have a purpose in life, and our destiny is to seek it out, whatever the cost, and make ourselves one with it. It is like brown eyes or blond hair or short and tall, it is there in us, and will come out no matter how much we try to hide it. I did not choose this life; it chose me. I think you understand, little bird, yes. You and I know."

Thalia thought about what he'd said all the way home. She tried not to imagine the old sow being tossed in a vat and stirred up in the boiling water until it started to separate into its different parts. Lucius scolded her for trying to take the Rendering Man to task, but she ignored him. She felt like a whole new world had been opened to her, a way of seeing things that she had not thought of before, and when she stepped out of the truck, at her home, she heard the crunch of the grass beneath her feet differently, the chirping of crickets, too, a lovely song, and a flock of starlings shot from the side of the barn just as she tramped across the muddy expanse that led to the chicken coops—the starlings were her sign from the world that there was no end to life, for they flew in a pattern, which seemed to her to approximate the scar on the left-hand side of the Rendering Man's face.

It was like destiny.

She climbed up on the fence post and looked down the road. A dust wind was blowing across to the Grass Widow's house, and she heard the cats, all of them, yowling as if in heat, and she wondered if that old witch had really poisoned the pig.

## II

Thalia was almost twenty-nine, and on a train in Europe, when she thought she recognized the man sitting across from her. She was now calling herself just Lia, and had not lived in Oklahoma since she left for New York in 1939 to work as a secretary—she'd taught herself shorthand and typing at the motel where her mother had worked. Then, during the war, Lucius died fighting in France, and her mother and father, whom she'd never developed much of a relationship with, called her back to the old farm. Instead, she took up with a rich and spoiled playboy who had managed to get out of serving in the military because of flatfeet, and went to live with him at his house overlooking the Hudson River. She went through a period of grief for the loss of her brother, after which she married the playboy in question. Then, whether out of guilt or general self-destruction, her husband managed to get involved in the war, ended up in a labor camp, and had died there not two weeks before liberation. She had inherited quite a bit of money after an initial fight with one of her husband's illegitimate children. It was 1952, and she wanted to see Germany now, to see what had happened, and where her husband of just a few months had died; she had been to Paris already to see the hotel where her brother supposedly breathed his last, suffering at the hands of the Nazis but dying a patriot, unwilling to divulge top secret information. She was fascinated by the whole thing: the war, Paris, labor camps, and Nazis.

She had grown lovely over the years; she was tall, as her father and brother had been, but had her mother's eyes, and had learned, somewhere between Oklahoma and New York, to project great beauty without having inherited much.

The man across from her, on the train, had a scar on the left-hand side of his face.

It sparked a series of memories for her, like lightning flashing behind her eyes. The stone house on the Post Road, the smokestacks, the mule in the front yard, an enormous breakfast that still made her feel fat and well-fed whenever she thought of it.

It was the Rendering Man from home.

On this train. Traveling through Germany from France. Now, what are the chances, she wondered, of that happening? Particularly after what happened when she was eleven.

Not possible, she thought.

He's a phantom. I'm hallucinating. Granny hallucinated that she saw her son Toby back from the First World War walking toward her even without his legs.

She closed her eyes; opened them. He was still there. Something so ordinary about him that she knew he was actually sitting there and not just an image conjured from her inner psyche.

He spoke first. "I know you, don't I?"

She pretended, out of politeness, that he must not be talking to her. There was a large German woman sitting beside her, with a little boy on the other side. The German woman nodded politely to her but didn't acknowledge the man across from them. Her little boy had a card trick that he was trying to show his mother, but she paid no attention.

"Miss? Excuse me?" he said.

Then it struck her: He spoke English perfectly, and yet he looked very German.

He grinned when she glanced back at him. "See? I knew I knew you, when I saw you in the station. I said to myself, you have met that girl somewhere before. Where are you from, if I may ask?"

"New York," she lied, curious as to whether this really could possibly be the Rendering Man. How could it? He would have to be, what? Sixty? This man didn't seem that old, although he was not young by any stretch. "I'm a reporter."

He wagged his finger at her, like a father scolding his child. "You are not a reporter, miss, I think. I am not saying you are a liar, I am only saying that that is not true. Where is your notebook? Even a pencil? You are American, and your accent is New York, but I detect a southern influence. Yes, I think so. I hope you don't mind my little game. I enjoy guessing about people and their origins."

She felt uncomfortable, but nodded. "I enjoy games, too, to pass the time."

She glanced at the German woman who was bringing out a picnic for her son. Bread and soup, but no meat. There was not a lot of meat to go around even six years after the war.

The man said, "You are a woman of fortune, I think. Lovely jewelry, and your dress is quite expensive, at least here in Europe. And I heard you talking with the conductor—your French is not so good, I think, and your German is worse. You drew out a brand of cigarettes from a gold case, both very expensive. So you are on the Grand Tour of Europe, and like all Americans with time on their hands, you want to see the Monster Germany, the Fallen."

"Very perceptive," she said. She brought her cigarette case out and offered him one of its contents.

He shook his head. "I think these are bad for the skin and the breathing, don't you?"

She shrugged. "It all goes someday."

He grinned. "Yes, it does. The sooner we accept that, the better for the world. And I know your name now, my dear, my little bird, you are the little Thalia Canty from Moncure County, Oklahoma."

She shivered, took a smoke, coughed, stubbed the cigarette out. She had white gloves on her hands; she looked at them. She remembered the German wife's apron, smeared with dark brown stains. She didn't look up for a few minutes.

"I would say this is some coincidence, little bird," the Rendering Man said, "but it is not, not really. The real coincidence happened in the Alsace, when you got off the train for lunch. I was speaking with a butcher who is a friend of mine, and I saw you go into the café. I wouldn't have recognized you at all, for I have not seen you since you were a child, but you made a lasting impression on me that morning we had breakfast together. I saw it in you, growing, just as it had grown in me. Once that happens, it is like a halo around you. It's still there; perhaps someone might say it is a play of light, the aurora borealis of the flesh, but I can recognize it. I followed you back to the train, got my ticket, and found where you were seated. But still I wasn't positive it was you, until just a moment ago. It was the way you looked at my face. The scar. It was a souvenir from a large cat which gouged me quite deeply. No ordinary cat, of course, but a tiger, sick, from the circus. The tiger haunts me to this day, by way of the scar. Do you believe in haunting? Ah, I think not, you are no doubt a good Disciple of Christ and do not believe that a circus cat could haunt a man. Yet I see it sometimes in my dreams, its eyes, and teeth, and the paw reaching up to drag at my flesh. I wake my wife up at night, just so she will stay up with me and make sure there is no tiger there. I know it is dead, but I have learned in life that sometimes these angels, as I call them (yes, dear, even the tiger is an angel, for it had some message for me), do not stay dead too long. Perhaps I am your angel, little bird; you must admit it is strange to meet someone from just around the bend on the other side of the world."

She looked at him again but tried not to see him in focus, because she felt the pressing need to avoid this man at all costs. "I'm sorry, sir. You do have me pegged, but I can't for the life of me place you."

He smiled, his cheeks red. He wore a dark navy coat, and beneath it, a gray shirt. When he spoke again, it was as if he had paid no attention to her denial. "My wife, Eva, she is in Cologne, where we live, and where I should be going now. We came to Germany in 1935, because Eva's parents were ill and because, well, you must remember the unfortunate circumstance. I was only too glad to leave Oklahoma, since I didn't seem to get along with too many people there, and Germany seemed to be a place I could settle into. I found odd jobs, as well as established a successful rendering business again. And then, well . . . " He spread his hands out as if it were enough to excuse what happened to Germany. "But I knew you and I would meet again, little bird, it was there on your face. Your fascination and repulsion—is that not what magnets do to each other, pull and push? Yet they are meant to be together. Destiny. You see, I saw your brother before he died, and I told him what was to come."

She dropped all pretense now. "What kind of game are you playing?"

"No game, Thalia Canty."

"Lia Fallon. Thalia Canty died in Oklahoma in the thirties."

"Names change through the years, even faces, but you are the little bird."

"And you are the Rendering Man."

He gasped with pleasure. "Yes, that would be how you know me. Tell me, did you run because of what you did?"

She didn't answer. "What about Lucius?"

The Rendering Man looked out the dark window as a town flew by. Rain sprinkled across the glass. "First, you must tell me."

"All right. I forgave myself for that a long time ago. I was only eleven, and you were partly responsible."

"Did I use the knife?"

She squinted her eyes. Wished she were not sitting there. "I didn't know what I was doing, not really."

"Seventeen cats must've put up quite a howl."

"I told you. I didn't know what I was really doing."

"Yes, you did. How long after before you ran?"

"I ran away four times before I turned seventeen. Only made it as far as St. Louis most of the time."

"That's a long way from home for a little girl."

"I had an aunt there. She let me stay a month at a time. She understood."

"But not your mama and daddy," he said with some contempt in his voice. "A woman's murdered, we all called her the Grass Widow. Remember? Those Okies all thought she was a witch. All she was was sad and lonely. Then all she was was dead. She and her cats, chopped up and boiled."

"Rendered," she said.

"Rendered. So they come for me, and thank God I was able to get my wife out of the house safely before the whole town burned it down."

"How was I to know they'd come after you?"

He was silent, but glaring.

"I didn't mean for you to get in trouble."

"Do you know what they did to me?" he asked.

She nodded.

He continued, "I still have a limp. That's my way of joking; they broke no bones. Bruises and cuts, my hearing was not good until 1937, and I lost the good vision in my right eye—it's just shadows and light on that side. Pain in memory brings few spasms to the flesh. It is the past. Little bird, but you think I am only angry at you. All those years, you are terrified you will run into me, so when you can, you get out for good. I was sure that little town was going to make another Bruno Hauptmann out of me. Killing a sad widow and her pets and boiling them for bones and fat. But even so, I was not upset with you, not too much. Not really. Because I knew you had it in you, I saw it that day, that we were cut from the same cloth, only you had not had the angel cross your path and tell you of your calling. It is not evil or dark, my sweet, it is the one calling that gives meaning to our short, idiotic lives; we are the gardeners of the infinite, you and I."

"Tell me about my brother," she pleaded softly. The

German woman next to her seemed to sense the strangeness of the conversation, and took her son by the hand and led him out of the cabin.

"He did not die bravely," the Rendering Man said, "if that's what you're after. He was hit in the leg, and when I found him, he had been in a hotel with some French girl, and was a scandal for bleeding on the sheets. I was called in by my commander, and went about my business."

"You worked with the French?"

He shook his head. "I told you, I continued my successful rendering business in Germany, and expanded to a factory just outside of Paris in '43. Usually the men were dead, but sometimes, as was the case with your brother, little bird, I had to stop their hearts. Your brother did not recognize me, and I only recognized him when I saw his identification. As he died, do you know what he told me? He told me that he was paying for the sins that his sister had committed in her lifetime. He cried like a little baby. It was most embarrassing. To think, I once paid him two dollars and a good sausage for a dead pig."

Lia stood up. "You are dreadful," she said. "You are the most dreadful human being who has ever existed upon the face of the earth."

"I am, if you insist. But I am your tiger, your angel," the Rendering Man said. He reached deep into the pocket of his coat and withdrew something small. He handed it to her.

She didn't want to take it, but grabbed it anyway.

"It is his. He would've wanted you to have it."

She thought, at first, it was a joke, because the small leather coin purse didn't seem to be the kind of thing Lucius would have.

When she realized what it was, she left the cabin and walked down the slender hall, all the way to the end of the train. She wanted to throw herself off, but instead stood and shivered in the cold wet rain of Germany, and did not return to the cabin again.

She could not get over the feeling that the part of the coin purse that drew shut resembled wrinkled human lips.

*III*

"He's here," the old woman said.

She heard the squeaking wheels of the orderly's cart down the corridor.

"He's here. I know he's here. Oh, dear God, he's here."

"Will you shut up, lady?" the old man in the wheelchair said.

An orderly came by and moved the man's chair on down the hall.

The old woman could not sit up well in bed. She looked at the green ceiling. The window was open. She felt a breeze. It was spring. It always seemed to be spring. A newspaper lay across her stomach. She lifted it up. Had she just been reading it? Where were her glasses?

Oh, there. She put them on. Looked at the newspaper. It was *The New York Times*.

March 23, 1994.

She called out for help, and soon an orderly (the handsome one with the bright smile) was there, like a genie summoned from a lamp. "I thought I saw a man in this room," she said.

"Mrs. Ehrlich, nobody's in here."

"I want you to check that closet. I think he's there."

The orderly went good-naturedly to the closet. He opened the door, and moved some of the clothes around. He turned to smile at her.

"I'm sure I saw him there. Waiting. Crouching," she said. "But he may have slipped beneath the bed."

Again, a check beneath the bed. The orderly sat down in the chair beside the bed. "He's not here."

"How old am I? I'm not very old, really, I'm not losing my wits yet, am I? Dear God in heaven, am I?"

"No, Mrs. Ehrlich. You're seventy-one going on eleven."

"Why'd you say that?"

"What?"

"Going on eleven. Why eleven? Is there a conspiracy here?"

"No, ma'am."

"You know him, don't you? You know him and you're just not saying."

"Are you missing Mr. Ehrlich again?"

"Mr. Ehrlich, Mr. Vane, Mr. Fallon, one husband after another, young man, nobody can miss them because nobody can remember them. Are you sure I haven't had an unannounced visitor?"

The orderly shook his head.

She closed her eyes, and when she opened them, the orderly was gone. It had grown dark. Where is my mind? She thought. Where has it gone? Why am I here at seventy-one when all my friends are still out in the world living; why, my granny was eighty-eight before senility befell her, how dare life play with me so unfairly.

She reached for her glass of water and took a sip.

Still, she thought she sensed his presence in the room with her, and could not sleep the rest of the night. Before dawn, she became convinced that the Rendering Man was somewhere nearby lurking; she tried to dress, but the illness had taken over her arms to such a great extent that she could not even get her bra on.

She sat up, half naked, on her bed, the light from the hallway like a spotlight for the throbbing in her skull.

"I have led a wicked life," Thalia whispered to the morning. She found the strength at five-thirty to get her dressing gown around her shoulders and to walk down the hall, sure that she would see him at every step.

The door to Minnie Cheever's door was open, which was odd, and she stepped into it. "Minnie?" Her friend was nearly ninety-three, and was not in bed. Thalia looked around, and finally found Minnie lying on the floor, on her way to the bathroom. Thalia checked her pulse; she was alive, but barely. Thalia's limbs hurt, but she used Minnie's wheelchair to get Minnie down the hallway, onto the elevator, and down to the basement, where the endless kitchen began.

\* \* \*

They found her there, two cooks and one orderly, like that, caught at last, Thalia Canty, all of seventy-one going on eleven, chopping Minnie Cheever up into small pieces, and dropping each piece into one of several large pots, boiling with water, on the stove.

She turned when she heard their footsteps, and smiled. "I know you were here, we're like destiny, you and me, Mister Rendering Man, but you'll never have me, will you?" She held her arms out for them to see. "I scraped off all the fat and skin I could, Mister Rendering Man, you can have all these others, but you ain't never gonna get my hide and fat and bones to keep useful in this damned world. You hear me? You ain't never gonna render Thalia, and this I swear!" She tried to laugh, but it sounded like a saw scraping metal. The joke was on the Rendering Man, after all, for she would never, ever render herself up to him.

It took two men to hold her down, and in a short time, her heart gave out. She was dead; when her body was taken to the morgue, it was discovered that she'd been scraping herself raw, almost to within an eighth of an inch of her internal organs.

It was a young girl, a candy striper named Nancy, going through Thalia's closet to help clean it out, who found the dried skins beneath a pile of filthy clothing. The skins were presumably from Thalia's own body, sewn together, crudely representing a man. Thalia had drawn Magic Marker eyes and lips and a nose on the face, and a scar.

Those who found Thalia Canty, as well as the candy striper who fainted at the sight of the skin, later thought they saw her sometimes, in their bedrooms, or in traffic, or just over their shoulders, clutching a knife.

She would live in their hearts forever.

An angel.

A tiger.

# The Night Before Alec Got Married

*I*

You can never be too sure or too stupid, but you can be too horny—Alec DelBanco, he was smart, but men are never very smart in that one area, and it got him right where you don't want to be got, not if you're twenty-four and on the run because something's after you, only it doesn't have a name and maybe it doesn't even have a face but you can see it sometimes in their faces looking out at you like it's some kind of tourist on a world cruise and you're one of the Wonders of the World to It. You call it an It because you don't know if It's been noticed by anyone else, and you can't really talk about It, because if you did, maybe that's when It would get you.

It got Alec that night, and he didn't even have talk to talk about it. Boy, was he smart, he was practically Phi-Fucking-Beta Kappa from Stanford, and then the job with Kelleher-Darden with an eighty-thousand-a-year salary for a twenty-two-year-old asshole you used to get drunk with—well, everybody figured Alec had just grabbed the golden ring and had not let go. And handsome! He'd been a stud since the age of twelve, if you remembered far back enough when every girl you'd ever had a crush on seemed to only want to get near you so they could get within breathing distance of your friend. Still, Alec DelBanco never forgot a friend, and you got some fringe benefits from knowing him all those years, beautiful girls who wouldn't normally give you the time of day all around you—you couldn't touch them, of course, not in the light of day, not with them in the room, that is, but, oh! when the lights were out and you were alone in bed with your hand and a little imagination—you had them all every which way but loose! You loved Alec, though, really loved him. Like a brother, I mean, because you'd practically grown up with him since you could remember. He was better than a brother, too, because your own brothers were kind of missing something in the compassion department. I wouldn't fuck a guy, no way, but if I had to fuck a guy—I mean, like the Nazis had me in this torture rack and told me I'd have to fuck a guy or get it cut off, well, I couldn't fuck just anyone—it would have to be Alec, and not just 'cause he was pretty, but because I have feelings for him—but not like you think. Once, in the showers after gym, he was leaning around to get his towel, and I swear to God this is true, I thought he was a girl, from the back, he's all lean and muscular, but I thought he looked like, you know, one of those Olympic women swimmers, taut and strong but kind of attractive, too. So, yeah, if pressed into it, I guess you could say I'd do him.

But this isn't about me or what I would do if the Fourth Reich came along—and it just might if you read the papers—it's about Alec and the night before he got married. His girl, Luce, was out with a whole gaggle down at the Marina getting toasted on margaritas and opening cute little presents, while you and me were over on Sunset trying to find just the right pro to come in and do a little dance over Alec's face when he least suspected it. I didn't like Luce too much—she was always kind of a bitch to me, almost like she thought I wanted Alec more than she did. I've got to be honest here, I would've preferred Alec to marry a hooker and at least be happy rather than wed Lucille C. St. Gerard, a fifth-generation Californian from Sacramento who debuted at every second-rate cotillion north of Bakersfield.

So we cruise Sunset, all the way from, say, La Cienega up to Raleigh Heights, and it's getting close to nine—you'd think every working girl in the world would be out by that time—Saturday night, party night, but we only see a bunch of tired old dogs pounding the pavement. You and me, we're doing St. Pauli Girl, but keeping the bottles low so the cops don't notice, when I see what I think is just about the most beautiful piece of work this side of the Pacific and I slam on the brakes and cross a lane to park.

"Look at her, holy mother of fuck, look at her," I say, and barely remember to put on the parking brake. I leap out of the Mustang—it's a convertible—and practically dive right over to her. She's got everything, and packed tight: a nice rack of tits, thin waist, and child-bearing hips. But what really gets me are the lips on her, big fat suckers that make me wonder if her labia's like that, too.

"Hey, little boy," she says, "you want some sugar in your coffee tonight?"

I've never picked up a whore, so I feel real tongue-tied.

"You want a date?" She's got teeth all the way down her throat, it seems, big white flashy teeth with a couple of gold caps in the way back. She's practically steaming there like an oyster out of the fish market, and I start to feel like a twelve-year-old of rage hormones and dripping wick.

"Listen," I say, "I got this friend. Alec."

She looks at you in the car. "That him? He's cute."

"No, no, that's not him. We're throwing a bachelor party tonight. We need a stripper."

"I can do that. I can do all of you boys."

"Well, more than a stripper," I say.

She shrugs. "I can do that, too."

"We want you to get him alone and, you know . . ." I say.

She smiles. "A dance and a fuck? It'll cost you."

"Not just a dance and not just a fuck, okay? We

want the Dance of Seven Veils, like Salome did, we want you to really get him to want you, and then it's got to be more than fireworks, more than an explosion, it's got to be the Big O."

"The Big O?"

"You know, the Orgasm at the End of the Universe. The Big One. The kind that guys dream about in their sleep, the kind that most of us never get."

She looks at me sideways, like maybe I'm some kind of creep with diarrhea of the mouth. "You just talking, ain't you? You don't really want the Big O, nothin like that, do you?"

I shake my head. "Every trick you got. Think you can do it?"

She has a look in her eyes like she's thinking, but cagily—she has a few secrets, I guess, and she guards them. Her eyes are muddy brown, and when she looks back at me, they look like tiny little pebbles, hard and round. "Baby," she says, "I think I can do anything. You pay, I'm gonna make sure it happens." She glances down the street. There's a big fat guy wearing a Hawaiian shirt—he looks less like a beach boy and more like a beached something else. "My manager," she says. "You need to talk with him, I think. I ain't too good at the business side of things."

Because I don't want to talk to him, I get you to do it, and the whole thing's arranged, even though it's going to cost us: four hundred bucks, plus whatever she makes in her dance, and if it goes over two hours, another four hundred. Two hundred in advance, so I pay the pimp, and we give him the address, to be there at eleven, all that shit, and then we head on back to the party.

Now, this is the part where I'm really stupid, I guess, but you can't have a stripper come to the party without giving somebody an address. But I guess this pimp looks at the money and figures there's more where that came from—so he must've gotten this idea—and I'm only assuming. You and me, we look like nice preppie kind of guys, shit, we practically have ties on from work, and I'm wearing five-hundred-dollar Italian shoes. So he decides that when he takes his girl over, he better pack something, because you never know how much cash you can get out of rich, scared, drunk guys at a bachelor party. I don't know a thing about guns, but this pimp probably had the automatic kind, and I figure that's how you got two of your fingers shot off before midnight.

## II

But I'm getting ahead of myself—it's easy to do when you're spilling your guts and you can't always remember the sequence of events; especially if you're trying to second-guess everyone around you. The thing with your fingers, it didn't happen until about eleven fifty-five, and the thing with Luce, that happened just before ten, after we'd gotten back, hoisted a few more St. Paulis and watched Long Jean Silver and her amazing stump-screwing of another woman in one of the six videos you rented from that scuzzy video store down in Long Beach. But something happened before even that, and that was when we stopped for more beer at 7-eleven and I bought a bunch of multicolored rubbers, all fancy, and then pricked them full of holes and you and I laughed our heads off thinking about Alec and Luce on their honeymoon, thinking they were doing some family planning by wearing the rubbers. I don't think I've ever laughed so hard.

So I stuff the rubbers in my jacket pocket. As I'm pulling out of the 7-Eleven, a car almost hits the Mustang, then swerves and crashes into a wall; the front half is all crushed, but the driver seems okay. "Should we call for help?" you ask, and I say, "Oh, right, like the cops are gonna love the beer in the car and all." So we pass this woman in the car, and she looks at us for a second, and I got to tell you, I will never, as long as I live, forget that look. Women are like this swamp or something, all dark and mysterious, but still you got to explore 'em, it's a guy thing. You know, I always say that if you were to put some fur around a garbage disposal, we'd all still take turns at it, even if it was turned on. But women, they have this power, that woman in the car, it was like she'd cursed us, you and me both. But we drive on, get to the house, ring the doorbell like twenty times before you remember you've got a key, and we get up to the party just in time to hear one of Ben Winter's dumb-blonde jokes. Billy Bucknell had been throwing up since about eight o'clock, and the bastard is still drinking. MoJo keeps stuffing his fat face with Cheet-os, every now and then burping or farting;

196

three guys I don't know are there, too, not that into the flicks, more into the poker game and cigars; Alec's little brother Pasco is sneaking peeks at the TV screen, but pretending to be more into a bowl of pretzels. And Alec—where the hell is he? Back in the can, ralphing his guts out—he's not too good at mixing the finer liquors with the baser variety, but our motto through college had always been that if you boot then you can keep on drinking. Alec was going to become a severe alcoholic, by the look of things, because within ten minutes of coming out of the bathroom, he's already mixing Zombies with Todd Ramey ("from Wisconsin," he kept telling everybody who gave a fuck). So Alec is battered and sloshed from the twin bombs of imminent marriage and bad booze, but he still has the classic smile and his dark hair still parts perfectly to one floppy side. "Hey, you," he flags me down with an overflowing plastic cup, "get it over here, man," he says, putting his arm out for a big hug. "Dude, you should've seen the mud getting flung at dinner, her sister's a major twat."

When I get close to him, his breath is like unto a toilet bowl; I pull back a little to let a breeze from the ocean beyond the open window protect me. You keep looking at your watch; you're nervous, I guess, about the whore. I say. "So, Lec, I saw Pasco. Getting tall these days, that boy is."

This brings a tear to Alec's eye. "My baby brother. Gettin' older. Already he's climbed into more panties than me. HEY!" shouting across the room, "PASQUALE!"

197

His brother glances over, shakes his head, maybe even rolls his eyes, and looks away.

"He's pissed 'cause he's taking her side in this." Alec makes some obscure but definitely obscene gesture toward his brother.

"Whose side?"

"Luce's. She and that sister—Jesus, is all I can say. Just Jesus. Hey, you wanna get stoned? C'mon, please? Wanna get stoned?"

I shake my head, but I can tell that you, you want to get stoned 'cause you're all shivering, and I'm afraid you're about to blow it and tell him this whore's coming from the city, the kind with a pimp. But you don't blow it; you go over to get another drink, and I think that's a good idea. "What's up with Luce?"

"Ah, that bitch. Thinks she owns me. God, this is a good party, all my friends." Alec begins crying; he was always verging on the sentimental, ever since I'd first met him. It was some Italian thing, I guess (he always said it was), about not needing to keep a tight rein on emotions, all the stuff. I kind of liked him for it, because I've never been a good one with the tears and open with anger. So, anyway, he tells me all about this thing with Luce, how she heard some story from her sister about Alec and this girl at a party from about a week back and suddenly she's claiming that he's doing everything that walks the earth. "She has this trust thing, it's something I don't understand," he says. "I mean, I trust her, hell, I'd trust her even if she was jawing some guy right in the backseat while I was driving, why the hell doesn't she trust me? It's not like I was unfaithful to her or anything, I was just, well, pursuing a little."

"Women." I shake my head, amazed that yet another woman failed to understand a man so completely. "And it's not like you were even married."

We both crack up at this, drunk as we are. "She even called me an asshole," he says, and we laugh some more.

"Of course," I say, coming down from the laughing high just like those kids in Mary Poppins when they came down from Uncle Albert's ceiling, "it's true. I mean, we're all assholes. Basically. All men are assholes."

"Basically," he concurs, and we crack up again.

As if this were the greatest cue in the world, the French doors open—we're at your folks' house at Redondo, with the cliff and the balcony and the moon-swept Pacific just out there—out there—and it's the door to the balcony, so whoever it is has to have climbed up the trellis or something to get to the second floor, and who do you think's standing there with a tight green dress and a big old ribbon tied around her waist looking like Malibu Barbie on a date, but Luce, more Nautilized and Jazzercised than when I'd last seen her, and she just keeps coming like a barracuda right toward Alec and spits in his face.

He's still laughing from the joke, too, so now he's all shiny and laughing and hiccuping like he might start throwing up again.

Luce looks at me. "When he sobers up, tell him there won't be a wedding, tell him I know all about it, and tell him he can go to hell."

Then she turns and sort of flounces out of the room, down the hall stairs, presumably to go out the front door now.

"What," Alec says, shaking his head, "she fly up here on her broom?"

"Must've," I say, "so, wedding's off?"

"Jesus, if I listened to her, the wedding would've been off for the past six months. Trust me, man, she's gonna be there tomorrow, it's costing her dad too much and her ego way too much—she'd rather wait and get divorced later on, I know her, I know my Luce." And it was true about Luce—she'd rather worry about divorce in a couple of years than NOT GETTING MARRIED. She attached a lot of status to Alec—his family was rich, he was rich, and they were going to live in Palos Fucking Verde Estates and have a house big enough for the two of them and any lovers that snuck in the back door.

But with love, who knows? Could be once that ring was on his finger, he'd be the most faithful little lapdog the world has ever known. Could be she would be, too, and then they'd sink into the marriage trap where sex is an outmoded idea, and lust gets swept between the rug and the floor.

But not the night of his Bachelor Party.

You keep drinking those Zombies, and I say to Alec, my arm around him, his arm around me, "We got this girl, Alec, oh, Christ is she a girl. She's got a nice rack of tits."

He giggles, and then dissolves into weeping again. "You're my best friend, you know that? You are my fucking-A best friend in the whole snatch-eating world."

"Yeah, yeah," I say, and the doorbell rings—I don't quite hear it, but you do, and you go to the door downstairs—I see you bounding down the stairs like a kid on Christmas. I decide to check out the poker game, but I can tell Alec's all hot for this stripper, and he watches the stairs expectantly.

You come up a few minutes later, the pimp and stripper in tow, and there's like dead silence—even the music stops, like the Bruce Springsteen CD knew when to end.

The stripper's changed clothes—she's in a kind of party outfit, something that Luce herself would wear, in fact, at a casual, by-the-sea kind of affair: it says glitz and glamour, but it also says throw me in the pool. Alec calls that kind of dress a French maid's outfit, a short skirt to show off legs, and lots of poofy ruffles, and those kind of fluffy short sleeves like the Good Witch had in *The Wizard of Oz*—in fact, she looks a little like the Good Witch, but with a very short dress and a nice rack of tits. But she's changed more than her clothes. I could swear her eyes had been brown when I'd spoken with her on the street, only now, they're Liz Taylor blue, and her skin seems sort of peaches and creamy, instead of the tanned and beat look she had before. But I know a good contact lens can do a lot, and maybe with makeup—I mean, women are so into changing their faces with paints and brushes, like they're all afraid we won't want to see their true faces (and I've seen a couple of chicks without their mascara and gloss and stuff, and let me tell you, it gets pretty scary when you're prettier than your date at four A.M.). Alec, he looked more fetching than Luce when she didn't wear a lot of makeup—I don't think I'm more into guys or anything, but give me Luce without makeup or Alec, and I'd rather see Alec's baby face down on my bone any day.

So the whore looks almost completely different than she had on the street. She looks like she could fit right in with the house and all of us, and I was thinking, boy, you did this right, you got the right girl.

I look over at you, and you wink at me, because we know that even if this girl costs us a thousand bucks or more, it's all worth it for Alec's last night before his doom.

Her pimp, who's still dressed like one of the Beach Boys on acid, is casing the place in a fairly obvious way, and I realize at this point that you and I have made a colossal mistake. We should've just got a stripper out of the phone book, but stupid me, I wanted a girl who would, for a little extra, take Alec into one of the empty bedrooms and sit on his face. The pimp sees me, comes over, grabs my drink out of my hand, and drinks it. Fairly turns my stomach. "Nice place," he says, his voice half gravel and half belch. "Name's Lucky. You boys gonna have a good time tonight?"

"Yeah, yeah," I say, wishing we'd wiped him off on the doormat out front.

Then he whispered, "You be careful with her, now,

boy, 'cause she's one of a kind, and I don't want nothing funny to happen to her. If there's gonna be sex, it's got to only be head or hand, no tail, you got me? It ain't safe for my girl to do tail, not with everything going around."

It dawns on me, drunk as I'm getting, that in some sewer-rat way, he cares for this girl. "We will, don't worry, man. Get yourself a drink, sit down, enjoy!"

"Naw," he says, "it's time to let the games begin."

I notice he's packing something under his flappy shirt—just the glimpse of some kind of revolver. I think, well, he's in a rough business, but I know he's got to protect himself. He sees me see the gun, and we stare at each other, but he says nothing. He's got eyes like a snake, all perverted looking and squinty—sometimes I think people with squinty eyes have squinty brains, and this pimp, if anyone has one, hell, he's got the most squinty-ass brain on the planet. I'm thinking of maybe turning the revolver into a joke, by saying, "So's that a gun in your pants or are you just happy to see me," but I know people with squinty brains aren't going to chuckle at that old standby. I keep my mouth shut.

And then the girl punches up a CD of Rod Stewart's song "Hot Legs" or whatever it's called, and she started a routine.

But you don't want to hear about how she writhed and spun, how she took everything imaginable off, lifted one leg above her head, how Alec played the Golden Shower game with her, drinking Molson Golden Ale from her pubes; how she squatted on my face and took a rolled-up fifty from between my lips just using her snatch—those are all the basics of a good party stripper.

What you want to hear about is how your fingers got on the floor in the bathroom, with you screaming bloody murder, and how she screamed even louder, right?

That's what you want to hear.

## III

I guess I'm going to digress a little here, but only for clarity's sake—the night before Alec got married was one of those nights where you have to piece a few things together later on. Like Pasco, Alec's little bro, giggling and blushing when the girl sat on his lap naked and beat his pretty face silly with her tits; or when MoJo got pissed off because she wouldn't sit on his face for a lousy ten bucks; he said, whining, "Doesn't she know any cheaper games?"—see, the girl was so hot and we were so loaded, that we were dropping hundreds and fifties on her like she was a bank. Cigar smoke was the only veil she had around her, in the end, just that stagnant smoke that stinks and sits in the air like it doesn't have anywhere to go, and all of us, through its mist, looking like ghosts. That's what I thought at the time: we were enshrouded by the gray smoke, and we looked like ghosts, or maybe old men with wrinkly skin, testicular skin, pale and blurry of feature. Horny bastards all, MoJo licking his lips like he was trying to taste her from three feet away, and Billy Bucknell grabbing his crotch without even knowing he was doing it. She really had us going, that girl did. You even kept trying to get your hand up her, and she kept pushing you away, until her pimp had to come over and tell you to knock it off, that nobody, but nobody touches her kitty. That's what he called it, her kitty. Might as well have called it her flesh purse, since she was making so much money out of opening it up. The pimp and I had a nice convo about how prostitution was a victimless crime and all that; his name was Lucky Murphy, a nice Irish boy as it turned out, from Boston, who had once been a fisherman off Dana Point, and as he spoke I could practically hear someone's Irish mother singing "Danny Boy," until I looked him in the eye and knew he was a fucking liar through and through, that he was Hollywood scum and if he could, he would've been peddling all our preppie asses for the twenty bucks per corn hole he could make.

And we keep looking at her kitty, too, all our eyes drawn back to the unholies of unholy, "little pouty petals," you called it. You were pretty adamant about getting your fingers up there, weren't you, you horny son of a bitch? It wasn't the pastrami labia of *Penthouse* magazine, or the mu-shu pork-dripping-with-plum-sauce of other, nastier skin mags—it was pink and sweet, almost like a Portuguese man-of-war turned on its back.

And finally, when it was over, all her dances, she took the party boy into the bedroom, and all I can say is, he didn't come out for over an hour.

In fact, by eleven-fifteen, he hadn't come out at all, and that's when you and I decided to storm the room.

## IV

Now, I had seen this room once before—it was your folks' master bedroom, and it was a good size, with kind of a faggy bed, you were to ask me, lots of silk and brass; a nightstand that looked like it was out of the Versailles; green-gold wallpaper, shiny and clean like they'd just had it put up the day before; a wall that was nothing but mirrors; and two walk-in closets, the sizes of my apartment in Westwood; a bathroom, all gold-plated fixtures, something I always thought was tacky about your folks—and I told you this a few times, too—with a big round Jacuzzi bath and a window so you could take a bath and watch your neighbors at the same time.

The door is locked, of course, but you know how to take a dime and very simply unlock it. So we get in, and the bed is perfectly made; no sign of hooker or trick. You go into the bathroom to look for them, giggling as always both of us are, because we think we're going to find them with her ass bent over a sink and his schlong pumping in like an oil drill; I check out the walk-in closets, but there's nothing but tons of Armani and Valentino and the smell of Red and L'Air du Temps.

As I'm about to go into the second closet, the pimp comes running in, out of breath because it's quite a hike up those stairs in your folks' house. "What you boys doin'?"

I cackle—sometimes, when I'm really bombed and in a party mood, I do this laugh that's like "snort-cackle-pop," and it sounds like I hurt myself or something.

Then I notice he's got his revolver out.

Oh, shit, I'm thinking. I sober up real fast. "Looking for the party boy."

He just stares at me with the gun drawn, and that's when I hear the girl in the bathroom, kind of moaning, and you, too, still giggling, and that wet sound like rubber and lubricant.

And another sound, while the Irish pimp from hell is staring at me, a sound in the walk-in closet.

My hand is on the door.

But someone else's hand is on the other side of the door.

"Alec?" I ask the door.

The sound that comes back isn't entirely human, but it's human enough. It sounds like the noises Alec used to make when he was doing like a feeb imitation: like his tongue got cut out and his lips are shredded. So I think maybe it's some kind of setup and joke on me, so I give the door a good pull, and it opens.

Dresses and coats, hanging, rustling, in a dark closet.

The sound of slow dripping.

I can smell the pimp's breath: He's real close to me.

I can tell he's a little scared, too, and he still has the gun out.

He's pointing it at the dresses, hanging.

Something clear and dripping from the corner of a full-length mink coat.

I switch on the closet light, but the pimp very quickly switches it off again.

But in that one second of light, I see something in the corner.

Something that left a trail of slime and human waste in its path.

Its ribs quivering.

Open, and quivering, like the skeleton of a boat, a slaughterhouse boat with the flesh and innards of animals dripping from its deck.

It's always through the eyes that you know someone. I once took care of a friend's dog when I was eight; and then, when I was nineteen, and had long before moved away from that friend, I was in New York, in Central Park, and I saw in the eyes of a dog an old friend, and sure enough, it was the dog I had known when I was eight, and in Orange County. It's always there in the eyes, the person, the animal, the creature, not in the skin or voice or the movements: It's in the eyes.

So I had seen in the brief light, his eyes, Alec's eyes, left in their sockets long after the skin had been torn from bone and skull to make the rest of him resemble a skinned possum.

And when it registers on my brain that it's Alec, that this girl did something to Alec, something inhuman, I hear your scream from the bathroom, and I turn and the pimp turns, and the girl screams, too, and there's the sound of breaking glass.

The pimp gets to the bathroom first, before me, and I hear him fire two shots; I'm just behind him, and when I see you clutching your hand with all that blood coming out, I figure the pimp shot your fingers off. For just a second, I see her, too, not as she was, pretty and tall and sexy, but some small tentacled thing, like a sea urchin, dropped from between her legs, released from the empty and ragged socket that had been her vagina, with a cut umbilical cord, loping on its wormlike feelers across the bathtub rim, out the broken window, into the night.

The pimp yells, "Goddamn it, that fucking bitch," then drops his gun, grabs me by the collar, "You bastards, you asked for it, you ain't supposed to get her down there, that's what she wants, you sons of bitches, you're supposed to get head or a hand job, didn't she tell you? She tricked you, and she was the best, you sons of whores!" He's weeping, and I'm thinking, Christ, he's in love with . . . that thing.

"Is that a fucking alien?" I'm screaming. "You brought some fucking outer space—"

But he cuts me off, spitting a wad of slime on my face. "I fished her out of the sea, asshole, down at Santa Monica pier, she got caught on my hook and she does things to you, she gets boys like you, but not like this, it's up to you, your buddies wanting to put it there, but I told you that ain't allowed! She's the best, but you can't touch her there, it's so hard to trap her, and now, look what you done!"

But you, you start screaming again and turning blue, so the pimp lets me go and goes running out of there in search of his escaped sea creature. That's when I figure it's time to call an ambulance.

## V

So now I know it wasn't the pimp shooting at you, but at that thing, that thing that you stuck your fingers up into. It was hell cleaning up the mess in the bathroom, getting rid of her skin. Funny thing about her skin and guts—they looked like they'd been spun with a fine silk, but they were all sticky, just like she was some kind of tar baby out of Uncle Remus. You were lucky to lose only your fingers. Think of what Alec lost, the night before he got married—not that he ever did get married. He's sort of a vegetable now, living off of machines at his folks' house, and Luce got married to Billy Bucknell last year, that scheming son of a gun.

You and me, we're rooming together these days. My new nickname for you is Fingers, and in the morning, when you bring me coffee, it's kind of nice, just the two of us. We get by. I tried to do it with a girl again, after that, but what if she's up inside there, what if that girl's just spun out of her silk, what if she's waiting to take me to the Big O and rip my skin right off my back and end up like Alec with wires and tubes all over him and his eyes, so weird and sad, like he had it, that orgasm at the end of the universe, like maybe it was worth it, what she did to him, but I got to tell you, Fingers, I got to tell you, I'm never getting close to one of those things again as long as we both shall live.

I keep seeing it in their faces, their eyes, the It that was the whore's core, the creature in the flesh purse, and I feel like It's coming for both of us, maybe to finish off the job. Alec, too, maybe even Billy Bucknell, and MoJo, and Pasco, and Ben Winter. Sometimes at night, when I can't sleep, I hear It's sloppy wiping at the windows, and I pull the covers up over the two of us just to feel safe. You and me, we'll take care of each other, we don't have to go out much, at least not till we get evicted, and then we can hide under the sewers or in the alleys, and if we see her, if we still got legs, we can run, you and I, I will not abandon you to It, and I promise, for better or worse, good buddy.

In sickness and in health.

# The Ripening Sweetness of Late Afternoon

Sunland City was the last place in the world Jesus was ever going to come looking for Roy Shadiak.

He returned to his hometown in his fortieth year, after he felt he could never again sell Jesus to the rabble. Something within him had been eating him up for years. His love for life had long before dried up, and then so had his marriage and his bitter understanding of how God operated in the world. He'd gotten off the bus out at the flats, and brushed off the boredom of a long trip down infinite highways. He stood awhile beside the canals and watched the gators as they lay still as death in the muddy shallows. He'd been wearing his ice-cream suit for the trip because it was what his mother liked him to wear, and because it was the only suit of his that still fit him. And it fit Sunland City, with its canals and palmettos and merciless sunshine. It was a small town, the City was, and they would think him mad to arrive on the noon bus in anything other than creamy white. He would walk down Hispaniola Street and make a detour into the Flamingo for a double-shot vodka. The boys in there, they'd see him, maybe recognize him, maybe the whores, too, and call him the King, and he'd tell them all about how he was back for good. He'd tell them that he didn't care what the hell happened to Susie and the brats and that doctor she took up with. He'd tell them he was going to open a movie theater or manage the A & P or open a boat-rental business. He'd tell them that anything you really needed, and all you could depend on in this life, you could find in your own backyard. Didn't need God. Nobody needed God.

God was like the phone company: You paid your bill, and sometimes you got cut off anyway. Sometimes, if you changed your way of thinking, you just did without a phone. Sometimes you switched companies.

Oh, but he still needed God. Within his secret self, he had to admit it. Roy Shadiak still needed to know that he could save at least one soul in the world. His feet ached in his shoes. He had only brought one suitcase. He had just walked out on Susie. It was in his blood to walk. His father had walked, and his grandfather had walked. They probably got tired of Jesus and all the damn charity, too. Even Frankie had walked, as best he could. All leaving before they got left. Roy had blisters on the bottoms of his feet, but still he walked.

He passed beneath the Lover's Bridge, and the Bridge of Sighs, with its hanging vines and parrot cages. He walked along the muddy bank of the north canal, knowing that he could close his eyes and still find his way to Hispaniola Street. All the street names were like that: Spanish, or a mix of Indian and Slave, named like Occala and Gitchie and Corona del Mar. Sunland City was a many-flavored thing, but in name only, for its inhabitants would've been pale and translucent as maggots if not for the sulfurous sun. All the canals were thick with lilies, and snapping turtles lounged across the rock islets. The water was murky and stank, but beautiful pure white swans cut across the calm surface as if to belie the muck of this life. Roy saw three men, old-timers, with their fresh-rolled cigarillos and Panama hats, on a punt. He waved to them, but they didn't notice him, for they were old and half blind.

After climbing the steep steps up to the street level again, he was surprised to observe the stillness of clay-baked Sunland City. As a boy, it had always seemed like an Italian water town, not precisely a Venice and something less than a Naples, thrust into the Gulf Coast like a conqueror's flag.

But now it seemed as ancient as any dying European citadel: It looked as if the conqueror, having pillaged and raped, had left a wake of buildings and archways and space. It had been a lively seaport once. It was now a vacant conch. The hurricane that had torn through it the previous year had not touched a building, but it had cleaned the streets of any evidence of life. When he found the Flamingo, he kissed the first

214

girl he set eyes on, a wench in the first degree with a
beer in one hand with which to wipe off that same kiss.
A teenage boy in a letterman's jacket sat two stools
over. The boy turned and stared at him for a good long
while before saying anything. Then, suddenly, as if
possessed, the boy shouted, "Holy shit, you're King!"

"And you, my friend, are underage."

The boy stood up—he was tall and gangly, with a
mop of curly blond hair, a face of dimming acne, and
cheek of tan. He thrust his hand out. "Billy Wright. I
swim, too."

"Oh."

"But you're like a legend. A fucking legend. The
King. King Shadiak."

"Am I?"

"You beat out every team to Daytona Beach. You
beat out fucking Houston."

"Did I? Well, it was a long time before you were
born."

"You ever see the display they got on you?" Billy
pressed his palms flat against the air. "The glass cabi-
net in the front hall, near the locker room. Seven gold
trophies. Seven! Pictures! Your goggles, too. Your
fucking goggles, man."

"If they do all that for you at your high school, you
should really be something, shouldn't you?"

Billy made a thumbs-up sign. "Fucking-A. You are
something, man."

"I'm nothing," Roy said, downing his drink and
slamming the glass on the bar for another. "No, make
that: I'm fucking nothing, man."

"What you been doin' all this time, man?" Billy asked, apparently oblivious to anything short of his own cries of adoration.

"Selling Jesus."

"Who'd you sell him to?"

Roy laughed. "You're all right, boy. You are all right."

"Thanks," Billy said, then glanced at his watch. "I better get going. Curfew soon. Listen, you come by and see me if you got car trouble. I work at night at Jack Thompson's. You know him? I can fix any problem with any car. I'm not the King of anything like you, but I may be the Prince of Mechanics."

"Why would anyone care if his car got fixed around here?"

The boy laughed. "That's a good one."

When Roy arrived at his mother's house a half hour later, he was three beers short of a dozen.

"The great King comes home." His mother's voice was flat, like the land. "You had to get drunk before you saw me. And you couldn't shave for me, could you?" Alice Shadiak asked. His mother wore khaki slacks and a white blouse. She had lost some weight over the past few years, and seemed whiter, as if the sun had bleached her bones right through her skin. A sun-visor cap protected her face. She had seen him from the kitchen window, and had come to greet him on the porch. "I suppose you need a place to stay."

"I can stay downtown."

"With your whores?"

"They all missed curfew, apparently." He attempted a light note. "Must've heard I was on my way."

His mother sighed as if a great weight had just been given her. "Some man of God you turned out to be. I just wish you'd've called ahead. I'd've had Louise fix up your old room. Lloyd's in Sherry's old room. The house is a mess. Don't act like such a foreigner, Roy, for God's sakes. Give me a hug, would you?" She moved forward. In all his life, he could count the times she'd hugged him. But he knew he needed to change, somehow. He had not hit on precisely how. He would have to listen to his own instincts, then disobey them to find out how he might change. He held his mother, smelled her saltwater hair. When he let go, she said, "Susie called. She wants to know when you're going to forgive her."

"Never," Roy said.

"What are you going to do?" Alice asked.

Roy Shadiak said, "Mama, I had a dream. It came to me one night. A voice said—"

His mother interrupted. "Was it Jesus?"

"It was just a voice. It said, 'Set your place at the table.' Something's trying to come through me. I know it. I can feel it. Like a revelation."

"It was just a dream," Alice said, sounding troubled. "What could it mean? Oh, Roy, you're vexing yourself over nothing."

"This is my table. Sunland City. I have to set my place here," Roy said. Then he began weeping. His mother held him, but not too close.

"A man as big as you shouldn't be crying."

"It's all I have left," he said, drying his tears on the cuffs of his shirt. "You live your life and make a few mistakes, but you lose everything anyway. Everything I ever had, it all came from here. Everything I ever was."

Alice Shadiak took a good hard look at her son and slapped him with the back of her hand. "You did it to yourself, what you are. Who you are. Don't blame me or your father or anyone else. All this big world talk and wife-leaving and crying. Don't think just because it's been twenty-two years that you can just walk back in here and pretend none of it ever happened." She raised her fist, not at him but at the sky, the open sky that was colored the most glorious blue with cloud striations across its curved spine. "No God who takes my boys away from me is welcome in my house."

"I told you, I don't work for God anymore," Roy said. He went past her, into the house. He found the guest bedroom cluttered, but pushed aside his mother's sewing and the stacks of magazines on the bed. He wrapped the quilt around his shoulders and fell asleep in his suit.

In the morning, he took a milk crate down to the town center. He set it down and stood up on it just as he would in other towns when he had preached the gospel. Folks passed by on their way to work, and barely noticed him. He spread his arms out as if measuring Sunland City and cried out, "I am King Shadiak and I have come here to atone for the murders of my brother Frankie and his friend, Kip Renner!"

A woman turned about as she stepped; a laborer in a broad straw hat glanced up from the curb where he sat with a coffee cup; an old Ford pickup slowed as its owner rolled down the window to hear.

As Roy Shadiak spoke, others gathered around him, the older crowd mostly, the crowd that knew him, the people who had been there when he'd drowned the two boys at the public swimming pool over on Hispaniola Street, down near the Esso station, by the railroad tracks.

"No need, Roy," one of the men called out. "We don't need your kind of atonement. We been fine all these years without it."

"That's right," several people added, and others nodded without uttering a word.

"No," Roy said, pressing the flat of his hand against the air in front of him as if it were an invisible wall. "All these years I've squandered my life in service to others. I owe Sunland City an atonement."

"You want us to crucify you, King?" Someone laughed.

Others chuckled more quietly.

"That is exactly what I want," Roy Shadiak said. "Two atonements, two murders."

A woman in the crowd shouted, "Two atonements for two murders!"

"Two atonements! Two murders!" others began chanting.

"Frankie Shadiak!" Roy shouted. "Kip Renner!"

"Two atonements! Two murders!" The crowd

became familiar now. Roy saw Ellen Mawbry from tenth grade, Willy Potter from the corner store, the entire Forster clan, the Rogerses, the Sayreses, the Blankenships, the Fowlers. As he chanted and as they chanted as the day loped forward, they all gathered— labor stopped, activity ceased, schools let out for a spontaneous holiday, until the town center of Sunland City was a sea of the familiar and the new. All turned out for the returning hero, their King, who passed among them to offer his life for their suffering.

"Two atonements!" they cried as if their voices would reach beyond that Florida sky.

It was what Roy expected from a town that God had turned his back on twenty-three years before.

And then Helen Renner, her hair gone white, stepped out of the crowd toward him. She wiped her hands on her apron, as if she'd just finished baking, and went and stood at the foot of the milk crate.

Roy crouched down and took her face in his hands.

"Don't do it," she said. "Roy Shadiak, don't you do it. Neither one of them was worth it. We all let it happen. We're all responsible. It may not even fix anything, Roy. There's no guarantee."

His kissed her on her forehead. "I've got to. It's something inside of me that needs room to grow, and I've been killing it all these years. I've been killing everyone of you, too. Two atonements," he repeated, "for two murders."

Joe Fowler was a crackerjack carpenter. He and his assistant, Jaspar, were at the Shadiak house within an hour of Roy's leave-taking of the makeshift podium. He stood on the porch in paint-spatter overalls, his khaki hat in his hands, looking through the screen door at Roy's mother. "We got some railroad ties from out the Yard," he said. "They got pitch on 'em, but I think they gonna be just fine for the job." His voice quavered. "We'd like to offer our services, Alice."

Alice Shadiak stood like stone. "You and your kind can get off my porch. I don't mean to lose two sons in this lifetime."

Roy came up behind her, touching her gently on the shoulder. "Mama, it's got to be done."

"Where is it written? Where?"

"On my soul," he said.

"Our kind has no soul," she said, pulling away from him. "I don't need God's forgiveness on my house. I don't want sweet Jesus' tears."

"It's Jesus that keeps you here."

"He doesn't even look on us, Roy," his mother said. "He doesn't even come to our churches. What does it matter? Does anyone in Sunland really believe there's a Jesus waiting to shine his light on us?"

"That's because of me."

"It's because your brother and his sick little friend were unnatural and perverted, and God cared more for them than for decency or nature or for any of us. I don't mind burning for that, Roy. I don't mind that sacrifice."

"I do," Roy said. "I saw Jesus out in the fields up north, and in the alleys of the fallen. Nobody else did. And you know why? Because Jesus was laughing at me, he was showing me that he was not going to be mine. He was going to belong to every fool who walked this earth."

Joe Fowler nudged the screen door open and stepped inside. "He's right, Alice. We ain't had Jesus or God for all this time, only those . . . things." He shivered a little, as if remembering a nightmare. In a softer voice, he said, "I'm getting tired of this life."

"I would advise you to get out of the light, Joe," Alice Shadiak said, sounding like the retired schoolteacher that she was. "I heard about your little Nadine."

All of them were silent for a moment, and Roy thought for a second he heard the cry of some hawk as it located its prey.

"Your boy knows what he's doing," Joe said, spreading his hands as if he could convince her with gestures. Still, he glanced briefly up at the empty sky. "We can't keep on like this." Then Joe grinned, but Roy could tell he was tense. "I'm prouder of you now, King, than I was when you won all those ribbons at the championship. Why don't we get on with this business?"

"Yes," Roy said, feeling an ache in his heart for Susie and the kids, but not wanting to retrace his steps. He glanced out on the porch, and beyond, to Joe's truck. "That's a sturdy-looking piece of wood, Joe."

"From the old Tuskegee route, before tracks got tore up. We're going to have to balance them good. That's why I brought Jaspar here." He nodded toward his assistant, who stood, mutely, on the porch. "We can get this going now, you like."

"Why wait?" Roy shrugged.

His mother retreated into the shadowy parlor. She called to him, but Roy did not respond.

Jaspar suddenly pointed to the sky and made a rasping sound in his throat.

Calmly, Joe Fowler said, "Come on in, Jasp, come on, it's okay, you'll make it."

As if too frightened to move, Jaspar stood there, sweat shining on his face. He stared up at the sky, pointing and shaking.

"Jaspar." Joe opened the screen porch slightly, beckoning with his hand.

Roy shoved Joe out of the way and ran out to the porch. He grabbed the young man by his waist.

The cry grew louder as the great bird in the sky dropped, blackening out the sun for a moment.


The smell was the worst thing, because they got it on their talons sometimes, from an earlier victim, that sweet awful stink that overrode all other senses.

Roy hadn't slept a night without remembering that smell. He couldn't get it out of his head for the rest of the afternoon.

"Where do they take them?" Roy asked.

Joe, who was still jittery, helped himself to the vodka. "Down to the shore. There's at least a hundred out there. And the rotting seaweed, too, and the flies, all the crawling things . . . it turned my stomach when I had to go down there to try and find Nadine."

"That's where it has to be."

"No, King. No. I won't go down there, no matter if it's midnight or midday."

"But how can you abandon her?"

Joe turned his face toward his glass. "She's ain't her. I saw her. I risked my sanity, and I saw her. It ain't her. It's a It, not a little girl. I told her not to go out between two and four. All of us know about the curfew. All of us know to stay inside. And you . . . " Joe shook his head. He raised his glass as if to toast Roy. "You're the luckiest son of a bitch alive, you can get out, and instead, you decide to come back. You fucked up once, King, you don't need to keep on doing it."

"How many are left?"

"First, have a drink." Joe pushed the glass across the kitchen table.

Roy picked it up. Downed the remainder. Set the glass down. "How many?"

"Twenty-six in one piece. The rest in as many as they leave us in. Some morning, you take a walk down there. Only, if any of them calls your name, you just run, you hear? You don't want to know who it is, believe you me."

Roy reached across the table and pressed his hand against Joe's shoulder. "That's where we need to do it."

"I ain't never going down there again."

"You'd rather all this continued?"

"Than go down there? You're damned right."

"I'll find someone else, then."

Joe stood up, pushing his chair back. He said nothing. He stomped out of the kitchen and went to sit with Jaspar and Alice.

Roy drank some more vodka. He glanced out the bay window. On the roof, two houses over, three of them had a woman pressed against the curved Spanish tile. Their wings had folded against their bodies, and they were digging with their talons into the soft flesh of her stomach.

He was sure that one of them saw him spying, and grinned.

That night, he found the teenager working at Jack Thompson's garage on the south corner of Hattatonquee Plaza.

"Billy?" Roy asked as he stood beneath a streetlamp.

The boy dropped the wrench he was using and bounded out to the sidewalk. "Hey, it's the King. How you doin'?" He snapped his fingers several times, as if he was nervous.

"I'm doing just fine. And yourself?"

"Hey, any day you get through the afternoon here's a good day. So I heard you're going to try something."

Roy nodded. "Let's go for a walk, Billy. Can you get off work?"

"Sure, let me just tell Mr. Thompson, okay?"

Several minutes later, they were walking down along Hispaniola Street toward Upper Street. Roy had been doing all the talking, ending with "And that's where you come in. Joe'll give me the ties, but I need someone to help."

"I don't know," Billy said. "You ever see how big those suckers are?"

"Yep. But we won't be out that late. We can do this at nine or ten in the morning. Hell, if you want, we can probably do it tonight."

"I heard the beach is really a bad scene. My dad got taken down there. I heard this guy at school say that they're like cracked eggs or they're all ripped up, only not quite dead yet. If I think about it too much, I get sick."

"It must be strange."

"What's that?"

"Well, you grew up in it. You never knew what the world was like before. You don't know what the rest of the world is like."

Billy stopped walking. "I thought it happened everywhere."

Roy shook his head. "Only here. Because of what I did."

"I don't believe you."

"Other places, you can walk around anytime of the day or night and those things don't attack. Honest. When I was the King here, I used to skip classes at two and take off with my friends to Edgewater to the McDonald's. Didn't anyone tell you? Not even your dad?"

Billy shook his head. "Well, if God did this, why didn't he do it just to you?"

Roy shrugged. "Who knows? It may not even have been God. I've never seen Jesus. Maybe there's just those things. The way I figured it, it's not just because of me killing those boys. It's because everybody here thought it was okay, no big deal. Nobody made a fuss."

"You loved your brother?"

"I did, but I didn't know it then. I wanted him and his friend to go to hell back then. I was the King back then. I thought I was God, I guess."

They came to the end of the Upper Street, which stopped at the slight dune overlooking the stretch of flat beach.

The full moon shone across the glassy sea. The sand itself glowed an unearthly green from the diatoms that had burst from the waves.

On the sand, the shadow of slow, pained movement as a hundred or more mangled, half-eaten Sunlanders struggled to die in a corner of the earth where there was no death.

Billy said, "I saw one of them up close. When they got my dad. She had long hair, and her eyes were silver. She had the fur, and the claws and all, and her wings, like a pterodactyl. But there was something in her face that was almost human. Even when she tore my dad's throat open, she looked kind of like a girl. Boy," he shivered, "I'm sure glad I'm up here and not down there. Down there looks like hell."

Roy said, "From down there, up here looks like hell, too. And it won't just end by itself."

Billy seemed to understand. "You swear you're not lying about what everywhere else is like?"

"I swear."

"Okay. Let's go down there. But in the morning. After the sun's up. I still can't believe it," Billy cocked his head to the side, looking from the moon to the sand to the sea to Roy. "I'm standing here with the King."

"Is that enough for you?"

"I guess. I got laid once, and that was enough. Standing here with you, that's enough." Billy pointed out someone, perhaps a woman, trying to stand up by pushing herself against a mass of writhing bodies, but she fell each time she made the attempt. "When I was little, we used to come down here and throw stones at some of them. But it's kind of sad, ain't it? Some of the guys I used to throw stones with, they're down there now. Someday, I'm going to be down there too, and if there are any girls left, they'll have babies, and they'll start throwing stones at me too. Where does it end?"

"Now," Roy said. "In the morning. You and me and a couple of railroad ties."

"There's going to be lots of pain, though, huh?"

"There's always pain. You either get it over with quick, or it takes a lifetime."

Billy rubbed his hands over his eyes. "I'm not crying or nothing."

"I know."

"I just want to get my head straight for this. I mean, we're both going to hurt, huh?"

"You don't have to. I do. I can find someone else to help."

228

"No. We'll do it. Then I'll be a legend too, huh? Maybe that's enough. We just drag those ties down there and set it up. One way or another, we all end up on that beach anyway, huh?"

It was easier said than done, for they had to borrow Joe's truck to get the railroad ties to the beach, which was the easy part. Lugging those enormous sticks across the burning sand, sliding them across the bodies, the faces . . . it made a mile on a Thursday morning at nine A.M. seem like forty or more. By the time they'd arrived at a clearing, Billy was too exhausted to speak. When he finally did, he pointed back at Sunland. "Look."

Roy, whose body was soaked, his ice-cream suit sticking to his skin, glanced up.

There, on the edge of Upper Street and Beach Boulevard was the entire town, lined up as if to watch some elegant ocean liner pass by. The chanting began later. At first the words were indistinct. Gradually, the boy and the man could hear them clearly: two murders, two atonements.

"Roy?" Billy asked.

"Yes?"

"I'm scared. I'm really scared."

"It's okay. I'm here. I'll go first."

"No. I want to go first. I want you to do me first. I might run if I go last. I can't do it right if I go last—I mean, I'll fuck it up somehow."

"All right." Roy went over and put his arm across Billy's shoulder. "Don't be afraid, son. When this is over, it'll all change again. Atonement works like that."

"I wasn't even born when you did it. Why shouldn't one of them do it with you? Why me?"

"Now, Billy, don't be afraid. If they could've done it before, they would've. I think Jesus brought you and me together for this."

"I don't even know Jesus."

"You will. Come on," Roy lifted up one of the smaller spikes and placed its end against Billy's wrist. "This one'll fit. See? It's not so bad. It's just a nail. And all a nail can do is set something in place. It's so you won't fall. You don't want to fall, do you?"

"Tell me again how you'll do it?"

"Oh, well, I set this rope up around my hand so I can keep it up like this . . . and then I press the pointed part of the nail against my hand and pull on the rope. My hand goes back in place, see? Like this, only I have to push a little, too."

"You won't leave me, will you?"

"No, I won't. I'm the King and you're the Prince, remember? I won't abandon you. Now, why don't you just lie down on it, like that, and your hand, see? It's going to pinch a little, but just pretend it's one of those things with the claws. Just pretend you won't scream, because you know they like it when someone screams. Okay? Billy, don't be afraid, don't be afraid . . ." Roy spoke soothingly as he drove the spikes through Billy's wrists.

By two, they'd both gotten used to the pain of the crosses. Roy tried to turn his head toward Billy to see how he was holding up, but his neck was too stiff and he could not.

"When's it going to happen?" Billy's voice seemed weak.

"Soon, I guarantee it. I had a dream from God, Billy. Something inside of me knew what to do."

Billy began weeping. "Just because of a couple of queers. What kind of God is that?"

"It's the only God."

"I don't believe it," Billy whimpered. "I don't believe that God would punish everyone just because of what you did. I don't believe that God would punish the unborn just because of what you did. It's all a lie, ain't it? We just did something stupid, building crosses and crucifying ourselves. Look at that, look up."

Roy tried to look up, but he couldn't. What he could see was the endless sea, and the shimmering sky as the sun crisped the edges of the afternoon. The smell was growing stronger from the bodies.

"I don't believe in God!" Billy cried. "Somebody! Get me down! Get me down! He's crazy! Somebody help me! Somebody get me down! Jesus!"

Roy tried to calm him with words, but Billy didn't stop screaming until an angel dropped from the sky and tore into him.

Roy remained, untouched, on the cross, amid the writhing bodies on the shore of the damned. He waited for some sign of his atonement, but only night came, and then day, and then the long afternoon set in.

# *Chosen*

*I*

When it was over, he remembered the picture.

Because of living in the big city all his life, his first-hand knowledge of nature had come from PBS documentaries, or Time-Life Books, or *Mutual of Omaha's Wild Kingdom.*

But he had forgotten about the picture all those years.

The caterpillar, its skin green and translucent and wet.

The wasp.

The bumps beneath the caterpillar's skin.

The caption: "As paralysis sets in, the wasp has proven her superior power."

He remembered what he thought, too, of the picture:

that in some awful way it radiated a beauty beyond conscience.

This was what he kept coming back to, later, when it was over, in his mind. Not his emotional life or his education or even his work, but that picture from a book he'd seen at the public library when he was only nine or ten. How, even in his forties, it could come back to him with so strong a memory.

## II

Rob Arlington awoke one morning and thought he felt something on his hand. He brushed at it but saw nothing there. A sensation left over from a dream, perhaps. He took a quick shower, crawled into his suit (he was so tired from being up late the night before), and grabbed his briefcase on his way out the door. It wasn't that he was late for work, it was just that for the fifteen years of his life that he had lived alone, he hated it. Not life, not work, not his loves and losses, but just the fact of knowing he was alone in the morning, that, at his age (forty), there was no one human being who shared his home with him.

The hallway, when he stepped into it, was hospital green, and smelled of paint. He locked his door, then thought he heard a noise from inside it. As if something were moving around in the kitchen. He looked at his door: to open or not? Could be just an echo from another apartment. Glancing down the hall, he saw, just this side of the fire doors, the super, papers in one hand, a dripping paintbrush in the other.

"Exterminator comes on Thursday," the super said. He was taping notes to doors; he came up to Rob and slapped a note to his door. The super, with his fat glasses and balding pate with its twin sprays of hair, looked like a large worker ant going about its business. Rob shot him a friendly grin—never hurts to be on good terms with management—and lifted the note off his door. It read: "Exterminator comes on Thursday. 10 A.M. He wadded the noted up.

"I don't want the exterminator," Rob said, still vaguely listening for the thing that might be moving around in his kitchen. Was it a rat?

"You don't got roaches?" The super, his glasses magnifying his small button eyes to enormous disks of glare, thrust out his lower lip in a middle-aged pout that meant disagreement. "Everybody in New York's got roaches."

"None that I've noticed," Rob lied. Of course he had roaches, but he also didn't like the idea of the super and his wife going into his apartment, looking through his things. He already had evidence of their last visit when he'd been on a business trip to California, how they'd gotten in and used his teakettle. He'd known it was the super, or perhaps Fanny, his wife, because they'd left behind a set of skeleton keys, which Rob returned to them hoping that embarrassment would be enough incentive to keep them from going through their tenants' homes again. "Look," Rob told him, "I've been fogging."

"You been what?"

"Fogging the apartment. I buy these foggers—you

know—and it kills them. I don't have roaches. Or spiders, for that matter."

Then 6C opened her door. She was clunky and large, like an old piano, with hair in her eyes from just washing, and an enormous towel wrapped around her middle, barely keeping her breasts bound up. "I don't want one either," she said. "A bug killer. Don't let him into my place. Let me chance being beloved of the flies, but I don't want no bug killer coming through my place. I like my privacy."

The super looked at her, then back at Rob. "Pretty soon, everybody's gonna tell me they got no roaches. Why in hell'd I call up the exterminator if suddenly nobody's got no roaches?"

The woman in the doorway glanced at Rob. Her eyes were wide and glassy, like she'd just had great sex and was now a zombie. She was not pretty, but still looked freshly plucked, which, to a man of Rob's years (just about forty) was just this side of alluring. She was less overweight than stocky, and her skin was pale from staying inside too much. When the super had gone on down the hall, through the fire doors, she said, "Do you really fog?"

She'd been eavesdropping at her door, he figured. "No," he said, "I just don't like the nosy couple going into my apartment without me around."

She let slip a smile and blushed, as if she'd just dropped an edge of her towel. "They do anyway. I'm here all day, and I see them. They go through all our apartments. All except mine. 'Cause I'm here all the time."

Then she drew herself back through the doorway, hands clutching the door and frame, as if her legs weren't quite strong enough. She seemed to drag them with her, one after the other.

On the weekend, Maggie came up. When she and Rob lay after the Great Event, him feeling sticky, and her feeling exhausted, he mentioned meeting the neighbor for the first time. Maggie said, "I've talked to her on the elevator. She seems nice. It's too bad about the accident, but I guess we all get smashed about once or twice before life is up."

He moved his arm around, because the back of her head seemed to cut into it at an uncomfortable angle. "She get hit by a car or something?" Remembering his neighbor's legs, how she barely moved them.

"She told me she's agoraphobic. Stays in all the time. Lives on disability. Sad little thing."

"Sad hefty thing. How the hell does she afford that apartment on disability?"

"That's not nice, the hefty part. It's her grandfather's old apartment—he had it since the building was built in 1906. He knew the Lonsdale family, in fact, when they were designing the place. And she's sweet, even if she is strange. She's only thirty-four—can you believe it? It's life that's aged her—in that apartment, all her grandparents' things around, antiques, and dark windows, and old shiny floors, she just sits there and collects her checks and . . . well, *ages*."

"Like a cheese left too long under glass," he joked. "She claims she's beloved of flies."

Maggie was beginning to look stern; she didn't appreciate disparaging comments about women. "Oh, stop, you. She's had a terrible life. She worked at a grocer's, but her back bent or something. And then she finally works up the courage to get out, into the marketplace, as it were. She went out one day, she told me, to see her mother, who's in Brooklyn, and when she was coming up from the subway, two men took her purse and pushed her down the steps. Twenty steps, she said. She woke up in the hospital, and couldn't move for three months. She's only been back in her place maybe two weeks. She said she had terrible nightmares in the hospital. She's scared of people, I think."

"No wonder I never see her. You heard all this in the elevator?"

"You'd be amazed how much information she can fit in between the fifth and second floors." Maggie paused and looked at the wall beside the bed. "You don't think she can hear us, do you?"

"Not unless she has a glass to the wall. Hey," Rob said, rapping his knuckles along the wall, "no spying."

Somewhere beyond the wall, the sound of shattering glass.

Then, after Maggie left at eleven, he took the elevator to the basement, the weekend's laundry in the machine, and counted quarters out. He thought he heard a noise. Figuring it was a mouse, he ignored it. There were cracks in the lower parts of the walls, right where wall met floor, all along the basement. He had seen fat roaches run into these hidey-holes when he'd flicked the laundry room lights on. Always gave him the creeps; but they're only bugs, he told himself.

He put his quarters in the machine and switched it on. He leaned against it, listening to the gentle humming as water sprayed down on his clothes. Rob always took a book with him when he did his laundry—and he never left the room while his wash was going, because the one time he did, his clothes had been taken out in midcycle and left on the dusty cement floor. At some point in his reading, above the sound of the machine, he heard a series of ticks, like a loud clock ticking. Assuming the laundry had set the machine off balance, he opened it; rearranged the soaked clothing; closed the lid. But the ticking continued. He lifted the machine lid again, and while it turned off, the ticking kept going. He identified the area of ticking as one of the cracks along the wall. Then he thought it might be coming from over by the trash Dumpsters, down the hallway—sometimes the noises in the shafts echoed through the basement. He walked down the narrow, dimly lit hall, its greenish light humming as if about to extinguish from unpaid utilities, and looked around the trash.

Something was tapping from inside one of the disposal shafts. Rob hesitated at first, wondering if a very large and angry rat might be inside it, but the tapping continued, and seemed too steady to be a rat. He went, and lifted the hatch up—

Something living, wriggling, wrapped in gauze and surgical tape, dropped, and he instinctively caught it, because he saw a bit of pink, like a human hand, from an undone section of the gauze and he knew as he caught it that it was a baby.

## III

He had the sense to call the police before he unwrapped the gauze, and was spared the sight of the dead infant.

"I think it was alive when I found it," he said. "I felt movement. Not for very long, though."

The officer, named Gage, shook his head. "Nope, she wasn't alive when you found her, Mr. Arlington. She'd been dead at least a half hour."

"I heard tapping. I think the baby was moving."

"It wasn't the baby," the officer told him.

The next morning, he read about it in the *Daily News*.

"Must be a slow week," he told one of his coworkers. In the paper they detailed the story: newborn baby, wrapped in gauze, skin chewed up by roaches, apartments under investigation, related to similar cases of babies left in Dumpsters and thrown down sewer drains, left in parks wrapped in old newspapers, covered with ants or flies or roaches or whatever scavenger insect had lucked into finding the fresh meat. There was his name: Rob Arlington. Advertising man. There was the building: The Lonsdale, Central Park West, where they refused to let the most famous rock stars live, even the ones who could pay the rent. It had another picture, older, of a man in his fifties, in the

style of the turn of the century, a stern-looking man
with a Rasputin beard and glaring eyes. The caption
read: "The Original Lonsdale Scandal of 1917. Horace
Grubb and his Theory of Nature." But nothing in the
brief article elaborated on this photograph.

Maggie came by that night with wine and fresh salmon.
"I thought you could use some cheering up," she said,
whisking past him in the doorway with her packages.
She smelled like gardenia, which he loved, and wore a
bustier under a short jacket, a translucent skirt, and
boots. He knew she would seduce him so that he would
feel better, and he loved her for the thought.

"You heard," he said.

"Yep. Did you actually talk to the *News*?"

"What do you think?"

She didn't answer; he realized that he was sounding
grouchy. She opened the kitchen drawers in search of
the corkscrew.

"It's in the basket on the fridge," he said. "My guess
is some poor bastard junior reporter is stuck down at
the precinct waiting for the dirt on a rape or riot, and
he looks at the schedule of events and sees a baby-in-
a-Dumpster story. My name's right there. He can't file
the story he's after 'cause nothing's in on it. So he ties
this in with all those other dead babies left out to die
stories and voilà—an urban legend begins. With my
name attached to the most recent one. The Man Who
Found A Dead Infant In The Laundry Room Of The
Famous Lonsdale Apartments Right Off Central Park
West."

"You're a star," she said, pouring the Merlot into two glasses.

"I didn't know about the bugs, about how they'd been . . . doing that to the baby's skin," he said, shivering a little, going over to her, taking the wine, reaching around her back with his free hand, between the jacket and her skin. "You smell good. Like a garden of earthly delights."

"Yeah, I've been gargling with cologne. It's not too strong?"

"Not at all," he said, smiling, loving her little insecurities because they made her seem less perfect, more human. He drew back, sipped wine, rotated his head around to relieve tension in his neck. "God, Maggie, a baby. They said it was less than a day old."

"It's a rough place, this world," she said, and drew him to her. "You ever wanted a baby, Robby?"

He almost was going to cry, thinking of the dead thing in his arms, whatever brief and terrible life it had to endure; but he held back. Kissed her with gentleness. "I don't know," he said.

"Someday I want a baby, but—don't get that fearful bachelor look—not yet, and probably not from you, unless you play your cards right."

After dinner they watched television, and as he lay on the couch with her, he saw a roach on the wall. He picked up his shoe and threw it across the room, but missed it. The shoe made two loud thuds as it hit the wall and then the floor.

A few seconds later, the phone rang. He leaned over

her head ("massive hair," he murmured, "like a scalp jungle") and lifted the receiver. "Hello?"

"Six D?"

He didn't recognize the woman's voice.

"Who's this?"

"Six C. Your neighbor. I got your number from the super. You all right? I heard a noise."

"Oh, hello. Yes. I lobbed a Bass Weejun at the wall."

She seemed to accept this.

Maggie looked up at him, her eyebrows knitting.

He shrugged and mouthed: *next-door neighbor.*

The woman on the line said, "It scared me. After all the news."

"Oh," he said.

"It was you who found it," she said.

He felt drained. "Yeah."

"Were they hurt?"

Rob pulled his ear from the phone and looked at it. What the hell?

"Were what hurt? You mean, the baby?"

But she'd hung up the phone.

"My neighbor lady is spooky indeed," he said as he rested the phone back in its cradle.

After midnight, he had a craving for frozen yogurt. There was this place down on the corner that made the best cappuccino nonfat yogurt, a favorite spot of his. So, while Maggie slept, naked except for her panties, her breasts creamy and lovely above her small, indented belly, her dark hair obscuring one side of her face, he slipped on his jeans and tucked his cotton shirt in, stepped into his shoes, and tiptoed out of the apartment. He forgot to lock the apartment from the inside, so he stuck the key (three strikes and you're out, bubba, he thought as he finally got the sucker in the keyhole on the fourth try) into the door on the outside, and turned it so it was locked twice over. Never be too sure, even in a building like the Lonsdale, seventeen hundred a month for a junior one bedroom, even if you've been here for ten years, he thought. Babies in the garbage chute, roaches on the wall, anything can happen. He was a little drunk from the wine, and the thought of frozen yogurt, even with the October coolness outside, sobered him a bit; by the time he got to the elevator, he was standing up straight, and wiped the grin of requited lust from his face.

He had to stand in line behind six others, all frozen-yogurt fiends like himself, and by the time he'd gotten up to make his order, he decided on the largest size possible. He got two plastic spoons, and tasted the treat on the walk back to the apartment. He fiddled with his pockets, because he couldn't locate the keys. Had he left them upstairs? Damn it. He'd have to wake Maggie up after all. He buzzed the apartment. Three times. The last one, a long sustained buzz. Finally, she picked up the intercom.

Her voice was sleepy. "Rob?"

He giggled, high on Merlot and frozen yogurt. "Hey, sweetie-pie, I locked myself out getting some dessert for the one I love and me."

As if she couldn't hear him, she asked again, "Rob?" She was still waking up, he could tell. He

243

looked at the small black plastic of the intercom as if he could maybe see her through it if he concentrated. "Is it you?" she asked.

He pressed the button on his side. "Yeah, yeah, I got melting yogurt, Maggie, and I'm starting to feel a draft."

"Rob?" she asked again, weakly, and it sounded, for just a second, like she wasn't sleepy at all but about to pass out. About to cry, or something, something almost whimpery and breathless. Not like sleepiness at all.

And then he remembered: He'd left the keys in the door to the apartment.

Don't panic, he thought.

Pressed the button. "Maggie? You okay? Buzz me in, okay?"

He let go of the button.

Waiting for her buzzer. The intercom finally got pushed, but there was just the *ch-ch-ch* sound of dead air.

He pressed the button for the super. "It's Rob Arlington, Six D. I left my keys inside."

The super, ever vigilant, buzzed him in with no further identification required.

Rob ran to the elevator, and, luckily, it was on the first floor. He got on and pressed Six. The elevator gave its characteristic lurch. He realized that he was clutching the frozen yogurt cup so tightly that it was all twisted, with dripping cappuccino yogurt spreading down his hand. He dropped it in the elevator. When he reached the sixth floor, he sprinted down the hall, tried the door. No keys. Locked. He rapped on it several times. "Maggie? Maggie! Maggie!"

He heard a noise, and glanced to his right.

The woman in 6C stood there, in a navy blue bathrobe. "She left."

"What do you mean she left?"

"She knocked on my door about ten minutes ago. She told me she had to go home, and she didn't know where you went. Here," the woman held her hand out, "she just left a second ago."

In her hand, his keys.

He looked at her, at the keys. "I just talked with her on the intercom. I came up on the elevator. I would've seen her."

The woman looked annoyed. "She comes banging on my door at God knows what hour and tells me you left the keys in the door and then we hear the buzzer go off and she goes back to the apartment, and mister, I can't tell you what else she did, because I came back inside kind of pissed off that I know have to wait up for you because your girlfriend wants to split. If she takes the stairs or something, I can't help it. She's a nice lady, seems like, but I can't read her mind. You want these or what?" she asked, finally tossing the keys to him. As she stepped back inside her apartment, he noticed the light blue bruises like polka dots on her pink legs.

Maggie's answering machine picked up for three days, and then he stopped calling. He dropped by her place one night with flowers, but she didn't answer the door. Even though the lights were out in her apartment, he sensed that she was standing behind the door, looking through the peephole.

Then, on Monday morning, she called.

"It's me."

"Jesus, Maggie, I've been worried sick. What happened to you?"

"What do you mean, what happened to me? What happened to you?"

"I went out for some yogurt. You were asleep. I didn't want to wake you."

Silence on the line.

"Something frightened me."

"What?"

"Oh, Rob," she sounded close to tears, "I can't talk about it. Not like this."

"Will you meet me somewhere? Café Veronese?"

He heard her slow breaths, as if she needed to calm down.

She whispered, "Okay. After work. Six."


When they met, she moved away as he tried to give her a friendly hug. Her eyes were circled with darkness, and bloodshot. Her lips were chapped. Something about her skin was shiny, as if she had a fever. They sat at a booth in the back, and she, uncharacteristically, withdrew a cigarette from her purse and lit it. "I didn't know where you went. The door was wide open. The lights were off. Someone was inside with me. I knew it wasn't you."

He noticed that she kept glancing down at her fingers; and then he knew why. She was afraid to look him in the face.

He said nothing.

"I was just about naked, and scared. I reached for my jacket, but . . . it . . . it grabbed my arm."

"A man," he said.

She shook her head.

"A woman?"

Maggie laughed once, bitterly. "None of the above. It crawled up my arm."

He looked at her, and couldn't help grinning. "It was a bug?"

She glanced up, saw his look, and her lips became tight. "Fuck you," she said.

"Sorry. But you got scared by a bug?"

"It wasn't just a bug, Robert. I knew I couldn't talk to you."

He sipped his coffee, she smoked her Camel. Her fingertips were yellow-brown from smoking.

As if suddenly inspired, she rolled the right-hand sleeve of her sweater up and thrust her arm under his face.

Dark bruises, in a diamond pattern.

He touched along them and felt thin blisters also.

"It attacked me," she said.

"Jesus," he gasped, "Maggie, you've got to see a doctor. This isn't just some bug."

"Exactly," she said, triumphant. Tears shone like jewels in her eyes. "It's like a disease. It feels like a disease. It's taking me with it. Whatever it is. Inside me. It did something. But this," she nodded toward the diamond bruise, "this was only where it held me. The others . . . "

"Others?"

Maggie's expression turned again to stone. "You don't believe me."

He said nothing.

She said, "They opened me up."

### IV

"She doing okay?"

Rob was checking his mailbox. He glanced around the corner, and there was the woman from 6C. It was eight o'clock, and he had walked Maggie home, put her to bed with a stiff drink, made her promise to see a doctor in the morning, and then walked home. He was hoping to just go to bed early, himself.

The woman said, "Your girl. I heard from the super she got attacked. He said it was a spider from South America or something. He started talking exterminating again—sounded like Adolf Hitler, you ask me."

"Better," he said, "she's doing better. I haven't talked with her since Monday, though. I think maybe she just needs to be alone for a while."

"You think she imagined it, don't you?"

"I don't know."

"She seemed nice. I don't think she'd lie. I seen spiders as big as birds at the natural history museum. She doesn't seem like the lying type, your girlfriend."

"I didn't say that. Something definitely happened."

"You was thinking it, though. Hard for guys to deal with things like that, I don't know why, happens every day in this city—bugs and thugs. You probably don't believe about the gators in the sewer, but I know two cleaning women who swear by them. Guys, they never believe it till it hits them butt first in the face. But you ain't like that, right? You half believe her, don't you?" The woman gave a hopeful smile. "I got attacked in the subway three months ago. My hip still ain't too good. You give me a choice between getting bit by a spider or jumped by a hoodlum, I choose spiders every time."

He managed a smile.

"My name's Celeste. Celeste Pratt. We talk a lot in halls and junk, but we never been introduced." She extended her beefy arm. It was the first time he'd actually seen her dressed, and it was all in black like some East Villager, but it made her pale face sparkle a bit. "I didn't know she got bit that night. I'm sorry I ragged on you so much. I was tired. Friends?"

He nodded. "Sure."

"Glad to hear she's doing better. You think it was a black widow or something?"

"I don't know. She won't see a doctor."

"I don't like doctors neither," Celeste said, shaking her head. "I believe in homeopathy and stuff like that. The mind, Rob. The power of the mind. And nature. It's weird to believe in nature when you live in a city like this, ain't it? But I always lived here, all my life, and you look for nature where you can find it. The law of nature, way I see it, is we got to sometimes give ourselves up to it, like we're part of this big system, and your legs—like, say, mine—get bashed, but you just let the pain of healing take over, you let nature run its course. It's like Grubb's Nature Theory, about survival and adaptation. Know what I mean? You tell your girlfriend I hope she gets better, okay? Do that for me? She's always been so nice and friendly to me, I hate to see nice people get hurt, but in this city, you know, it happens every day, but better some spider or something instead of a guy with a butterfly knife, right?"

Rob stared at her as if he could not quite believe she existed. He blinked twice.

"What's wrong?" she asked.

"Nothing," he said, then departed for the elevator. Celeste got on it with him and smiled, but didn't volunteer another river of conversation. On their floor, he let her off first, then got off, stood just on the other side of the elevator door, and watched Celeste go to her apartment.

When she had put her key in the lock and turned it, he said, "Excuse me, Celeste."

She turned to him, beaming.

"Downstairs, did you mention something about someone named Grubb?"

"Grubb's Nature Theory. Yes."

"Is that Horace Grubb?"

She nodded, blushing.

"My grandfather," she said.

\* \* \*

She invited him into her apartment, to show him her grandfather's books. Rob accepted out of curiosity, as much to see the large apartment as the texts. The apartment was a three-bedroom, "although it was once this entire floor, a fourteen-room affair, but it was divided up in late '29, when everyone with anything lost it. My grandmother was from New Orleans, and redecorated accordingly," Celeste pointed out the French touches, "and the apartment, what's left of it, has largely remained as she left it in 1964, when she died. 'Course, she ruined the floor, the beautiful dark wood floor, what with her wheelchair scraping along, it's why I have the oriental carpets and runners all over the place. My mother never wanted to live here ever since she married back in '48, to my dad, Rice Pratt, but Grammy left it to me, because she knew I'd take the right kind of care of it. But I ain't much of a housekeeper. The bedrooms are disaster areas—I do all my crap in them—but, here, we can have a nice martini at the window." She guided him over to the kitchen, which was dark and wooden like the rest of the place; the floors were dark with a layer of dust and crumbs, as if she never cleaned up after herself; the windows were dark, too, painted black, supposedly because her grandmother, at the end of her life, could not abide light because of an ocular problem. But Celeste pressed the small latch to the left, then pushed the larger of two windows open.

The view was of the park, shrouded in night, and was not blocked by the Cavanaugh Building, as it was from Rob's small apartment.

When both martinis were made, she sat down opposite him and raised her glass. He clinked his to hers and sipped. Strong.

He said, "I saw in the papers a picture of your grandfather."

She rolled her eyes, and flapped her hand in a gesture of dismissal. "Oh, God, that business. Grampy's book was called *De Naturis* and it basically expounded his theory. Oh, right, right, you want to know about it, don't you? It was that man's role in Nature was as a farmer and facilitator. We ain't here to enslave nature, he said, but 'cause we got to ease the birth, so nature can keep on keeping on, or something like that."

"How'd he get in trouble over that?"

She *tsk*ed. "It was about the time of World War One, and it had something to do with soldiers going to France, and some literature Grampy gave out. It was a mob thing. Terrible. Would've killed him, too, but things worked out eventually. But it made the news here for about ten minutes before the war took over. Put the Lonsdale on the map, too."

"Was he antiwar?"

"Oh, no," she said, her breath strong and gin-soaked, "just the opposite. He supported war, he said, 'cause it meant more human flesh got put in the ground, which was good for crops throughout the world. He believed that the best use of human beings was as compost or incubators. That's really where the trouble was, in his big fat mouth. He cheered the deaths of soldiers, because he felt the death of a youth was the best food nature knows. He had people, you know, who agreed with him, listened to him and stuff. Wrote a lot of pamphlets. They called themselves Grubbites. He was definitely weird. He wasn't a cannibal or anything like that, even though they said he was. He was a . . . what do you call it?"

"Misanthrope?"

"Yeah, in a big way." She drank down the rest of her martini and went to get another. Her back to him, she said, "Maybe something different, too. He had this whole spiritual side to him, like he believed there was a god in everything alive, trees, birds, even the air."

"Sort of a pagan transcendentalist, then," Rob amended.

She was drinking her martini at the sink, half turned to him, looking out the window. "Everything. Even unto the smallest," she whispered.

Rob noticed that there was a trail of ants running from a crack near the top of the kitchen wall, all the way down beneath the sink. No wonder, he thought, she leaves crumbs and scraps everywhere.

She was watching the ants, too, but she made no move to kill them. As he followed the trail from its highest point, he noticed that the ants went down to the corner of the shelf where the sink was, and were trooping across the shiny tile to within an inch of her hand.

He lay in bed that night with his reading light on. He thought about Maggie, which was pleasant after the martini, about her gardenia smell, garden of earthly delights—and somehow this reminded him of the ants in Celeste's apartment, for he wondered what kind of urban garden they made their nest in. Finally, he turned out the light and fell asleep.

He awoke, sometime in the night, hearing the sound of a woman moaning from nearby.

Through the wall.

Celeste. Having a nightmare. But the moaning continued, escalating to muffled cries, and he knew it was not a nightmare but a private pleasure. He heard the humming buzz of what could only have been a vibrator, and he thought: good for her.

Strangely, it aroused him, and the more he listened, the less aware he was of his own left hand slipping down beneath the elastic of his Jockey shorts.

Just as he was closing his eyes, dreaming about a faceless but beautiful woman, the moaning from the other side of the wall turned into a scream.

The screaming went on for nearly a minute, and then died.

He threw on his bathrobe and dashed to the hall, but by the time he was knocking on Celeste's door, it was silent. The hallway light flickered and buzzed; the bulbs would need replacing. He stood there, looking around at the other apartments, wondering if anyone else had heard the woman's screams. He started knocking again, and this time he heard her moving around, as if drunk, knocking things over as she made her way to the door. Maybe she'd had another martini or two after he'd left; she'd certainly gulped them down fast enough.

He saw her shadow beneath the space between the

floor and the door. She was standing on the other side of the door, looking through the peephole at him.

"Celeste? Are you all right?"

She must've been scraping her nails on the door.

"Celeste?"

The shadow beneath the door vanished; he heard noises as she moved back down the corridor.

From within the apartment, the chime of a clock.

Two A.M.

He turned to go back to his place, shaking his head.

As he climbed back into bed, he thought he heard the buzzing of her machine again, just at the wall. A little louder than before. He closed his eyes, wondering if he should investigate further. Maybe she'd just tripped on something and screamed, maybe she was drunk, maybe she didn't even scream with pain, maybe it was the way she climaxed, who the hell knew?

He was asleep, probably dreaming, he knew, but he imagined that a big cockroach was riding Celeste's ass, its feelers stroking the back of her neck, and its face turning slowly to look at Rob as it diddled with his neighbor, its face all brown and callused, with flecks of dirt across the broad platform between its eyes, and its eyes looking just like the Rasputin eyes of Horace Grubb.

The phone rang, both in the dream and out of it; in the dream, Rob went running down a long corridor in search of the phone; in reality, he snarfled himself awake and reached to the table by the bed.

"Yello?"

He heard static on the line.

Then: "Help me."

A woman's voice.

Its very weakness shocked him awake.

"Celeste?"

"Help me," she said, and then a sound like high-pitched humming, like the Vienna Boys Choir humming one note without taking a single breath, filled the phone, and it felt like a needle thrust in his ear.

He dropped the receiver.

V

The door to 6C was open.

The sun was still not up, although he could hear the honkings and screechings of morning traffic.

Her apartment was lit with red lights, like a bordello, and he thought of Celeste's grandmother decorating the place with her New Orleans touches. The furniture seemed bloodied by the light, and it made him queasy as he walked through the front hallway. He had a sense that there was movement all around him, just on the periphery of his vision, but every time he glanced at the red-shrouded furnishings, there was nothing out of the ordinary.

The phone, off its hook, lay in the kitchen.

A smell, too, there, like clothes that had been sweated in and discarded in a heap to rot for months. The window that had formerly held the view of the park had been blackened over with dark cellophane.

Again, he sensed a slithery movement, and glanced around the floor, but saw nothing.

He glanced down the slim hallway that led to the three bedrooms.

"Celeste?" he asked.

A sudden noise, as of someone rushing to a door, and throwing herself against it, sliding down to the floor. Sobbing. Muffled, as if a mouth were taped over.

His first instinct was to walk back to the door, go to his apartment, and call the police.

He took one step back, and stood still when he heard another sound: a repetitive vibrating sound, like monks chanting *aum* over and over.

But it was a woman; it sounded like a synthesis of a woman and a machine, for the vibration of her voice seemed to increase beyond what a human might be able to, and he felt the vibrations in the floor and walls.

Someone threw herself at the door again.

Door Number Three.

He could not turn around and run for cover.

It was Maggie's voice that was humming, louder, until he wanted to cover his ears.

Then it was as if he were being swept along with a tide, for he found himself moving toward that door, that dark red-stained door, moving smoothly straight forward, moving his feet, not one after another, but together, as if he were in a dream and was not touching ground at all. His heart was beating loud; it was not his heart, but her humming; his mouth had dried up; he swallowed dryness.

When he reached the door, he twisted the knob, opened it.

The room was dark.

The stench came at him in waves of heat; it smelled like a compost pile.

He stepped into the darkness and reached for a light switch.

The switch was low, as if made for someone in a wheelchair (her grandmother had been in a wheelchair, she'd said, and had left tracks all along the floor).

The light came up, also red, from the solitary bulb that dangled from a thin chain in the center of the room.

The room was small, and covered with dark earth and wet leaves.

Maggie lay in mud just a few feet in front of him.

She was naked.

She stared at him, and he could see the vibrations of her lips as she hummed.

Bruises, too, all along her arms, stomach, breasts, legs.

Her humming increased to a shattering pitch.

There was a twitching, almost, no, a wriggling of skin along her arms and belly, too, and as he leaned forward to touch her . . .

As the humming seemed to vibrate the entire building . . .

He felt the edge of an antenna stroke featherlike down the back of his neck.

Celeste whispered in his ear, "Isn't she beautiful?"

He turned around, and Celeste was dressed in a gown made entirely of wasps, all with wings twitching, diamond heads, their thousand legs clinging to her. "I am their chosen, Rob. For what my grandfather did for them, his many kindnesses, I got chosen as their midwife. They won't hurt you, Rob, I wouldn't let that happen, as long as you don't try to hurt me, you're gonna be fine."

The wasps moved along her shoulders, over her breasts, her living clothes shimmering in the light.

He gasped, "What did you do? What in God's name?"

"Nature is God," Celeste said, "we are here to serve. People build cities like this, and what, do you think it's all for us? It's for them. We're just part of the colony, Rob. God's a maggot, Rob, turns the flesh to earth. We're less than maggots, don't you get it?"

"What about Maggie? What did you do to her?"

Celeste shook her head, clearly disappointed that this was his interest. "It ain't like she's in any pain, you know, one of the mothers paralyzes her while they lay their eggs under her skin. I ain't gonna make anybody go through pain. Not what's not natural, anyways."

The scream on the other side of the wall.

Maggie's scream.

Maybe. Maybe.

Maybe it was Celeste, maybe she was mating with a wasp, maybe the scream was pleasure, maybe it's her eggs inside Maggie's body.

It was then that Rob felt his mind leaving his head, as if it were leaking out of his ears and drifting smoke-like to dissipate in the hall. Something short-circuited for him; he could not easily remember words or how to make his arms or legs move right; for a moment, he wondered if he knew how to breathe.

Celeste reached out and took his hand in hers. He watched her do this and felt like an infant, unable to make sense out of the world in which he'd found himself. She stroked his hand. "If I want, they'll choose you, too, to help. I want you to help. I feel like you're a friend," she said, drawing his hand to her bosom. "It's so lonely sometimes, being chosen. It's so lonely sometimes being the one that the gods pick."

He watched the wasps travel from her hand to his, then up his arm, sometimes biting, but it didn't bother him, he didn't mind, he didn't mind. He felt them everywhere, all over his skin, and when he listened carefully he began to understand what they were saying, all of them at once, through their vibrations and feelers and bites.

## VI

The season was a hard one, for the earth needed turning, and there needed to be others, for once these young came up, the mothers would need to lay more eggs after the mating time.

When it was over, he remembered the picture.

He remembered the picture when he looked at Maggie as they were coming out.

The caterpillar, its skin green and translucent and wet.

The bumps beneath the caterpillar's skin.

Beauty beyond conscience.

The cruel face of nature.

But as he was watching it happen, Maggie's eyes on him, her humming at a pitch, he knew it was the most glorious and selfless act that any human being could ever perform, and he wept with the intense and silent beauty as her shiny skin ruptured with conquering life.

# "The Little Mermaid"

The beach house was large, and an entire glass wall looked out upon the flat brown sand below the hill, to the brief line of pavement for the boat landing, down where the pelicans and gulls cracked their clams and oysters and crabs.

Alice didn't see the birds or the beach much. That first year she kept the curtains drawn shut. Sometimes she opened them, standing at the window, smoking a cigarette. The ocean was a haze most of the winter, but that was fine by her. She wasn't an ocean person. She could not even swim, and she never waded. She considered herself more of an isolationist, and that is precisely what the beach house offered. She drank a lot of her father's stored wine (a wood bin had been converted into a wine cellar), and left the house only twice a week to go see a therapist in Nag's Head.

Molly came down for a visit that lasted approximately six hours before the mother-daughter anger got out of hand; Molly still didn't understand the divorce, and being a mother now herself, and perhaps (Alice surmised) in a bad marriage, Molly was young enough to still believe in staying together for the sake of family.

Alice read a lot of books, particularly long fat ones that took her mind off life and her miserableness at it. When she thought of it, she practiced her own brand of yoga based on having watched a morning television show once. When the hangovers from the red wine became unbearable, she slacked off drinking and became a coffee addict. This prompted her to frenetic activity in the winter; she began jogging on the beach, finally unable to avoid the outdoors and health (which she kept in check by smoking and drinking coffee sometimes into the wee hours), and thus she met the old man who collected shells.

He was, at first, barely a face to her, for while her jogging was slow enough to distinguish features on the few beachcombers who came down her way, she had stopped looking anyone in the face. She noticed his hands, actually, and the cracked, wormholed shells he held in them. His hands were tanned and rough. Then, another day, she noticed his knees: rather knobby, with fat blue veins down the sides of them. Finally, she met him the day she sprained her ankle at a place where the sand sank. She sat on a large piece of driftwood—moving the red kelp to the side—and rubbed her ankle.

He walked right up to her. "You okay?"

She nodded. She still could not bring herself to look at his face. She looked at his feet: he was barefoot, as was she, with a particularly nasty looking ingrown toenail on his big toe.

"If you run, you should wear shoes," he said. "The sand tugs at your heel. It's very bad for your arches. It's made for crabs and seaweed, not people, this beach is."

"I'll take that into consideration next time," she said testily. She rubbed her foot.

"Here," he said, dropping to his knees. She could no longer avoid his face. He was probably in his late sixties; old enough to be her father by a hair. He had brown eyes and thin lips. He must've been handsome, but it had turned to sand, his skin had, and his nose, the shiny red of a lifelong drinker.

He took her foot in his hands and rubbed.

"Please," she said, pulling her foot back. It hurt when she did it.

"I'm a doctor," he said. "Retired now, but I know something about feet. We'll just massage it a little."

"Well," she said noncommittally. No one was around to watch, and it did feel good. He pressed his thumbs into the soft flesh at her ankle; the sensation burned at first, but then, as he continued, it felt warm and pleasant. She had had a headache; it melted.

He watched her. "You need to keep off this for a few days. I can wrap it for you, if you like."

Because she was financially broke from countless therapy sessions and the divorce itself and would not be able to afford any medical expense if her foot's condition worsened, she agreed to this. She leaned against his shoulder, and he guided her back to her house.

In the master bathroom, he heated torn rags of old towels in the sink with hot water. Then he squeezed them, and tied them around her ankle and foot. "The heat," he said, "it helps. They say it's ice that helps, but not for this. It'll swell up from the heat, but it needs to."

Alice, who knew nothing of medicine, nodded as if she did.

"Sometimes we need fluids to collect. They carry away the bad stuff."

She almost laughed. "Sorry, sorry," she said, "it's just that it sounded so undoctorly."

He grinned. He was a warm man, she decided. Not like her ex. This old man, he was a good country doctor who cared. He was a house call kind of doctor. He said, "I try my best. I find that all that medical jargon gets in the way of patient care. Sometimes nature knows best."

"I couldn't agree more."

He continued to massage her foot through the warm wet rags.

"You collect shells?" she asked, not wanting him to stop.

"I'm rather aimless these days. Since my wife died."

"I'm sorry."

"Oh, we had quite a life together. Life, while it lasts, has its own secrets."

Alice didn't quite understand him, but she really didn't want to get into the dead wife as a topic of conversation any more than she wanted to start prattling on about her husband.

"So I walk the beaches like I'm waiting for a ship to come in or something. Like an old salt. Do you believe in mermaids?" His eyes glistened a bit, as if he practiced this question and its anticipated response.

"No."

"I used to, when I was a boy." He grinned dopily. "Do you know that when a man becomes old, he begins to remember what he believed in as a child and it all comes back to him?"

Something sweet in his voice; that boy that was him thousands of years before, that little boy, was still there in his eyes. She smiled. He rubbed.

"I believed that out in that ocean was a lovely mermaid. She and I knew each other, and when I was four, I would go down to the beach early in the morning, before anyone else was up, and stand on the edge of the land and sing mermaid songs to her. I imagined her fins and her tail, how if she were on land I would carry her to a safe place, and how she would tell me all the secrets of the sea. And I, in turn, would tell her how much I loved her, how much I wanted to be with her," he said.

Alice began weeping upon hearing this. She could not control it, and it was not just about the pathetic little four-year-old who sang to the nonexistent mermaids; it was about everything she'd wished for as a child, all within her grasp, gone now, like sand, like seawater, the way memory always left her bereft and longing for innocence. He slid his hands from her feet and placed them on either side of her face. They were comfortingly cold.

"A beautiful woman should never cry," he said.

"I'm sorry."

"No, don't say that either. Your tears are like the mermaids'."

She opened her eyes to him and felt that lustful heat of first love again, just as if he were not old and she were not middle-aged.

He caressed her, and they fell across the bed, her ankle's throbbing becoming a distant and occasional pinching. They kissed, weeping, both of them, and then he kissed her every arch and turn and curve.

Afterward, she fell asleep.

When she awoke, the pain was excruciating. The room, shrouded in darkness. The curtains were still drawn shut. She gasped; a light came on.

Her doctor-lover stood over her.

The pain was in her foot. She wasn't thinking clearly because of the pain.

She reached down to touch her foot, anticipating a throbbing ankle.

But her hand, sliding down her leg, ended at a stump.

She touched the air where her foot should've been.

He said, "I had to operate, Alice." He knew her name now, even though she didn't know his.

His words seemed meaningless, until on the third try to find her foot where it should've been, she suddenly understood.

Her screaming might've been heard had the night surf not boomed, had the winter not brought with it a tree-bending wind.

The operation was not completed for six days; it was a blur to Alice, for he kept her drunk and on painkillers.

When she awoke, clearheaded, she felt nothing but a constant stinging all up and down her spine, as if her skin had been scraped and she'd been rolled in salt.

There was dried blood on the sheets. Several hypodermic needles lay carelessly beside her. Fish scales, too, spread out in a vermillion and blue desert, piled high, as if every fish in the ocean had been skinned and thrown about. The smell was intolerable: oily and fishy. And the flies! Everywhere, the blue and green flies.

She tried to sit up, but her back hurt too much. She fought this, but then parts of her body, including her arms, felt paralyzed. She wondered what drugs he'd been administering to her—strangely, she felt euphoric, and fought this feeling.

She lay back down, closed her eyes, willing this dream to depart.

She awoke again when he came back into the room.

"One last thing," he said, holding the serrated knife up to her neck, "one last thing."

The blade had been warmed with the fire on the gas stove. She felt no pain as he took the knife and scored several slits just below her chin. Afterward, she could not even speak or scream, but could only open her mouth and emit a bleating noise.

He lifted her up into his arms, kissing her nipples as if they were sacred, and carried her out to the beach. "I will take you out to your city, my love, and set you free," he said as he laid her down in the bottom of a small boat. She could only stare at him. She felt resigned to death, which would be better than the results of the torture he had put her through.

Out to sea, he rolled her over the edge of the boat.

At first she wanted to drown, but something within her fought against it. She managed to grasp hold of some rocks out beyond the breakwater. She held on to them for over an hour as the freezing salt water smashed against the back of her head.

She grasped at the edge of a rock; it cut at her hands, but she held on. If I just hang on for another minute, she thought, just another ten seconds, I'll be fine. God will rescue me. Or someone will see me. Will see what he's done to me, this madman. I haven't lived all my life to come to this. I know something will happen. Something will pull me out of this.

The waves crashed around her, like glass shattering against her face. Please, God, someone, help me. All she could taste was the stinging salt. Something animal within her was clinging to all that she knew of life now, not her marriage or her family or her career, but this serrated rock and this icy sea.

269

From the shore she heard him, even at the distance. His boat already docked. The old man stood there, singing.

Alice held on to the rock for as long as she could.

Then she let go.

The old man stayed on the shore for hours, his voice faltering only when dark arrived. He had a great and lovely baritone, and he sang of all the secrets of the sea. A couple, walking along the beach that evening, held each other more tightly, for his song sparked within them a memory of love and regret, and such beautiful and heartrending longing.

They watched from a distance as the old man raised his hands up, his songs batting against the wind, against the crash of the surf, against all that life had to offer.

# *Damned If You Do*

Calhoun was sweating up a storm, and it was only ten, but this was La Mesa in summer, and he actually found the talk radio soothing while he worked. He could hear, beyond the chattering radio, the children in the schoolyard across the street, all yelling and pounding the blacktop while they played dodgeball. He could smell the jaw-aching sweet stink of the fat lemons in the trees that Patsy had planted when they'd first moved into the bungalow ten years before. The old shepherd, Vix, was chawing on a lemon, which made the dog whine with sour hurt as the juice got into his gums—and still, he wouldn't let go of a lemon once he got hold of it.

Cal's beard itched, too, another annoyance on a particularly annoying day, and his shovel struck the flat rock again, or maybe it was a pipe this time—for sure the sewage system ran this way and that across the back of the property, and who the hell knew why since the toilets were always backing up, and the garbage disposal ran rusty brown nine times out of ten.

"Mother—" he began, then held his tongue, laughed because Patsy didn't like strong language or strong drink in her house.

Her house.

It's my house as well as yours.

He had been digging for twenty minutes—the ground was dry and hard, and there weren't many places left.

Not that he'd left any markers, but he had a memory like a trap, and once he saw something, he always remembered it.

I remember you, you, and you, he thought, blinking his eyes in the sun, looking from one patch of garden to another, or there, in the mulch pile.

He went back in for a Pepsi and one last piece of apple pie—she had baked it the night before, and he had had one too many pieces, but he loved her pies. The radio was louder in the kitchen, echoing, and a man was on it talking about his problems with his wife, and how he wanted to leave but couldn't because he loved her.

The call-in dj, who claimed to be a therapist, although she doled out advice about as bad as any Cal had ever heard, the Radio Lady, as Patsy called her, said, "Love is not just a state of being, but an active, everyday thing, you know—know what I mean? Like you maintain your house and your car, you also have to every day maintain your relationship, like a tune-up . . ."

Patsy always had that thing blaring, always talk radio, from morning till night till morning.

The Radio Lady jabbering, nattering, bantering.

He wanted to turn it off, but if he did then they'd know.

The neighbors.

They'd know.

Old Fat Broad over the high wall with her arms of beef and face of jug, always leaning over and saying, "Whatcha doin'?" Or that brat of hers trying to get over to pick lemons, looking in the windows, trying to slide through the casement windows into his wood-shop.

Mr. Erickson, whom Patsy called Ear-Ache, complaining about the volume of the radio, wouldn't he think it strange when the radio went off? Ear-Ache once came over to be neighborly, and asked Cal, "So, you're retired now, what was your business, anyway?"

And Cal had told the truth, although he sometimes lied because he hated when people pried. "I used to be a principal of a school down in Dauber's Mill, back before they consolidated. I liked teaching better, more hands-on work, but they needed a principal more than they needed a woodshop teacher, so I had at it for a good fifteen years."

Ear-Ache and Fat Broad, eyes ears and mind on him all the time, wondering if they were looking, if they were watching.

He never did his work at midnight or in the wee morning hours, because he had learned in his sixty-three years that you could do anything you wanted in life as long as you did it in broad daylight, when nobody believed what they saw anyway.

He took a bite of pie and a swig of soda, and looked out across the lawn at the shallow trench he had begun.

Maybe I'll just put her with that pigtailly girl, in the mulch.

The problem with the mulch pile, or with any mulch pile, is you couldn't put anything salty in it or you'd ruin it for sure. No bacon drippings, no skin, nothing that had a high salt content. The pigtailly girl was easy enough to scrape, and even though she still had plenty of salt in her, he just had to bury her deep and hope for the best. Dead mice you could put on the mulch, and even dead birds, but nothing too much larger or you had a pile of shit that was just a pile of shit.

Cal set the can of soda down, stroked his walrus mustache, scratched his chest through his sweat-stained T-shirt.

Can't scrape Patsy, though. Can't do it.

Take much too long, and then I'd have to flush too much scrapings. More backup in the toilets, maybe too much, and maybe they'd have to come out and dig up the lawn to check on the sewage pipes, and then what?

"No more woodshop, for sure," he said aloud.

He whistled for Vix to come inside, then he turned

and went down the narrow hallway with its family pictures tattooed on the wall, all the kids they'd had in all those years. The radio noise got louder, this time just a commercial. He hated the way on TV and radio, how they made the commercials louder than the shows. They were advertising for Squeaky Kleen, a deodorant. Cal didn't use deodorants, although he made an excellent natural soap in his woodshop, using an old recipe he'd found in a book from the turn of the century. It was a little bit of lye and a little bit of animal fat, and it got skin so clean it practically took the hair right off, with a fresh smell, like children on their birthdays.

He went into Patsy's room—they had separate rooms, ever since he'd retired, because she wouldn't put up with his night fears anymore. So he had the little guestroom, what used to be the nursery off the second bathroom, and she kept the master bedroom, which looked out over the backyard. She was simple in her tastes, which is what he always liked about her anyway, and difficult in her emotions. She had a bed, a table with a reading light, her mother's rocking chair, and the radio. It was an old one, a big jobbie that she'd had since the fifties, hell, it took four big fat batteries to run it, and like his old Royal typewriter, she had it repaired constantly rather than replace it with something newer and easier to use.

On the radio, a woman began crying, and the dj lady said, "It's all right, it's good to cry, hey, I'd cry, too, if that happened to me. But you do have a choice, sweetie, you can walk right out that door and get a life!

It's the thing to do in the nineties, get . . . a . . . life. It's easy. When you do it, you'll see. You'll call a friend, or a family member, and see if you can't stay with them for a while, until you've got your feet on the ground, and then you'll get a life. Sound good?"

The woman on the line said, "I guess. I thought this was my life."

"What you described is not a life. I know it hurts to hear this, but it's why you called in, isn't it? It's not a life, I repeat. A life is something you participate in and draw some satisfaction from. Capisce?"

Cal wanted to shut that damn radio off more than anything, but he knew if he did, someone somewhere nearby would think something, would wonder about something, might even look in a window somewhere.

Patsy's eyes were wide, but the tape had held on her mouth. The wire around her ankles had cut into the flesh, but not too far, and they held well, strung around the frame of the rocker. She'd exhausted herself all night rocking back and forth, trying to get over to the window; he'd had to pick her up twice between eleven and two when she'd spilled forward and slammed her head into the parquet. He'd wiped the blood from her nose, and kissed at her tears, and used his heart to try and unscramble a message to her, to help explain what he was doing and why he had to, but she was too busy listening to talk radio. She never got the messages he sent from his heart, but he always followed his heart and tried to get her to understand the direction it took him. It was no use talking to her, because she only understood normal everyday problems and emotions, not the kind that made a man do what he had to do, a place beyond words, a territory of pure obligation.

Maybe if she still went to her job downtown, maybe she never would've noticed.

But she, too, had retired, just had the retirement party at the Sportsman's Lodge down on Edison and Fourth last Friday night. He was going to wait until she went to run some errands or whatever—and maybe if she hadn't given up liquor so suddenly, and gotten religion in one lightning bolt of revelation, maybe she would've been so self-involved she would've missed what he did.

What he'd been doing for twenty-five years.

He remembered his mother's words, so many years back, on her deathbed. Her advice, her comfort. He repeated them, whispering, although Patsy would not hear them, she would hear the radio, radio, nothing but radio. "I know it's terrible to watch your mother die like this, Cal. But far worse is it for me to go to my glory without knowing that you are taken care of. I want you to be happy, but I know the pain life brings. We've all had it visited upon us. Happy is the man who buries his own children, for in his pain, in his burden, is the care and comfort that he laid them to rest before their spirits could be crushed."

The sunlight burned the windowsill, beneath the translucent shade, and he heard old Vix whining from the kitchen—still chewing that lemon.

Patsy smelled, and her face glowed with sweat.

Nine children in twenty-five years.

Someone was bound to find out, one day, but he never imagined it would be his wife. She had used the soap, she had used the candles, she had blown on the whistle he made out of bone, the whistle with the little sparrow carved into the side, the whistle like ivory. She had stood by him when he spoke with the police about each one running away, about the troubles boys and girls like that faced, not feeling that their biological parents had claimed them, not feeling at home, not feeling safe.

Not feeling cared for.

On the radio, a teenaged girl giggled and talked about not having her first period until she was sixteen.

He had promised Patsy, too, that he would care for her until death. Perhaps this was Providence stepping in and making sure he was as good as his word, although he didn't believe in fate or God or karma.

Soon, he'd have to stop old Vix's breath, too, for what would a dog do if his master were to die?

I've been dying for years, Patsy, his heart said, and I've cared for my own.

It wasn't fun, never, he wasn't one of those who enjoyed doing his duty. It was like being a soldier, shooting his brother, but the weight of his obligation was great.

His mother, too, he had taken care of her in her last moments.

He had no choice back then, when he was sixteen, because she had been the one with the gun in her hand, and it had taken a good half hour to wrestle it from her.

Mother was trying to take care of him, but Cal had known, even then, that it was a man's job. He knew he was damned, but it was a damned if you do, damned if you don't sort of proposition when you came into this world.

Patsy's eyes were bulging, and he never liked to see her worried or in pain, but he had wanted to give her time to think it over and make her peace. Life is meant to work out the way it works itself out, and maybe Patsy, maybe she would die within the next decade anyway, and if something happened to him, who would care for her?

The weight of duty was heavy, for sure.

The Radio Lady said, "We are given free choice when it comes to our own behavior, and we can only change someone else insofar as we can change ourselves, you know?"

He looked around for her needles, the long thick ones.

He didn't like to prolong pain, and he remembered how peaceful his mother had been, how the gasp from her bosom, and the stench, and the relief in the act itself, were like opening a sewer pipe of flesh to release gas and what was trapped inside the gutter of the body.

It was noon before her heart stopped, and nearly one when he'd taken her down to his woodshop. He laid her across the bench, her neck in a vise because it helped keep the rest of the body stable if the spine held.

Then he went to work, and he cried, as he always did, and he drowned out the sound of talk radio with his instruments.

The sky clouded over by two-thirty. The children were let out of school, and he had to wait until the last yellow bus took off, and the last child had finished walking home, peeking over the wall to taunt Vix into barking, before he could go out and dig some more. He went to the mulch pile, which was still moist and humid with dead grass and sour milk and the fish heads from Tuesday's supper. Vix lay down beside him and let a lemon roll from his mouth. The old dog looked at the lemon and pawed it. Cal noticed there were ants crawling across it. He bent over, his back hurt, picked it up, was about to toss the rotting, chewed, ant-cursed lemon into Fat Broad's yard, when he figured, what the hell, and dumped it down beside him. Then he pitched the shovel in deep, trying to keep in mind where he'd buried the pigtailly girl from two years back. When he felt he had dug down far enough, he went and got several of Patsy's parcels, and plopped them in, and then checked the wall for a spy, saw no one, and went and got the rest.

Vix sniffed the hole he'd dug, but the dog was more attached to lemons than anything else out in the yard. "Find another one, Vix, this one," Cal nudged the rotting lemon by his foot, "this one's all wormy. Good boy."

He took the radio, too, shut it off, finally, and dropped it in, kicked in the wormy lemon and some fish heads, and covered the whole mess up.

Then he went into the kitchen, sat at the small glass table, and actually missed the sound of talk radio for once in his life. He went and turned on the little Japanese radio he'd bought for Patsy, the one she'd never used. He turned it to the talk radio station and kept the volume up.

"I just loved that last call—didn't you?" the Radio Lady said. "It's a day brightener to hear something like that in these times. Imagine, rescuing a cat and someone's grandmother in the same hour. Gosh, sometimes life is difficult, but it's always fascinating, isn't it?"

Cal looked at the telephone hanging from the wall.

At the radio.

Wonder if Patsy ever called in.

She wasn't one for discussing her life.

Miss her, even so.

The Radio Lady announced the number to call in, and Cal went and dialed it.

After seven rings, a man picked up, and Cal hung up quickly.

Then he dialed again, got the man who mentioned he was screening calls, and asked Cal what his problem was.

"It's about my wife and kids. I have trouble, sometimes, taking care of them."

The man on the phone told him he'd be on in about two minutes.

Two minutes turned to four, when the Radio Lady came on. Cal had to turn the radio down to hear her. "What can I help you with?"

"Well," he said, then thought he might hang up.

"Don't be shy," she said.

"I've been listening to you for a long time. Years."

"Well, I've been here four years so far, so thanks for the compliment."

"Hmm. I thought it was longer. Well, it's about my wife and my kids."

"Is it good or bad?"

"Neither. Just about life. What I've learned. I'm sixty-three, you know."

"Congratulations. Hey, isn't it great that you people still call in?"

"My wife, I miss her, and the kids. Most of the kids."

"How many do you have?"

"Nine."

"Holy cow, nine kids. And you raised them all?"

"I cared for each and every last one of them to the best of my ability."

"Well, you deserve a pat on the back for that. These days, too many people are abandoning their children."

"That's right," Cal said, "most of my kids were like that. Foster kids. But my wife and I took them in. Loved them. Gave them a home. And I fulfilled my obligation to them, too."

"I wish I could meet a man like you," the Radio Lady said. "I'll bet a lot of women in my audience would. So what are you calling about, you catch?"

Cal paused. "I'm tired of burying them. I miss them."

The Radio Lady said nothing.

Cal said, "Oh, they live on, in things, in day-to-day objects, when I wash sometimes, I can smell their skin.

Fresh. So fresh, the way only a child can smell."

The Radio Lady said nothing.

And then Cal realized why.

She was crying. "Oh, you poor wonderful man. God bless you, God bless you."

"Thank you," Cal said, and hung up.

He went and turned off the little Japanese radio. He couldn't cry anymore. Except for taking care of Vix, he had fulfilled his obligations. He just couldn't take care of Vix, not yet.

In the morning, the roses needed hosing down because he had been hoping it would rain and had left them dry for days. He washed with the sunken-eyed boy soap, and remembered the tight little curl to the child's fingers (although he couldn't for the life of him remember names much anymore). Then he went outside, turned the hose on, and sprayed down Vix while he flooded the roses. Ants crawled out from the soaked earth, and crawled up the garden wall. Fat Broad was out in a muumuu and barbed-wire curlers with her Yorkshire terrier, getting the ball of stringy fur to yap, yap. Before he could take cover, she'd spotted him and called out, "Your wife—is she all right?"

Cal kept the hose spraying and pretended not to hear.

She thinks I'm ancient, so being deaf isn't much of a stretch.

Fat Broad, and her Yorkie, toddled over to the wall, and he smiled, then dropped the smile like a turd.

She said, "I don't hear the radio. The talk shows."

"Radio broke. Wife won't listen to any other radio. She's a peculiar woman. Thirty-five years of marriage."

"I'm not surprised it broke. Good heavens, she played it night and day. You must be happy it broke."

He scrunched up his face angrily. "Not at all, woman. I was used to it."

"Well, it's nice to have the quiet so I can hear my wind chimes."

"Doesn't get too windy," Cal said, stepping as far from the wall as he could without getting too muddy in the puddles he'd created with the garden hose. Vix put his forepaws up on the wall and began barking at Fat Broad and her Yorkie, so she went back to her own business.

He went and checked the bougainvillea, which hadn't been growing well this year, although the Mexican trumpet vine was in full bloom, with hummingbirds darting in and out of its blossoms.

I take care of my own. My family, my garden.

My obligations.

Oh, but he missed them, their kisses, their hands, their love.

Even his mother, with that friendship of blood that transcended all others.

It's over, he thought. It's done.

Someone, in another yard, somewhere, he thought, just beyond Fat Broad's, turned up their radio loud as if to fill the void left by Patsy's blaster.

He could faintly hear the Radio Lady say, "You're on the air, caller? You're on the air."

A child's voice said, "Hi . . . um . . . I don't know if I'm s'posed to call you . . . but I listen to you all the time."

The Radio Lady said something, although Cal couldn't quite hear it.

The boy said, "I ain't—I mean, I guess, I haven't ever called in. Not like this."

Another voice, a girl's said, "Hello? Wow. This is cool. Hello? Is someone there?"

"You're talking with the Radio Lady," the other voice said, and although faint, Cal recognized it. It was Patsy.

He went and called Fat Broad back over to the wall. She came over, shuffling like she was all bound up inside that oversized dress, and curled up her nose at him like he stank.

"You hear that?" he asked her.

"What?"

"Listen." He held a finger to his lips.

Fat Broad was silent for a moment, cocking her head to the side like she was trying to roll that last marble right out from her eardrum.

Another boy, about six, said, "I scared."

The girl, the pigtailly girl, Cal was sure, said, "Don't be scared. We're all taken care of. Aren't we?"

The Radio Lady said, "That we are."

Fat Broad interrupted Cal's listening. "I don't hear nothing. Is it a siren or something? If you tell me what I'm listening for, maybe I can hear it."

Cal was angry that she was talking so much while the talk radio was going on. "No," he said. "I won't tell you. If you don't hear it, I won't."

"I hear things sometimes," Fat Broad said, nodding. "Maybe you're hearing a ghost."

Cal looked at her sharply. "I don't believe in ghosts."

"I don't mean that kind, I mean like on TV when you have a ghost image. Or now that your wife's radio broke, you're so used to hearing it that you still think it's playing." But the woman saw that Cal was paying no attention to her, so she tramped across her own pansy bed to reprimand her son for leaving his trike out overnight.

Cal listened, and noticed that Vix, covered with mud in the garden, seemed to be listening, too.

He couldn't fall asleep. He went to Patsy's room and rocked back and forth in the chair, smelling her smell. He had the curtains pulled to the window, and he looked out at the backyard. The radio had gotten louder, just a bit, but still not to the volume it had been up to when Patsy had been around. He listened to each of his nine children talk with their mother, and he listened to her words of comfort, but he was still very sad.

At least I have one comfort, he thought, at least I can hear them.

And then, around three A.M., just as he was nodding off, he heard a voice on the radio that did not belong to any of his children, nor to his wife.

It was a woman with such an impediment to her speech, it sounded like a toad was sitting beneath her tongue. "Ca-hoo, Ca-hoo, heh-up mee, Ca-hoo."

He got out of the rocker and went to the window. He rolled the side windows open wider, smelled the sweet rosewater and the scent of moist earth.

"Mother?" he asked, peering out into the dark.

"Cay-uh, cay-uh," she said, and then was lost in the static of the radio.

She had said "care," he was sure.

Care.

Even though she wasn't buried in the yard, but in a cemetery twenty-five miles away, she had traveled through the ground waves, through the sewage pipes of the dead, to speak to him.

He knew why her voice was strange, because of what he'd had to do to her mouth.

He wished now he hadn't. He would like to understand her better, for she was a person of enormous wisdom.

He watched the darkness, listening for her voice again on the radio, but all was silence.

He drank several shots of whiskey, not his style at all, and slept late. He dreamed of the sound of machines roaring and dogs barking, and awoke at nine-thirty when someone tapped him on the shoulder.

He smelled mud and flowers, and looked into the empty eyes of his mother, her face dripping with mud and sewage. She opened her scarred mouth, the one

287

that had burned so well when he stretched the electric cord across her lips, between her teeth, and switched on the juice. The scars took the form of a star pattern, and when she parted her lips, dry leaves and dead grass dropped out.

She took his hand and led him to the woodshop, where the sound of talk radio drowned out the other sounds, the sounds of the care one human being shows for another.

The Radio Lady said, "Happy is the man who fulfills his obligations in this life."

# The Hurting Season

The wind had a taste to it, for Leona hung out the wash on the rope strung between the willow and the sapling, down by the river, with the smell of shad, dead on the water's surface from running, and the clean of soap powder and bleach; the Sack was strung up and bounced with each windblow; and Mama was boiling meat in back before the flies would be up to bother her; and it was a rough wind, a March wind even in late April, coming ahead of a storm. The river was high, threatening flooding if the storms kept up, which they were wont to do, but Theron had done all the clearing, and the chairs and table from the levee were already in the springhouse, the old springhouse that no longer flooded, and he was almost to the shed now, because the horses were kicking at the stall. The sky was its own secret blue, unnatural, with blue clouds and blue winds and blue sun, all signaling a squall coming down from off-island. He could see the oyster boats rocking across the bay, two miles from the house, just like mosquito larvae wriggling, and he wondered how it was on Tangier, of that girl he met at Winter Festival—he was fourteen, and she was nearly seventeen, but he had seen it in her eyes, those flatland island dull eyes, a flicker of what could only have been fire when she had let him touch her the way Daddy touched Mama.

The horses, prophesying storm, kicked the wood, and the shed trembled. Mama cried out at the noise, surprised, but Leona, in her earthly wisdom, just kept hanging sheets and shirts as if the impending storm mattered not one whit, for it would come and go quickly, a final rinse for the laundry. Theron kept buttoning his shirt; the screen door banged with the wind; the blue sky turned indigo and then gray, with flashes of lightning between. First drops of rain, sweet and cold.

He ran like a horse himself, back to the shed, for he loved the horses and could not bear their distress. The ground was damp but not muddy, and he galloped across it barefoot in spite of the biting chill. He could feel the rain spitting at his back as he got there, to the door, which he drew back. The smells of the horses, the manure, the cats, too, for they roamed among the piles and hay for mice and snakes, strong but not unbearable.

His father was there, at the mast that centered the shed, around which the horses were knocking and frenzied. The mast had a great length of chain hanging from it, and the leather strops of discipline, too, wrapped about its middle. Carved notches marked the days of the season, from Winter Festival to May Day, the days when Daddy did his penance, the hours of his atonement for a sin long ago forgotten. His father wore no shirt; his chest was covered with kudzu hair that sprawled across his shoulders and connected to his belly like inflamed moss; trousers were dirty, shit-stained; boots, too, with blood near the toes for they were tight and he would wear them all during the hurting season.

"You got Naomi upset," Theron said, not meaning to scold, but it was hard to avoid. Naomi was not yet a year, and needed gentleness; the old horse, her sire, Moses, was used to the season, the frantic pain that Daddy put himself through, but Naomi was barely more than a foal.

His father's eyes were not even upon him, but gazing through him, beyond him, to some richer meaning, listening to the words, but decoding them. The man's face was yellow jaundice, and the hunger was showing in the sunken cheeks; the thin blond hair, cut short like a monk's, Theron thought, was slick and shiny, the sweat, pearls of mania. "That's not good," his father said, "you take her out, then, take her out, boy."

Theron nodded, glad, and ran around the mast to grab Naomi's bit. He tugged at her, but her eyes were still wild. Theron looked around the shed. "It's the chain. Daddy," he said, for he knew that a horse, unless tempered to a rope, would take fright at anything that resembled one; the silver chain swung lightly about the thick wood. On its end was a rusty hook, from one of the oyster trawlers that had dry-docked over in Tangier, and there was blood on it. He registered this for a moment, wondering what his father did with the hook that drew blood from him. It was frightening, sometimes, the hurting season, at least to him; he was sure it frightened Mama, too, for she was moody during those months; Leona, older than Daddy or Mama, didn't seem to notice or care; and Milla, being so young, accepted it the way Theron had up until he'd become aware that it was only his daddy who did it, that when he went to Tangier, nobody else had a mast or the chain and strops, nobody else had a daddy that slept with the horses from February to May.

The boy brought the horse out of the shed, into the slapping rain; the smell of bleach and soap stronger, and he looked up to see the wash swimming in the wind, but their stays holding tight to the rope; Naomi tugged away from him, but he kept his grip, watching for the horse's teeth. He spoke to her, calmly, and led her over to the springhouse. It would be small for the horse, but she'd be safe and fairly dry, and the darkness of it would calm her. He tied her to the upturned patio chair and wiped at her forelock and nose with the red bandanna the girl over at the Festival had given him, smoothing down the horse's mane, and withers, to settle her. The horse had the thick hair of the island horses—it was said that they could be traced back to the Spanish ships wrecking off the islands, and his father had told him that the harsh winters in the wild had developed the breed to the point of hardiness and hairiness. Something Theron had learned in school, too, a phrase, "survival of the fittest." That had been the island horses, for they swam every spring around the time of May Day from Tangier over to Chite Island, which was here. Here, beneath my feet. Centuries of horses coming to mate on Chite in the spring, and to swim back in October when winter came too harsh here first. Here. Chite was a small island, although the river that ran through it connected it through the wetlands to the Carolina Isthmus, so it had not been a real island since sometime long before Theron was born. Old Moses, he had been a Chiter, and his dam, a wild horse that had never been tamed on Tangier, had died and left the one foal, Naomi. Mine. Naomi had a bad fetlock, the back left, and she raised it a little, so he squatted down beside her and massaged it. The wind through the cracks in the old gray wood bit around his ears, but the whistling sound it made seemed to steady his horse. "Good girl," he said, and wrapped the bandanna around his neck the way the girl had. It smelled of horse now, and perfume, and fish, as all things on Tangier smelled of fish.

Theron waited out the storm in the springhouse, and when it was over, in just a few minutes, he led the horse out to the rock-pile road that spanned the wetlands to the west of the house, and took her at a canter.

The horse slowed toward the middle of the rock pile, for it became less smooth here, and there were small gaps in the rocks. The sky cleared, but the sun was still not up in the middle of it, but back in the west, over Tangier. A red-winged blackbird flew up and out from the mesh of yellow reeds and dive-bombed at Theron's hair. "Hey!" he shouted. "Didn't do nothin' to you!" He flapped his hands at the descending bird, and dug his heels into Naomi's side until she galloped some more. His butt was sore from the pounding, for he didn't have his seat yet, at least not with Naomi, for she was an erratic bounder, but he rose fell rose fell with her, his leg muscles feeling stronger, and he tried to pretend that he and the horse were one animal, just like his daddy had taught him. The bird left him alone once he was out of its territory, and he guided Naomi down to some fresh water for a drink. He saw their reflection, the horse's long neck, its thick shaggy mane hanging down, and then his own face in the cold brown water— the red bandanna tied smartly just under his chin, and some whiskers on his upper lip. He smiled at himself; she had liked him, that older girl in Tangier, the pretty one. She was brown eyed just like everybody else on the islands, and brown hair, and freckles. Her hands were like little brushes on his, for they scratched and tingled and smooth when she had slid them across his palms. "Lookit," she'd said after she'd done it, and he had looked at his hands. At the palms of his hands. All red, the palms, like they were blushing and warm. "You got skin like water," she said, "see-through hands. I can see you through your skin, boy. Boy." She said "boy" like it was a dare, so he had kissed her behind the booth, where nobody could see them. He had known what the other boys did, the ones in school, even over in the Isthmus, for they bragged about tit touching and pussy stroking and diving and plunging and gushing. He had felt the electricity in his body, and in hers, and her lips were—gold warm hot sting bite taste smell wet mud—sensations had gone through him that words did not even come near, for it was his first kiss ever, and she had seen his excitement when she drew back from it. She had looked down at his trousers and said, "I guess that means you like me."

Embarrassed, he had dropped a hand in front of him and clasped it with the other, "Huh?"

"Rising like that. In your pants. It means a boy likes a girl. It's nature," she had said, the teacher of his flesh. She drew a line with her finger down his belly to his pants, and circled the knob that thrust forward from the denim. It grew wet, a spot. She grinned. He leaned forward and kissed her again, but she pushed him away this time and said, "Nuh-uh." But it led him, this feeling, just like the boys had told him it would, it led him without a thought in the world to anything else.

The horse leaned down, disturbing the water, and Theron's reflection whirled and broke in the water. She had liked him, that girl, that day. He had changed since then, he knew it.

He was a man now, even if the others called him boy.

The rock-pile road ended at the Isthmus Highway, rising out of reeds and swamps and curly-down trees like an altar of the true religion. Theron wasn't supposed to take Naomi up on it, for even though few cars traveled it until summer, when the summer people from the cities came down, and when Daddy blocked the rock-pile road to keep them off his property, the highway could be dangerous, for an occasional truck roared through in nothing flat, and a girl's mother got hit a long time ago trying to push her daughter out of the way and to safety. But Theron, a man now, and cocky, rode Naomi up the brief, steep hill, batting back the sticks and dead vines that had not yet greened since the winter, and clopped up onto the potholed blacktop. Naomi was faster on the highway, riding down the centerline, for it was completely flat, and where it dipped could be seen, and avoided, for several yards.

As he slowed her down at a bend in the road, there was a car stuck in mud on the shoulder. Theron was not big on cars, not like the other boys, but this one was pretty and sporty, a two-seater. A man stood beside it, kicking the bumper and cursing to high heaven. He was a lot younger than Daddy, but maybe only Mama's age. He wore a tan suit, and had rolled his slacks up almost to his knees, which were black with mud. He was soaked head to toe, caught, no doubt, in the storm. His eyeglasses were fogged in exertion and frustration. Cars were like that, which is why Theron's family didn't own one.

Theron dismounted, and led Naomi up to the man. "Mister, 'scuse me, but what kind of car is that?"

The man looked at Theron as if he could not hear. Almost like his father in the shed. Then he said, "It's a Miata, Mazda, kid. Right now it's a shitkicker."

"Pretty nice. Never seen one before," Theron nodded. "You're stuck."

"You must be the local genius," the man said, and then grinned. "Sorry, but you ever get so pissed off at something you can't see straight, kid?"

"I guess."

"So, kid, you live nearby? You got a phone or something?"

"Yeah, only we don't let strangers use it."

"Okay. Anybody else around here? A drugstore?"

Theron laughed, and covered his mouth to keep from making the man feel too bad. "Sorry—sorry—don't mean to laugh. Don't mean to. But you're twenty-five miles from town center." He pointed toward the direction that the man must've already come.

"That piss hole? Christ, kid, that's a town? I thought it was a mosquito breeding ground. Nothing the other way? You sure?"

Naomi whinnied, and Theron patted her nose. "She's shy. Just shy of biting, sometimes, I think." Then he tugged at the bandanna around his neck, self-consciously. There was something about this man he didn't feel comfortable about. "You're not from around here."

The man shook his head. "No, kid, I'm a damn Yankee. Make that a goddamned Yankee. But don't hold it against me." The man said his name was Evan, and he was from Connecticut, and that he wrote magazine articles and was supposed to meet his wife up in Myrtle Beach, but he was doing some kind of article on Lost Byways of the South.

"You write," Theron said, smiling, "that's wild. Wild. Me, I barely read. I watch TV. Anything you write ever get on TV?"

Evan shook his head. "Yeah, I once did write for the TV news. CBS."

"I watch that. Dan Rather. My daddy thinks he's from another parish, if you know what I mean, but Daddy thinks anybody on TV is."

"Well, kid, I don't know about that, but I know I hated it. I hate this. What a way to make a living, huh?"

Theron shrugged. "Survival of the fittest, I guess."

The wind, which had died, picked up again, rattling the dead reeds, shagging at the budding trees, dispersing the petals of those that had blossomed early. He could smell honeysuckle already, up here on the Isthmus, and it wasn't even May. The man had a kind look to him, a wrinkled-brow honesty, and Daddy had always told him that when someone needed help, there was only one thing to do. "Look, mister," Theron said after watching the man pace his car, "if you don't mind walking down there," he pointed down the gully, over the wetlands, to the stand of trees that separated Chite from the mainland, "it's about two miles. I'd let you ride her, but she's shy. My daddy's got a phone, only I got to warn you about one thing."

Evan said, "What's that, kid?"

"We keep to ourselves most of the time. I go to

school up in Isthmus, but we don't really mix. My baby sister, Milla, she never even seen a mainlander."

The man named Evan seemed to grasp this immediately. "Let's go."

Evan got a camera and a tape recorder out of the back of his car and strung both of them around his neck like ties. His shoes were brown and would be uncomfortable for the trip—Theron smiled inside himself when he thought of crossing the land on the other side of the rock-pile road, where the mud would surely suck him to his ankles if he wasn't careful. Evan asked, as they descended from the highway, down to the road between the wetlands, "Are there snakes down here?"

"Too cold still. There'll be plenty by June. I once saw a man from Tangier bite the head off a cottonmouth. You ever see that? He just chomped, and spitted it out like it was tobacco." Theron rode Naomi, but walked her slow so the man could keep up with them. He wasn't sure how Daddy or Mama, or even Leona for that matter, would take having a stranger over; Daddy was normally friendly with outlanders, but this was the hurting season, and it might be embarrassing for someone to walk right into the middle of that. Theron assumed that other fathers had their own hurting seasons, although he'd been too awkward to ask any of the boys over in the high school, both because they always seemed smarter than he, and because he was already teased enough as it was for being so different.

The sun was just past noon when they reached sight of the house, and the wind had pretty much died. The sky was white with cloud streaks, and the earth was damp, the moss that hung from the trees sparkled with heaven's spit, as Mama called rain when she was feeling poetic. Naomi tried to pick up speed, for the shed was close by, but he kept her slow out of courtesy to the stranger. "How you doin'?" he asked Evan.

Evan wagged his head around and said, "Hey, kid, can I get a picture? You and the horse and the house and that thing—what is that? Some kind of bag?"

Theron looked in the direction where Evan indicated, as the man unscrewed his camera's lens cap. Dangling from the willow, with the wash, was the Luck Sack. "It's for good luck," Theron said. "It keeps away hurricanes and floods in spring."

"How's it work?"

"So far, so good." He posed for a picture, sitting up proudly on his horse, keeping his chin back so the man could get a clear shot of the red bandanna that girl in Tangier had given him. Theron wished he had a hat—his father had a hat, and now that Theron had crossed the border between boyhood and mandom, he would've liked something brown with a broad brim to keep the sun out of his eyes, to make him feel like a horseman.

"So," Evan said, snapping several pictures, "you have other good-luck charms?"

Theron struck pose after pose, attempting a masculine look for this one, a shy look, a rugged, tough pose.

"We're not much into good luck. It's what we call tradition. Say, how much film you got in there?"

"Lots." snap—snap—snap. "What's in that sack, anyway?"

"One of the cats. We got seven. Kittens on the way," Theron said. "I love kittens, but cats I ain't so fond of. You gonna put my pictures in a magazine or· something?"

"Maybe," Evan said, lowering the camera. He let the camera swing around his neck. He reached beneath his glasses and rubbed his eyes. His face glowed with sweat—the two miles had been hard on him, because he was a Yankee. The man seemed to be taking in the house and the river, maybe even the bay if his eyesight was any good with those thick glasses. "Are you people witches or something?"

Theron straightened up and grunted, "Nahsir," his pride a little hurt by such an assumption, "we're Baptists."


"Ronny, honey," Leona said, her eyes lowering, not even looking at the stranger; she kept the screen door shut, and her massive form blocked the way. "I don't think you should be bringing people home right now."

"This's Evan. He's a Yankee," Theron said. "He needs to use the phone."

Leona looked at Evan's shoes. Theron saw the squiggle vein come out on her forehead, like when she was tense over cleaning. "Mister, our phone's out of order." She said it lightly, delicately, sweetly. Then she looked him in the eye.

Evan blinked. "That's okay," he said, patting Theron on the shoulder.

Leona arched her eyebrows and stared at the small tape recorder and camera around his neck. "You a traveling pawnshop, mister?"

"Nah'm," Theron butted in, "he writes for magazines. He's a famous writer, Leo, he used to write for Dan Rather."

"Not really," Evan said.

"I'm sorry, sir, but you can't come in the house. The little girl's sick, and like I said, the phone's not working. We had a big storm this morning. Always knocks out the power lines and such." She kept her hands pressed against the screen door as if the man would suddenly bolt for it. And then, to Theron, "Now, Ronny, why'd you bring this nice man all the way out here when you knew the line was down?"

Theron said, " 'Cause I thought it'd be up by now," turning to look up at Evan, who kept staring at Leona. "It's usually up in a hour or two," and, as if this were a brilliant idea, he clapped his hands. "I know, Evan, you can stay and have some sandwich and pie, and then maybe the phone'll be up."

A groan from the shed out back, and Evan and Theron both glanced that way. It was Daddy with his hurting. Leona groaned, as much to cover up the other noise as anything, and she clutched her stomach. "I tell you, mister, what little Milla's got, we all seem to be coming down with. You'd be wise to get on back up to Isthmus."

302

"Some kind of flu," Evan said.

"That's right. That one that's been going around." She nodded, looking pained.

Evan grinned, as if this were a game. "Had my flu shots, ma'am. And anyway, even if I hadn't, I'll survive it."

Leona lost all semblance of pretend kindness. "Just get off this property right now, and Ronny, you take him back up to the highway." She stepped back into the gray hallway and shut the big door on both of them.

"She always this sweet?"

Theron shook his head. "I don't know what's wrong with her today. She's almost a hundred, but all age done for her is make her ornery." He went and tied Naomi around the sapling.

"I thought you had your marching orders," Evan said, following him.

"I don't listen to Leona. She's just the hired help. You take orders from servants, my daddy says, and you end up a shit frog. We got them in the springhouse. You ever see a shit frog? They go from the stable to the river, but they still can't get it off them." Theron grabbed the laundry rope with both hands and clung to it, letting his knees go slack. "You gonna take more pictures?"

"I don't know," Evan said, but he lifted his camera again, snapped some more of the boy, and then of the river, and the house, and the tire swing, and the Lucky Sack hanging on the willow. He looked all around, through his camera, as if trying to see something else worth photographing, when he seemed to freeze. He lowered the camera and turned to face Theron.

Theron shivered a little bit because of the man's look, all cold and even angry, maybe.

"Where are the lines?" he asked.

"Huh?"

"Kid, if you got a phone, where's the pole? Where're the lines? If the line's down, you got to have a line in the first place, kid. What kind of game is this?"

Theron didn't haven an answer, not yet anyway. He said, "Dang."

From the shed, a series of shouts, cusswords as strong as Theron had ever heard from the boys at Isthmus.

The stranger named Evan turned around at the sound, took in the whole landscape, the house, the river, the shed, the springhouse, the laundry rope, the bay, the boats, the way the grass was new and green and damp. He walked over to the Lucky Sack, and Theron shouted, "Mister! Evan! Hey!"

But the man had already opened the sack, his face turning white, and he looked at Theron, his eyes all squinching up, and Daddy began screaming at the top of his lungs from the shed, and Old Moses, the horse, started thumping at the wood.

"You sick fucks," Evan said, weeping, "you sick fucks, you said it was a cat, you sick . . ." But the sobbing took him over, racking his body, the convulsions of sadness shaking him.

Theron blurted, "It's bad luck to look in the Sack, mister."

"Who is it, you sick fuck, who is this?"

Theron tugged at the red bandanna around his neck. "It's private."

"Listen, you." Evan raised both fists and brought them down on the boy, knocking him to the ground.

Theron was angry, and knew he shouldn't, but told him anyway because he hated keeping the secret. "It's the first girl I ever kissed. It's the part of her that's sacred. It's the part that made me a man!"

But then Mama was there, behind the man, and hit him with the back of the hoe, just on his skull, and the glasses flew off first, and then his hands wriggled like nightcrawlers, and he crumpled to the ground.


Milla held on tight to Mama's skirt, her brown eyes wide, her hair a tangly weedy mess. She looked like an unmade bed of a baby sister; when Theron got up from the ground, he went and lifted her up. "It's okay, it's just fine, Milla-Billa-Filla," he said as he bounced her around. She was only three, and she looked scared. Theron loved her so much, his sister. He had prayed for a brother when the birthing woman was in their house, but when he had seen Milla in the shed, lying there in his mother's arms, while the birthing mother screamed as Daddy tied her to the mast, he knew that he would love that little girl until the day he died, and protect her from all harm.

305

Mama said, in her tired way, "Ronny, why'd you bring him down here?"

Theron kissed his sister on the cheek and looked up to his mother. He was always frightened of his mother's rages, for they, like the hurting season, came in the spring and lasted until midsummer. "I—I don't know."

"That ain't good enough. And don't lie to me, or you shall eat the dust of the earth all your days and travel on your belly."

"I—I guess. I guess because I wanted Daddy to stop hurting for a while. I want us all to stop hurting for a while, Mama," and then he found himself crying, just like the man named Evan had been, because he didn't like the hurting season, and he didn't completely understand the reason for it.

For a moment, he saw the temper begin to flare in his mother's eyes, and then she softened. She bent down, dropping the hoe at her side, and gathered him up in her arms, him and Milla both, hugged tight to her bosom. "Oh, my little boy, you may be a man now, but you will always, always be my little boy." She threatened to weep, too, and Theron figured they'd be the soggiest mess of humans in the county, but Mama held back. Daddy was silent in the shed, no doubt exhausted.

Theron thought it might be the right time to ask the question he'd had on his mind since he first discovered about the hurting season. "Why, Mama?"

"Ronny?"

"Why does it have to be us?"

"You mean about the season?"

"Not just the season," he said, drying his tears, "but us here, and them," he looked across the bay to Tangier, "over there. We don't mix."

His mother reached over to his forehead and traced her finger along the brand that had been put there, a simple X. He felt her nail gently trace the lines of the letter. "It's our mark," she said, "from the beginning of creation. Passed through the fathers to the sons."

Theron looked at Milla. "What about the daughters?"

"Uh-huh, that, too, but no birthing, no creation. Our womb must not bear fruit. You remember the scripture."

He did: "And your seed shall not pollute your womankind, but shall be passed through the women of the land to bring your sons and daughters into lesser sin. And of your daughter, the fruit of her womb shall be sewn shut, and neither man nor beast may enter therein. Behold, you and your seed shall sin that the world may be saved."

But when he told the lines to one of the boys in Isthmus, the boy laughed and said he knew the Bible by heart and that wasn't in it. But in the hide-covered Bible that Leona kept above the bread box, it was right there, in Genesis.

The man on the ground began to stir, his hands twitching.

"I'm gonna take him to the shed," Theron said, pulling away from the warmth of his mother's arms.

\* \* \*

The man was heavy.

Dragging him through the mud was made more difficult because of the way he was moving, for the legs now kicked a bit, and the man was groaning, but the blood had stopped from the wound on the top of his skull. Theron felt muscles in his arms and legs begin to plump with this effort; he was sore from riding, too, which didn't help, and when he was halfway to the shed, he wished he'd been smart enough to have just thrown the man over Naomi and get him to the shed that way. He smelled the stewpot, for Mama let it cook all day long, and then when the men, meaning him and Daddy, were hungry, they could just ladle out a hefty portion into the bowl themselves, for men were too busy with work to sit down at table until suppertime. When he got to the shed, Evan looked up at him, although the glasses had fallen somewhere along the way. Theron could tell by the way he was squinting that he wasn't seeing much right in front of his face.

"It's okay, mister," the boy said, "don't worry."

Evan, scrunching up his face, not quite sure where he was, coughed up some spit, which dribbled down the side of his chin. "Uh-awh" was the noise he made.

Theron rapped on the shed door, not wanting to let go of the man's shoulder with his other hand. "Daddy!" he called, "open up, Daddy!"

The door opened inward, and his father seemed to know what to do. He bent down on one knee, cradling Evan's face between his hands. His father's face was slick with greasy sweat, and there was blood around his eyes where he'd driven the fish hooks beneath the lids. He brought his face close to Evan's and kissed the sputtering man on the lips.

Theron knew then that he had done the right thing, for it would mean that spring would come fast now, and that Daddy didn't have to suffer through the hurting season alone. While he kissed the man, Daddy brought the oyster boat hook with its length of chain down beside their lips, and began pressing its rusty point into the man's forehead to carve the X of their mark upon him so that the transfer of hurting could begin.

Laundry dried by three, with Leona taking it down, and laying it out across the basket. Milla was playing on the tire swing, head first through it, her small fingers clutching desperately at the black sides as she twirled around on it. Mama was napping, as she did in the spring afternoon, and the horses were calm again, after the first wave of screeching. Theron sat out on the dock, twiddling his toes in the icy water, and soon, Daddy came and sat down beside him.

"Give him some rest," Daddy said, but the pain was gone from his eyes, for the first time since Winter Festival.

"No more storms, I reckon," Theron said, feeling the weight of his father's arms around his shoulders. A bird was singing from one of the trees, and there were ducks bickering out on the river. Across the bay, the solitary Tangier, so close, so distant.

"You may be right."

"Daddy?"

"Boy?"

"Why does it have to hurt?"

"What do you mean?"

"This life. Why does there have to be a hurting season?"

His father had no reply.

That was what disturbed him about life, the very mystery of it, the deepness of its river, where on the surface all was visible, but beneath, something tugged and grabbed and drowned, and yet the current flowed, regardless.

"Look there." His father pointed off toward Tangier.

Theron squinted but could see only the island and the emptiness beyond it.

"The curvature of the earth," his father said. "Why does it go in a circle? Who knows? It's for God to decide. But we have our task here. We follow the rituals so the circle remains unbroken."

Theron was fourteen, a man now, he had been kissed, he had helped his father with the serious work of life, he had the mark, but he thought, looking at the eastern horizon, that one day he would go beyond Chite and Tangier and even Isthmus, and see the places that the Yankee had seen, in some yonder springtime. He would take what he knew of his task, of his mark, and show the world what it meant.

The stories came like dreams, like flights of ravens, like a ravening wind.

# *I am Infinite; I Contain Multitudes*

First off, I'll tell you, I saw both their files: Joe's and
the old man's. I had to bribe a psych tech with all kinds
of unpleasant favors, but I got to see their files. I want
you to sit through my story, so I'll only tell you half of
what I found. It was about Joe. He had murdered, sure,
but more than that, he had told his psychiatrist that he
wanted only to help people. He wanted only to keep
them from hurting themselves. He wanted to love.
Remember this.

It makes sense of everything I've been going
through at Aurora.

Let me tell you something about Aurora, something
that nobody seems to know but me: it is forsaken. Not
just because of what you did to get there, or how hay-
wire your brain is, but because it's built over the old

Aurora. Right underneath it, where we do the farming.
I heard this from Steve Parkinson, right underneath it
is the old Aurora. I saw pictures in an album they keep
in Intake. It used to be a dusty wasteland. The old
Aurora was underground. Back then they believed it
was better, if you were like us, to never see the light of
day, to be chained like animals and have your food
shoved to you in a slot at the bottom of your door.
Back then, they believed that nobody in the town outside the fence wanted to know that you were there. But
that's not why it's forsaken. You will know soon
enough.

There was a town of Aurora once, too, but then it
was bought out by Fort Salton, and 'round about 1949
they did the first tests.

I heard, from local legend, that there were fourteen
men down there, just like in a bunker at the end of the
war.

They did the tests out at the mountain, but some
people said that those men in Aurora, underground,
got worse afterward.

I heard a story from my bunkmate that one guy got
zapped and fried right in front of an old-timer's eyes.
Like he was locked in on the wrong side of the
microwave door.

The old-timer, he's still at Aurora; been there since
he was nineteen, in 'forty-six. Had a problem, they
said, with people after the war. He was in the Pacific,
and had come back more than shell-shocked. That's all
I ever knew about him, before I arrived. You can safely

assume that he killed somebody or tried to kill himself or can't live without wanting to kill somebody. It's why we're all here. He's about as old as my father, but he doesn't look it. Maybe Aurora's kept him young.

He was always over there, across the Yard. He knew everything about everyone. I knew something about him, too. Actually, we all pretty much knew it.

He thought he was Father to us all. I don't mean like my father, or the guy who knocked your mother up. I mean the Father, as in God The.

In his mind, he created the very earth upon which we stood, his men, his sons. He could name each worm, each sowbug, each and every centipede that burrowed beneath the flagstone walk; the building was built of steel and concrete and had been erected upon the backs of laborers who had died within the walls of Aurora; the sky was anemic, the air dry and calm; he could glance in any direction at any given moment and know the inner workings of his men as we wandered the Yard, or know, in a heartbeat, no, the whisper of a heartbeat, where our next step would take us. There was no magic or deception to his knowledge. He was simply aware; call it, as he did, hyperawareness, from which had come his nickname, Hype. He was also criminally insane by a ruling of the courts of the state of California, as were most men in Aurora.

I watched him sometimes, standing there while we had our recreation time, or sitting upon the stoop to the infirmary, gazing across the sea of his men. His army, he called them, his infantry: they would one day spread across the land like the fires of Armageddon.

The week after Danny Boy got out was the first time he ever spoke to me.

"Hey," he said, waving his hand. "Come on over here."

I glanced around. I had been at Aurora for only four months, and I'd heard the legends of Hype. How he called on you only after watching you for years. How he could be silent for a year and then, in the span of a week, talk your head off. I couldn't believe he was speaking to me. He nodded when he saw my confusion. I went over to him.

"You're the one," he said, patting me on the back. You couldn't not look him in the eye, he was so magnetic, but all the guys had told me not to look him in the eye, not to stare straight at him at any point. They all warned me because they had failed at it. They had all been drawn to his presence at one time or another. He was pale white. He kept in the shade at all times. His hair was splotchy gray and white and longer than regulation. His eyes were nothing special: round and brown and maybe a little flecked with gold. ("He milks you with those eyes," Joe had told me.) There were wrinkles on his face, just like with any old man, but his were thin and straight, as if he had not ever changed his expression since he'd been young.

"I'm the one? The one," I said, nodding as if I understood. I had a cigarette, left over from the previous week. I offered it to him.

He took the cigarette, thrust it between his lips, and

sucked on it. I glanced around for an orderly or psych tech, but we were alone together. I didn't know how I was going to light the cigarette for him. They all called me Doer, which was short for Good-Doer, because I tended to light cigarettes when I could, shine shoes for one of the supervisors I'd ass-kiss, or sweep floors for the lady janitors. I did the good deeds because I'd always done them, all my life. Even when I murdered, I was respectful. But since there was no staff member around, I couldn't get a light for the old man.

Hype seemed content just to suck that cigarette, speaking through the side of his mouth. "Yeah, you know what it means, but you're it. Danny Boy, he would've been it, but he had to pretend."

"You think?"

He drew the cigarette from his mouth and held it in his fingertips. "He was a sociopath, you must've recognized that. He had to perform for his doctor and the board. He studied Mitch over in B—the one who cries and moans all the time. Mitch with the tattoos?"

I nodded.

"He studied him for three years before perfecting his technique. Let me tell you about Danny Boy. He was born in Barstow, which may just doom a man from the start. He began his career by murdering a classmate in second grade. It was a simple thing to do, for they played out in the desert often, and it was not unusual for children to go missing out there. He managed to get that murder blamed on a local pedophile. Later, dropping out of high school, he murdered a teacher, and then, when he killed three women in

Laguna, he got caught. The boy could not cry. It was not in him to understand why anyone made a fuss at all over murder. It was as natural to him as is breathing to you." He paused, and drew something from his breast pocket. He put the cigarette between his lips. He flicked his lighter up and lit the cigarette. Although we weren't supposed to have lighters, it didn't surprise me too much that Hype had one. As an old-timer he had special privileges, and as something of a seer, he was respected by the staff as well as by his men. It's strange to think that I was suitably impressed by this, his having a lighter, but I was. It might as well have been a gold brick, or a gun.

He continued, "Danny Boy is going to move in with one of the women who work in the cafeteria. She's never had a lover, and certainly never dreamed of having one as handsome as Danny Boy. Within six weeks, he will kill her and keep her skin for a souvenir. Danny Boy would've been it, but he wasn't a genuine person. You are. You know that, don't you?"

"What, I cry, so that makes me real?"

He shook his head, puffing away, trying to suppress a laugh. "No. But I know about you, kid. You shouldn't even be here, only you come from a rich family who bought the best lawyer in L.A. I assume that in Court Ninety, he argued for your insanity and you played along 'cause you thought it would go easier for you in Aurora or Atascadero than in Chino or Chuckawalla. Tell me I'm wrong. No? How long you been here?"

"If you're so smart, you already know."

"Sixteen weeks already. Sixteen weeks of waking

up in a cold sweat with Joe leaning over your bed. Sixteen weeks of playing baseball with men who would be happy to bash in your head just for the pleasure of it. Sixteen weeks hearing the screams, knowing about Cap and Eddie, knowing about how all they want is the taste of human flesh one more time before they die. And you, in their midst." He seemed to be enjoying his own speech. "You're not a sociopath, son, you're just someone who happened to kill some people and now you wish you hadn't, and maybe you wished you were in Chino getting bludgeoned and raped at night, but at least not dealing with this zoo."

The bell rang. I saw Trish, the rec counselor, waving to us from over at the baseball diamond. She was pretty, and we all wanted her and we were all protective of her, too, even down to the last sociopath.

"Looks like it's time for phys. ed.," Hype said. "She's a fine piece of work, that one. Women are good for men. Don't you think? Men can be good, too, sometimes, I guess. You'd know about that, I suppose."

"What am I 'it' for?" I asked, ignoring the implication of his comment.

He dropped the cigarette in the dust. "You're the one who's getting out."

I thought about what the old-timer'd said all day.

In the late afternoon, I was sitting with Joe on the leather chairs in the TV room after we got shrunk by our shrinks, and said, "I don't get it. If Danny Boy wasn't it, and 'it' means you get out, why the hell am I it?"

Joe shrugged. "Maybe he means 'you're next.' Like

you're the next one to get out. That old guy knows a shitload. He's God."

Joe had spent his life in the system. First, at Juvy, then at Boys' Camp in Chino, then Chino, and finally some judge figured out that you don't systematically kill everyone from your old neighborhood unless you're not quite right in the head. But Joe was a good egg behind the Aurora fence. He needed the system and the walls and the three hots and a cot just to stay on track. Maybe if he'd been a Jehovah's Witness or in the army, with all those rules, he never would've murdered anybody. He needed rules badly, and Aurora had plenty for him. He had always been gentle and decent with me, and was possibly my only friend at Aurora.

I nudged him with my elbow. "Why would I be it?"

"Maybe he's gonna break you," Joe whispered, checking the old lady at the desk to make sure she couldn't hear him. "I heard he broke another guy out ten years ago, through the underground. That old man's got a way to do it, if you go down in that rat nest far enough. I heard," Joe grabbed my hand in his, his face inches from mine, "he knows where the way out is, and he only tells it if he thinks your destiny's aligned with the universe."

I almost laughed at Joe's seriousness. I drew back from him. "You got to be kidding."

Joe blinked. He didn't like being made fun of. "Believe what you want. All's I know is the old man thinks you're it. Can't argue with that."

And then Joe kissed me gently, as he always did,

or tried to do, when no one was looking, and I responded in kind. It was the closest thing to human warmth we had in that place. I pulled away from him, for a psych tech was trolling in with one of the shrinks. Joe pretended to be watching the TV. When I looked up at the set, it was an ad for tampons. I laughed, nudging Joe, who found nothing funny about it.

I wanted to believe that Hype could break me out of Aurora. I spent the rest of the day and most of the evening fantasizing about getting out, about walking out on the grass and dirt beyond the fence. Of getting on a bus and going up north where my brother lived. From there I would go up to Canada, maybe Alaska, and get lost somewhere in the wilderness where they wouldn't come hunting for me. It was a dream I'd had since entering Aurora. It was a futile and useless dream, but I nurtured it day by day, hour by hour. I could close my eyes and suddenly be transported to a glassy river, surrounded by mountains of pure white, and air so fresh and cold it could stop your lungs; an eagle would scream as it dropped from the sky to grab its prey.

But my eyes opened; the dream was gone. In its place, the dull green of the walls, the smell of alcohol and urine, the sounds of Cap and Eddie screeching from their restraints two doors down, the small slit of window with the bright lights of the Yard on all night. Only Joe kept me warm at night, and the smell of his hair as he scrunched in bed, snoring lightly, beside me, kept alive any spirit that threatened to die inside me. I had never been interested in men on the Outside, but in Aurora, it had never seemed homosexual between us. It had seemed like survival. When you are in that kind of environment, you seek warmth and human affection, if you are at all sane. Even if sanity is just a frayed thread. Even the sociopaths sought human warmth; even they, it is supposed, want to be loved. I knew that Joe would one day kill me if I said the wrong thing to him, or if I wasn't generous in nature toward him. He had spent his life killing for those reasons. Still, I took the risk because he was so warm and comfortable, and sometimes, at night, that's all you need.

The next morning I sought Hype out, and plunked myself right down next to him. "Why me?"

He didn't look up from his plate. "Why not you?" His mood never seemed to alter. He had that stoned look of one who could see the invisible world. His smile was cocked, like a gun's trigger. "Why not Doer, the compassionate? Doer, the one who serves? Why not you?"

"No," I said. "It could be any one of these guys. Why me? I've only been here four months. We don't know each other."

"I know everybody. I'm infinite. I contain multitudes. Nothing is beyond me. Besides, I told you, you don't pretend."

"Huh?"

"You don't pretend. You face things. That's important. It won't work if you live in your own little world, like most of these boys. You've got the talent."

"Yeah, the talent," I said, finally deciding the old fart was as loony as the rest.

"I saw what you did," he said. As he spoke, I could feel my heart freeze. In the tone of his voice, the smoothness of old whiskey. "I saw how you took the gun and killed your son first. One bullet to the back of the skull, and then another to his ear, just to make sure. Then your daughter, running through the house, trying to get away from you. She was actually the hardest, because she was screaming so much and moving so fast. You're not a good shot. It took you three bullets to bring her down."

"Just shut up," I said.

"Your wife was easy. She parked out front, and came in the side door, at the kitchen. She didn't know the kids were dead. All she knew was her husband was under a lot of pressure and she had to somehow make things right. She had groceries. She was going to cook dinner. While she was putting the wine in the fridge, you shot her and she died quickly. And then," Hype shook his head, "you took the dog out, too. Who would take care of it, right? With everybody dead, who would take care of the dog?"

I said nothing.

"Who would take care of the dog?" he repeated. "You had no choice but to take it out, too. You loved that dog. It probably was as hard for you to pull the trigger on that dog as it was to pull it on your son. Maybe harder."

I said nothing. I thought nothing. My mind was red paint across black night. His words meant nothing to me.

He patted me on the back as my father had before the trial. "It's all right. It's over. It wasn't anything anyone blames you for."

I began weeping; he rubbed his hand along my back and whispered words of comfort to me.

"It wasn't like that," I managed to say, drying my tears. Although we had been left alone, I looked across the cafeteria and felt that all the others watched us. Watched me. But they did not; they were preoccupied with their meals. "It was . . ."

"Oh. How was it?"

I wiped my face with my filthy hands. I was so dirty; I just wished to be clean. I fought the urge to rise up and go find a shower. "I wanted it to be me. I wanted it to be me."

"But you wanted to live, too. You killed your family, and then suddenly—"

"Suddenly," I said.

"Suddenly, your life came back into focus. You couldn't kill yourself. You had to go through all of them before you found that out. Life's like that," he said. "The bad thing is, they're all dead. You did it. You are a murderer. But you're not like these others. It wasn't some genetic defect or some lack of conscience. Conscience is important. You couldn't kill yourself. That's important. I don't want to get some fellow out who's going to end up killing himself. You need to be part of something larger than yourself. You need God. Tell me, boy: How do you live with yourself?"

I couldn't look him in the eye. I was trying to think up a lie to tell him. He reached out and took my chin in his hand. He forced me to look at him.

I remembered the warning: he milks you with those eyes.

"I don't know how," I said, truthfully. "I wake up every morning and I think I am the worst human being in existence."

"Yes," he said. "You are. But here's the grace of Aurora. You're it. You will get out. You will live with what you did. You will not kill yourself or commit any further atrocities." He let go of my chin and rose from the table. "Do you love your friend?"

"Joe?"

"That's right." He nodded. "Joe."

"Two guys can't love each other," I said. "It's just for now. It's surviving. It's barely even sexual."

"Ah." He nodded slowly. "That's good. It would be hell if you got out and you loved him and he was here. You must be careful around him, though. He is pretty, and he is warm. But he has the face of Judas. He will never truly love anyone. Now, you, you will love again. A man, perhaps. Or a woman. But not our friend Joe. Do you know what he did to the last man with whom he shared his bed? Has he ever told you?"

I shook my head slightly.

"Ask him," Hype said. He walked away. From the back, he didn't seem old. He had a young way of walking. I believed in him.

\* \* \*

"Tonight," Hype said to me during Recreational Time. "Two-thirty. You must first shower. You must be clean. I will not tolerate filth. Then wait. I will be there. If your friend makes trouble, stop him any way you can."

Joe could be possessive, but not in the expected way. He was not jealous of other men or women. He simply wanted to own me all the time. He wanted me to shower with him, to sit with him, to go to the cafeteria with him. Our relationship seemed simple to me: we had met about the third week in, when he caught me masturbating in the bathroom. He joined in, and this led to some necking, which led to a chill for another week. Then I got a letter from my mother in which she severed all connections with me, followed by one from my father and sister. I spent two days in bed staring at the wall. Joe came to me, and took care of me until I could eat and stand and laugh again. By that time, we were tight. I had been at Aurora for only two months when I realized that I could not disentangle myself from Joe without being murdered or tortured—it was a Joe thing. I didn't feel threatened, however, because I had grown quite fond of his occasional gropings and nightly sleep-overs. In a way, it was a little like being a child again, with a best friend, with a mother and lover and friend all rolled up into one man.

That night, when I rose from my bed at two A.M., Joe immediately woke up.

"Doer?" he asked.

"The can," I said, nodding toward the hallway.

Because Joe and I weren't in the truly dangerous category, we and a few others were given free rein of our hallway at night. Knowing, of course, that the Night Shift Bitch was on duty at the end of the hall.

"I'll go, too," Joe whispered, rising. He drew his briefs up—he had the endearing habit of leaving them down around his ankles in postcoital negligence.

I tapped him on the chest, shaking my head.

"Doer," he said, "I got to go, too."

I sighed, and the two of us quietly went into the hall.

In the bathroom, he said, "I know what's going on." He leaned against the shiny tile wall. "It's Hype. Word went around. This is the night. Are you really going?"

I nodded, not wanting to lie. He had been sweet to me. I cared a great deal for him. I would be sad without him for a time. "I'll miss you," I said.

"I could kill you for this."

"I know."

"If you leave I'll be lonely. Maybe it's love, who knows?" He laughed, as if making fun of himself. "Maybe I love you. That's a good one."

"No you don't." I knew that Joe was fairly incapable of something so morally developed as love, not because of his sexual leanings, but because of his pathology.

"Don't go," he said.

"For all I know, Hype is full of shit."

"He's not. I've seen him do this before. But don't go, Doer. Getting out's not so terrific."

"I want freedom," I said. "Plain and simple."

"I want you." Joe seemed to be getting a little testy.

"Now, come on, we're friends, you and me," I said, leaning forward to give him a friendly hug.

I didn't see the knife. All I saw was something shiny, which caught the nearly-burnt-out light of the bathroom. It didn't hurt going in—that was more like a shock, like hearing an alarm clock at five A.M.

Coming out, it hurt like a motherfucker.

He pressed his hand against the wound in my chest. "You can't leave me."

"Don't kill me, Joe. I won't leave you, I promise. You can come too." This I gasped, because I was finding it difficult to breathe. I felt light-headed. The burning pain quickly turned to a frozen numbness. I coughed, and gasped, "Get help, Joe. I think you really did me."

Joe pressed his sweaty body against mine. I began to see brief tiny expolosions of light and dark, as if the picture tube of life were going out. Joe kissed the wound where he'd stabbed me, as blood pulsed from it. "I love you this much," he said.

Then he drew his briefs down, a full erection in his hand. He took his penis and inserted it in the wound, just under my armpit. As I worked to inhale, he pressed the head of his member into the widening hole of the wound.

He pushed farther into my body.

I passed out, feeling wave after wave of his flesh as he ground himself against my side.


I awoke in the infirmary three days later, barely able to see through a cloud of painkillers. My stomach ached with the antibiotics that had been pumped through me.

I stared up at the ceiling until its small square acoustic tile came into focus.

When I was better, in the Yard, I sought Hype out. "I tried to make it," I said.

He said nothing. He seemed to look through me.

"You know what he did to me," I said. "Please, I want to get out. I have to get out."

After several minutes, Hype said, "Love transformed into fear. It's the human story. The last man Joe befriended was named Frank. He grew up in Compton. A good kid. He tore off another man's genitals with his bare hands and wore them around his neck. His only murder. Sweet kid. Twenty-two. Probably he was headed for release within a year or two. He had an A-plus evaluation. A little morbid. Used to draw pictures of beheadings. Joe latched on to him, too. Took care of him. Bathed him. Serviced him. Loved him, if you will. Then rumor went around that Frank was getting some from one of the psych techs. Totally fabricated, of course. Frank was taking a shower. Joe knocked him on the head. Strapped him to the bed, spread-eagled. Don't ask me how, but he'd gotten a hold of a drill—the old kind, you know, you turn manually and it spins. He made openings in Frank. First in his throat to keep him from screaming. Then the rest of him. Each opening . . . "

"I know," I said, remembering the pain under my arm. Then something occurred to me. "Where did he get the knife?"

Hype made a face, like he'd chewed something sour.

"The knife," I repeated. "And the drill, too. Everything's locked up tight. You're supposed to be God or something, so you tell me."

Without changing his expression, Hype said, "Joe gets out."

The enormity of this revelation didn't completely hit me. "From here?"

Hype nodded. "It's not something I'm proud of. I can open the door for about three hours, if I use up all my energy. Joe knows it. He was the first one I took out. But he didn't want to stay out. He only wanted out to get his toys. Then he wanted back. He's the only one who manages to get back. Why he wants to, I couldn't say." For the first time ever, I watched worry furrow the old man's brow. He placed his hand against his forehead. A small blue vein pulsed there, beneath his pale skin's surface. "I created the world, but it's not perfect."

"Joe knows how to get out?"

"I didn't say that. I can get it open. I just can't keep him from going back and forth. And then it closes again."

I wasn't sure how to pose my next question, because there was a mystery to this place where men got out. I had figured it to be down in the old underground, where Hype would know the route of the labyrinthine tunnels. "Where does it go?"

"That," Hype sighed, "I can't tell you, having never been through it. I just know it takes you out."

Back in my own bed that night, trying to sleep, I felt his hand. Joe's hand. On my shoulder. He slipped swiftly between the covers to cradle my body against his. "Doer," he said. "I missed you."

"Get off me." I tried to shrug him away. He was burning with some fever. A few drops of his sweat touched the back of my neck.

"No." He tugged himself in closer. I could feel his warm breath on my neck. "I want you."

"Not after what you did."

He said nothing more with words. His mouth opened against my neck, and I felt his tongue heat my sore muscles. All his language came through his throat and mouth, and I let him. I hated him, but I let him.

Afterward, I whispered, "I want out."

"No you don't."

"Yes. I don't care if you stab me again. I want out. You going to get me out?"

I waited a long time for his answer, then fell asleep.

I was still waiting for his answer three days later.

I cornered him in the shower, placing my hands on either side of him. I could encompass his body within my arms. I stared straight into his eyes. "I want out."

He curled his upper lip; I thought he would answer, but first, he spat in my face. "I saved you. You don't even care. Out is not where you want to be. In here's the only safe place. You get fed, you got a bed." He leaned closer to me. "You have someone who loves you."

I was prepared this time. I brought my fist against his face and smashed him as hard as I could. His head lolled to the side, and I heard a sharp crack as his skull hit the mildewed tile wall. When he turned to face me again, there was blood at the corner of his lips. A smile grew from the blood.

"Okay," Joe said. "You want out. It can be arranged."

"Good. Next time, I kill you."

"Yeah." He nodded.

As I left the shower room, I glanced back at him for a second. He stood under the showerhead, water streaming down—it almost looked like tears as the water streamed in rivulets across his face, taking with it the blood at his lips.

An hour later, Hype found me out by the crude baseball diamond we'd drawn in the Yard, under the shade of several oak trees that grew just beyond the high fence.

"Your lover told me we're moving up the schedule. Shouldn't do this but once every few years. You should've gotten out that night. Joe shouldn't have stopped you. Any idea why he did?"

I kicked at home plate, which was a drawing in the dirt. Aurora was a funny place that way—because of things being considered dangerous around the inmates, even home plate had to be just a drawing and not the real thing. The real thing here were the fences and the factorylike buildings. "No," I said. "Maybe he's in love with me and doesn't want to lose me. I don't care. He can go to hell as far as I'm concerned."

"I once tried to get out," Hype said, ignoring me. "It was back in the early fifties. I was just a kid. Me and my buddies. I tried to get out, but back then there was only one way—a coffin. Not a happy system. I didn't know then that I'd rather be in here than out there."

"Make sense, old man," I said, frustrated. I wanted to kick him. The thought of spending another night in this place with Joe on top of me wasn't my idea of living.

"A little patience'll go a long way, Doer," he said. It felt like a commandment. He continued, "Then they started doing those tests—bombs and all kinds of things, twenty, thirty miles away. Some closer, they said. Some this side of the mountain. We lived below back then. Me and Skimp and Ralph. Others, too, but these were my tribe. We were shell-shocked and crazy, and we were put in with the paranoid schizophrenics and sociopaths and alcoholics—all of us together. Some restrained to a wall, some bound up in straitjackets. Some of us roaming free in the subterranean hallways. Skimp, he thought he was still on a submarine. He really did. But I knew where we were—in the farthest ring of hell. And then, one morning, around three A.M., I heard Skimp whimpering from his bunk. I go over there, because he had nightmares a lot. I usually woke him up and told him a story so he could fall back to sleep. Only, Skimp was barely there. His flesh had melted like cheese on a hot plate, until it was hard to tell where the sheets left off and Skimp began. He was making a noise through his nostrils. It was like someone snoring, only he was trying to scream. Others, too, crying out, and then I felt it—like my blood was spinning around. I heard since that it was like we got stuck in a microwave. The entire place seemed to shimmer, and I knew to cover my eyes. I had learned a little about these tests, and I knew that moist parts of the body were the most vulnerable. That's why insects aren't very affected by it—they've got exoskeletons. All their softs parts are on their insides. I felt drunk and happy, too, even while my mouth opened to scream, and I went to my hiding place, covering myself with blankets. I crawled as far back into my hiding place as I could go, and then I saw some broken concrete and started scraping at it. I managed to push my way through it, farther, into darkness. But I got away from the noise and the heat. Later, I heard that it was some test that had leaked out. Some underground nuclear testing. We were all exposed, those who survived. Never saw Skimp or Ralph again, and I was told they were transferred—back in those days, no one investigated anyone or anything. I knew they'd died, and I knew how they'd died. There were times I wished I'd died, too. Every day. That's when I learned about my divinity. It was like Christ climbing the cross—he may or may not have been God before he climbed onto that cross, but you know for sure he was God once he was up there. I wasn't God before that day, but afterward, I was."

Hype was a terrific storyteller, and while I was in awe of that ability, I stared at him as if he were the most insane man on the face of the earth.

"So I found a way out," he concluded.

"If that's true, how come you don't get out?"

"It's my fate. Others can go through, but I must

stay. It's my duty. Trust me, you think God likes to be on earth? It's as much an asylum out there as it is in here."

I was beginning to think that all of this talk about going through and getting out was an elaborate joke for which the only punch line would be my disappointment. I decided to hell with it all: The old man could not get me out no matter how terrific his stories were. I was going to spend the rest of my life with Joe pawing me. I went to bed early, hoping to find some escape in dreams.

I awoke that night, a flashlight in my face.

Joe said, "Get up. This is what you want, right?" His voice was calm, not the usual nocturnal passionate whisper of the Joe who caressed me. He hadn't touched me at all. I was somewhat relieved.

"Huh?" I asked. "What's going on?"

"You want to get out. Let's go. You've got to take a shower first." I felt his hand tug at my wrist. "Get the hell up," he said.

The shower was cold. I spread Ivory soap across my skin, rubbing it briskly under my arms, around my healing wound, down my stomach, thighs, backs of legs, between my toes, around my crotch. Joe watched me the whole time. His expression was constant: a stone statue without emotion.

"It doesn't have to end like this," I said. "I'm going to miss you."

"Shut up," he said. "I don't like liars."

When I had toweled myself off, he led me, naked, down the dimly lit hall. The alarm was usually on at the double doors at the end of the hall, but its light was shut off. Joe pushed the door open, drawing me along. The place seemed dead. Hearing the sound of footsteps in the next ward, he covered my mouth with his hand and drew me quickly into an inmate's room. Then, a few minutes later, we continued on to the cafeteria. He had a key to the kitchen; he unlocked its door. I followed him through the dark kitchen, careful to avoid bumping into the great metal counters and shelves. Finally, he unlocked another door at the rear of the kitchen. This led to a narrow hallway. At the end of the hallway, another door, which was open.

Hype stood there, frozen in the flashlight beam.

"Hey," I said.

Hype put a finger to his lips. He wore a bathrobe that was a shiny purple in the light.

He turned, going ahead of us, with Joe behind me. I followed the old man down the stone steps.

We were entering the old Aurora, the one that stretched for miles beneath the aboveground Aurora. We walked single file down more narrow corridors, the sound of dripping water all around. At one point, I felt something brush my feet—a large insect, perhaps, or a mouse. The place smelled of wet moss, and carried its own humidity, stronger than what existed in the upper world. For a while it did seem that Hype had been right: This was the farthest ring of hell.

But I'm getting out, I thought. I'll go through any sewer that man has invented to get out. To go through. To be done with all this.

Joe rested his hand on my shoulder for a brief

moment. He whispered in my ear, "You don't have to do this. I was wrong. I love you. Don't get out."

I stopped, feeling his sweet breath on my neck. Even though I had been in Aurora only a little over four months, I had begun getting used to it. If I stayed longer, I would become part of it, and the outside world would be alien and terrifying to me. I saw it in other men, including Joe. This was the only world of importance to them.

"Why the change?" I asked.

"You don't want to go through. I want you here with me."

"No, thanks." I put all the venom I could into those two words. I added, "And by the way, Joe, if I had a gun I'd shoot your balls off for what you did to me."

"You don't understand." He shook his head like a hurt little boy.

Hype was already several steps ahead. I caught up with him while Joe lagged behind.

"I'm going out through that hiding place you talked about," I guessed.

"No," he said. When he got to a cell, he led me through the open doorway.

A feeble light emanated within the room—a yellow-ish-green light, as if glowworms had been swiped along the walls until their phosphorescence remained. It was your basic large tank, looking as if it had been compromised by the several earthquakes of the past few years.

Joe entered behind me. "This is where Hype and his friends lived. This is where it happened." He shined the flashlight across the green light. I shivered, because for a moment I felt as if the ghosts of those men were still here, still trapped in the old Aurora. "Tell him, Hype. Tell him."

Hype wandered the room, as if measuring the paces. "Ralph had this area. He had his papers and books—he was always a big reader. Skimp was over there," he pointed to the opposite side of the cell, "his submarine deck."

"Tell him the whole thing," Joe said.

In the green light of the room, as I glanced back at Joe, I saw that he had a revolver in his right hand. "Tell him," he repeated.

"Where the hell did you get that?" I pointed to the gun.

"You can't ever go back," Hype said. "Once you're out, you can never go back. I won't let you back. Understood?"

I nodded. As if I was ever going to want to return to Aurora.

"Tell him," Joe said to Hype. This time he pointed the gun at Hype. Then, to me, he said, "The gun was down here. I get all my weapons here. We get all kinds of things down here. Hype is God, remember? He creates all things."

"To hell with this," I said, figuring this bad make-believe had gone too far. "You can't get me out, can you?"

Hype nodded. "Yes, I can. I am God, Joe. Those underground tests, they made me God. They were my cross. I'm the only survivor. The orderlies, the doctors, the patients, I'm the only one. That's when I became God."

"You want to get out, right?" Joe snarled at me. "Right?" He waved the gun for me to move over to the far wall.

Hype turned, dropping his robe. Beneath it he was naked, the skin of his back like a long festering sore. The imprint of hundreds of stitches all along his spine, across the back of his rib cage. To the right of this, a fist-size cavity just above his left thigh, on his side.

"Tell him," Joe said.

The old man began speaking, as if he couldn't confess this to my face. "Inside me is the door. The tunnel, Joe. To get through, you've got to enter me."

The must vulgar aspect of this hit me, and I groaned in revulsion.

Joe laughed. "Not what you think, Doer. Not like what you like to do to me. Or vice versa. His skin changed after the tests. Down here, it changes again. Look—it's like a river, look!"

At first I didn't know what he was pointing at—his finger tapped against Hype's wrinkled back.

Then, before I noticed any change, I felt something deep in my gut. A tightening. A terrible physical coiling within me, as if my body knew what was happening before my brain did.

I watched in horror as the old man's skin rippled along the spine. A slit broke open from one of the ancient wounds. It widened, gaping. Joe came closer, shining his flashlight into its crimson-spattered entry. It was like a red velvet curtain, moist, undulating. A smell like a dead animal from within. The scent, too, of fresh meat.

Joe pressed the gun against my head. "Go through."

My first instinct was to resist.

Seconds later, Joe shot a bullet into the old man's wound, and it expanded further like the mouth of a baby bird as it waits for its feedings.

Joe kissed my shoulder. "Goodbye, Doer."

He pressed the gun to my head again.

The old man's back no longer seemed to be there; now it was a doorway, a tunnel toward some green light. Green light at the end of a long red road. His body had stretched its flesh out like a skinned animal, an animal-hide doorway, the skin of the world. . . .

With the gun against my head, Joe shoved me forward, into it. I pushed my way through the slick red mass and followed the green light of atomic waste.

Once inside, the walls of crimson pushed me with a peristaltic motion farther, against my will. Tiny hooks of his bones caught the edge of my flesh, tugging backward while I was pressed into the opening.

We are all in here, all the others who got out through him. Only, "out" didn't mean out of Aurora, not officially. We're out of our skins, drawn into that infested old man. When I had rein of him for an afternoon, I got him to go down and bribe the psych tech on duty. I pulled up both of their files, Joe's and Hype's.

Joe was a murderer who had a penchant for cutting

wounds in people and screwing the wounds. This was no surprise to me. Joe is a sick fuck. I know it. Everyone who's ever been with him knows it.

Hype was a guy who had been exposed to large amounts of radiation in the fifties. He had a couple of problems, one physical and one mental. The physical one I am well aware of, for the little bag rests at the base of my stomach, to the side and back. Because of health problems as a result of the radiation, he'd had a colostomy about twenty years back.

The mental problems were also apparent to me once I got out, once I got through. He suffered from a growing case of multiple personality disorder.

I pulled my file up, too, and it listed: ESCAPE.

I had a good laugh with Joe over these files. Then God took over, and I had to go back down into the moist tissues of heaven and wait until it was my turn again.

There are prisons within prisons, and skins within skins. You can't always see who someone is just by looking in their eyes. Sometimes, others are there.

Sometimes, God is there.

*"I am infinite," the old man said. "I contain multitudes."*

Alice lay on her back gasping for air—it was dawn, she knew. She felt it. The little boy lay next to her, curled up in some dream of his own. The blue and white flickering of the work lamps above . . .

She looked about the room—the stains on the walls, the breaks in the old plaster that covered the older brickwork. The flies, still humming along the far wall, where the troughlike sink sat half on and half off its fixture, where the water slowly drip-dropped into the porcelain basin.

A quick glance at the boy: still sound asleep, snoring softly. The handcuffs had cut into his small wrists slightly. There was something more familiar about the boy than she cared to admit. She tried to focus on him, but her head throbbed with the visions from the previous night. Pushing herself to her elbows, and then up to a sitting position, she looked about—the wheelchair, still overturned, just feet away. One hand, then the other, she dragged herself across the damp mattress, toward the wheelchair. Looking back—the boy remained asleep, dreaming, his hands twitching lightly like a puppy.

Alice raised herself up again to a full sitting position when she reached the fallen chair. As quietly as she could, she tried to bring it up so that it was on its wheels again, but could not. She was too weak, and the chair was too heavy for her.

Perspiring as much from the nightmares as from effort, she lay back down on the cold concrete floor.

Where was Charlie? Where was Stephen? She looked at the door, and wondered if she could drag herself to it, open it, and be out of there before the little devil woke.

A glance at the boy: now she knew why he looked familiar to her. His hair was cut the way she used to cut Stephen's when he was a little boy not much older than this one. A bowl cut, he used to call it, and the boy had the same black hair of her Stephen. Asleep, he seemed sweet, but from the hallucinations of the previous night, Alice knew this was no sweet innocent boy, not like her Stephen.

She reached her hand forward, pressing it against the concrete floor. Pull. Then the other. Pull. Then the other. Pull. Then the other. Pull.

A glance at the boy. Asleep. Hands and feet cuffed.

Hand forward, pressing. Pull. Then the other. Pull. Then the other. Pull.

If only my legs worked. If only there'd never been an accident, she thought. But there was no use wishing for things that could not be. She'd learned that lesson hard, years before the Rolls Royce had hit her at the crosswalk. Years before she lay there in agony, hearing the driver of the car say to someone, "She's crazy. You saw her jump out in front of my car. You saw it."

She reached down to touch her knee. Once she could walk.

A glance at the boy. Fingers twitching in a dream—a dream she was happy to not be part of.

Where were Charlie and Lana? They were supposed to do mornings with the boy. Where were they?

Pull. Then the other. Pull. Then the other. Pull.

Alice was nearly at the door. When she slid up to it, she reached up for the knob, turning it. It had an old, large keyhole, and she glanced through it, into the darkness of the corridor. Nearly out. Nearly away. If she could crawl this far, hell, she could crawl all the way down the corridor to the elevator. It was morning.

The nightmares were over.

But through the keyhole she saw a blue and white flickering, and another room with a little boy lying on a mattress, his hands and feet cuffed, his fingers twitching in dream.

Alice blinked, and looked again.

A glance back to the boy on the mattress, whose eyes opened wide.

"Alice," the boy said. "You don't want to go out there. It's a worse place than my dreams."

"What?" she asked, fever growing in her as she frantically turned the knob. "You nasty monster from hell, let me go!"

The door flew open, and she pulled herself out into the hallway. There was nothing there. Nothing.

"Stephen!" she called. "Charlie!"

Her voice echoed down the dark hall.

From the casement windows from other, empty rooms of the building, the pale morning poured like fire across the open doorways.

Alice glanced back at the boy, who sat on the mattress, a forlorn look on his sleepy face.

"I won!" she shouted, laughing. "I won! I spent the night with you and your demons, and I'm still here!"

A sly smile crept across the boy's face as the blue and white lights slowed in their flickering. "Yes," he said, "you did. And you are changed because of it."

Alice continued laughing, feeling foolish for ever believing the nightmares, for ever thinking that this boy had some special and terrifying magic. When her laughing ceased, the boy said, "You can walk."

"Just shut up, you," she said. "I've had it up to here with your dreams and stories and nastiness. Something must be wrong with a boy who can make up those awful things in his head."

The boy turned his face into the mattress, ignoring her.

When Alice was fully out the door, she shut it again. Reaching for the knob, she pulled herself up.

She stood beside the door, leaning on it for support, for several minutes.

The boy shouted something at her, but with the door closed she couldn't understand him.

Alice rode the elevator up, and tried not to let her emotions overtake her. The miracle of her walking seemed to be small payment for what the boy had made her see all night long.

It did not surprise her when the elevator doors opened on the eighth floor and the bodies lay in front of her.

She could not weep for her sons, nor for Lana, and she chose not to investigate the multiple stab wounds on their bodies.

The blood was too much.

The knife she needed was on the parquet floor, not far from her son Stephen's hand. She wiped it off in a towel hanging in the bathroom. She washed her face in the rusty water.

Alice felt calm as she rode the elevator back down to the basement.

Her calm did not vanish until she'd opened the door to the small room again and the blue and white flickering lights came up—

And the boy, handcuffed to the mattress watched her, his small eyes wide.

The duct tape held on his mouth.

"I saw what you did," Alice said, stepping into the room. She shut the door behind her. Holding the knife up to show him. The blue and white lights flickered across it like heat lightning. "I don't know how you did it. I don't know why. But it's over now. The night-mares. The games. The childish games."

As she approached the mattress, she swiped at the air with the knife.

She watched the boy's eyes.

The duct tape held on his mouth.

His eyes held some terror, but she knew he was an abnormal monster.

Alice knew he was not a little boy.

He was an It.

She knelt down beside him. "It's morning. You don't have so much power at dawn, do you?"

Alice lifted his head slightly and brought the edge of the blade just under his chin. "It's a dull blade, this one. This might take a while. I might have to hack a bit. But, whatever gets the job done, right?"

Pressed the cold metal slightly into his flesh, not enough to cut, but almost.

"You gave me my legs back," she said without emotion. "I don't believe it's real yet, so I'm not going to thank you. It may just be another trick of yours."

The boy's eyes seemed impossibly wide. Tears poured from them.

"You murdered my sons and their friend. Somehow. And you gave me a miracle. Why?"

The boy moaned, choking.

Alice reached up and ripped off the duct tape. "Oh, lose the charade, you devil. Why did you do this? Why did you choose me?"

The boy coughed, sputtering, spit drooling from his mouth.

"Because," he said, coughing through the words, "because . . . I knew . . . I knew you'd . . . love me . . . if I did."

She kept the knife beneath his chin, letting his words echo in the blue and white flickering.

She brought her other arm behind his head, cradling him. "I will cut your throat with the same mercy you showed my two sons."

The boy closed his eyes. "Last request," he gasped. "One last request."

"Sorry, no last requests," Alice said. Now! she told herself. Do it now!

But holding him like that, it was so much like holding Stephen when he'd been little, and sick with some fever. Cradling his head in her arms.

Something inside her relaxed.

"All right, then," she said. "One last request. What is it?"

He looked up at her, no longer afraid, and no longer the monster of the previous night. A small boy hand-cuffed to a filthy mattress. "Could you tell me a story?"

"A story? Haven't we had enough?"

He shook his head.

Something about him—now, in the morning— seemed less terrifying. All the previous night, looking back, Alice could clearly see was just a night of stories, nothing more. Even the bodies upstairs—might they be part of some story too?

"All right, then. I'll tell you a nice story about a mother raising two sons."

Do it now, she thought. Slit his throat and be done with this creature!

"No," he said. "Not that one. I know that one. I want to hear something from your dreams."

"Oh," Alice said. "But when the nightmares are told, people die, don't they?"

The child nodded. "They're only stories, Alice. Just tell me one. Show me."

She closed her eyes and began. She was no longer in the blue and white flickering room, or even in her flesh, but in a world far greater and more terrifying and vivid than any she had ever experienced as she let the child wander through her nightmares.

Alice lay there dreaming, knife in her hand, child curled like a kitten beneath her arm.

The world in her mind opened, like a flower, its petals spreading wide beneath the light of white and blue flickering.

Outside, in the world of metal and concrete and flesh and blood, terrible things happened.

Awful things, beyond imagining.

But within the room, wonder and nightmares.

# *Afterword*

Here are some notes on these stories, for those interested. First, none of these stories was written with publication in mind, since I didn't really think (at the time I wrote them) that I was writing for anyone other than myself—with two exceptions.

"White Chapel" was written for Poppy Z. Brite, a good friend and a fine writer who also has edited a couple of anthologies. I had begun a story about Jane Boone, and when Poppy mentioned to me that she was editing an anthology to be called *Love in Vein,* I wondered if Jane's life would be something Poppy would want to read about. As it turns out, Poppy liked the story and it went into the anthology.

"O Rare and Most Exquisite" was written for my friend Claudia O'Keefe. Prior to writing it, I had mentioned to my friend Edward Lee that I'd had a dream about prolapsing genitalia that became a flower. Then I remembered my summer working in a nursing home, and running into two different elderly people who still haunt me. One was in her nineties, and was really sweet until we were alone and then she'd say, "You're an evil boy, aren't you." She was quite serious. And a guy was there, who, like the old man of the story, despaired of all love he'd ever been given. It all bubbled up—one of those sudden Proustian rushes, I guess.

"Underworld" came about from a few things. I have an old friend, Mary Connally, who used to live at Thirty-third and Third. I always liked that address. I have a friend, Stefan, who used to work at Matthew Bender. I heard stories about people who rented apartments in the city and then walked in on a drug deal in their new apartment and were killed. And then I was in this Chinese restaurant once and looked through one of those portal windows in the door that led to the kitchen and I thought I saw someone who I knew to be dead looking at me from the other side. But, of course, it wasn't her.

I consider short-story writing to be my little love affairs while I'm writing my novels—I can cheat on my novels by taking a few days or a week or so to write a short story. When I look back at some of them, I can see solidly where I was. "Damned If You Do" came about when my friend Robbie Koch and I were walking through her neighborhood and a guy was digging holes out back in his yard, listening to talk radio while a school nearby let out and all the kids were screaming as they ran to the bus. The guy was drinking lemonade for a second, and I wondered if he was burying kids back there.

"I Am Infinite; I Contain Multitudes" came from my proximity to Patton State Hospital in San Bernardino, California. I was doing a little research about the place, and discovered that there was an underground area that had once been used as a sort of prison for the occupants.

"The Night Before Alec Got Married" came about after I was in a friend's wedding party (Tim Long, where are you?) and attended a bachelor party that actually shocked me. Not that anything nefarious went on. I'm just fairly easily shocked. It was in southern California, a place I sorely miss while I write this in Manhattan (which I also love), and the same weekend, I heard a story about a nightmare bachelor party in which a hooker had been hired to strip, only some thugs showed up at the nice suburban gathering and shot this guy's fingers off as he answered the door.

I like that kind of tale.

"Chosen" is really a story about my love affair with insects. I was a summer worker at the Insect Zoo at the Smithsonian Institute when I was sixteen when that section of the museum was still fairly new. I used to have a pet tarantula in college named Abraxas. That was a weird pet, but it was just a spider, after all. Sometimes I think we're just fodder for the bug kingdom, and so Celeste and her apartment were born. Oh yeah, and another thing that has haunted me since childhood: an image from one of those Time-Life books on insects I saw as a kid. I think my brothers and I passed it around, getting happily horrified. There was this huge picture of a wasp injecting a sweet little green caterpillar with its eggs.

"The Ripening Sweetness of Late Afternoon" arrived one morning when I saw Roy Shadiak, in my mind, walking along a sun-flattened southern town in a white suit while swans glided down a murky canal. The angelic harpies just sort of arrived on the scene. This is probably my most overtly religious story, and I'm sure some really good psychologist could figure out everything about me from it. The story was original called "The Swimming Pool," but the final title suggested itself to me as the town of Sunland City grew inside me.

"The Rendering Man" came from a couple of things. I wanted to write a short story that began in the 1930s and followed a woman into her old age. I also wanted to pick three significant, deciding moments for her—the times in her life when she "woke up." I think most of life is a struggle to continually wake up and be alive. So Thalia Canty came to be, and the Rendering Man arrived in short order. It became more of a character sketch than story, but I just went with it.

351

# Douglas Clegg

"The Fruit of Her Womb" came out of one of the many places I've lived in my life. I was born in Virginia, but by the time I was six I had also occupied space in Hawaii and Connecticut. Then, at eight, I was back in Virginia, where I grew up and lived until I was in my early twenties. At that point, I moved to Washington, D.C., traveled overseas a bit, then to Los Angeles, and then, in my late twenties, to a town out near the desert of California called Redlands. (Now I'm closer to Manhattan. Go figure.) Redlands is a terrific place, and the house there was precisely the house I describe in this story. It was an adobe ranch house, but there were no nasty or haunting surprises there. But right next to it was an enormous field with scattered trees around it. I'm also a big fan of ancient Greek myth, so this Persephone story suggested itself to me.

"The Little Mermaid" was my way of going back in my mind to a friend's family's place on Sea Island, Georgia, as well as my recalling how I would sing to mermaids at the edge of Virginia Beach at dawn when I was a little boy—and all of this with a debt to that most wonderful of storytellers, Hans Anderson.

"The Hurting Season" came out of my love for Tangier Island, off the coast of Virginia. I flew to that island in a couple of small planes back in my mid-twenties and loved the idea of such an isolated existence—not far from civilization but far enough to be cut off. I also saw the story as a metaphor for the secret rituals all families have that would seem insane to outsiders but are perfectly normal within a household. And then I was writing in many ways about the childhood of a boy who would one day become one of those monstrous killers we all read about but all of whom were once—after all—little boys, someone's kid, trying to understand the world.

"Only Connect" is really about Nora, whom I saw most clearly, and about New London, Connecticut, where I lived for two years—and its train station, which is beautiful and I hope will not be destroyed anytime soon. Place has a lot to do with these stories and with most of my novels. My parents were nomads, and I'm a nomad, but I'm always trying to find the place that feels most like home. I have a feeling that the Southwest is it, even though I am, right at this moment, looking out over the island of Manhattan. Home for me is truly where the heart is, and my heart is apparently where the wind takes me.

You may notice more than one Alice in this book, including the woman who leads her sons to kidnap the little boy who produces all the nightmares. The name Alice is one I love primarily because of the tales from Lewis Carroll of Alice and her underground adventures. I think names are magic, and Alice is one, along with Wendy, that retains an echo of my favorite books from childhood.

I appreciate you coming along on this journey through these short stories, as many of you have for my novels.

My novel *You Come When I Call You*, which has taken me about ten years to write, will be coming out in paperback in the spring of 2000, and I hope you enjoy that ride, as well. Here is a brief glimpse of it:

*It came to the High Desert of California at the onset of summer with the dying of the dried-blossom joshua trees, with the deflowering of the desert, in the form of a man. He had once been called Michael Southey, although he hadn't used that name for over ten years. Not since he'd caught it at his father's tent revival in some desert shit-dust town. It had been passed to Michael by a little girl whose mother claimed she was possessed by demons, a little girl who swore with such passion, screamed the vilest obscenities, barked like a dog, even tried to bite. In those days, Michael had himself believed that the girl was inhabited by a nest of demons. It was the mid-sixties, and devil worshipers were everywhere: in the growing hippie communes and the LSD psychedelic culture. He had laid his hands on the girl to cast out her demons, and cast them out he did.*

*When Jesus cast out demons, he sent them into swine, and sent the swine to their deaths.*

*But the demons Michael Southey cast from this girl came into himself: she bit him on the arm as he laid the flat of his palm against her forehead.*

*He became the vessel.*

*Michael Southey learned that what had gotten inside him was a glimpse of the Eternal. He thirsted for the knowledge God had bestowed upon him. As it took hold and became part of him, he acquired a new name through its baptism.*

*He called himself the Juicer.*

*The man stood five feet eight inches and wore a smile across his face like Alfred E. Neuman, with the gap right in the middle. His eyes were yellow with disease; a brownish, scaly crust had already begun to seal them half shut around the lids. His face was the color of summer squash, and seemed to have dried out as much from lack of spirit as from the desert air that he had been living in for the past six months. When he smiled that What, me worry? grin, he didn't seem to have any lips at all, just deep red gums engulfing gray teeth. He wore the clothes he'd torn from his fourth victim—torn those clothes off with his bare hands while the terrified man stood paralyzed with fear. Stood there, waiting for what was to come. What he knew would be his destiny.*

*'Cause I am a fucking celebrity, the man on the highway giggled to himself. And that dumbass bastard was just waiting for me to give him The Squeeze.*

*The clothes were filthy. They'd been that way since the day he'd taken them, almost a year and a half ago. But the man with the gap-toothed grin loved the smell of them: those folks he'd*

355

*squeezed like an orange, their pungent odor when they brushed against his shirt, against the crotch of his pants.*

*Dried blood caked the polo shirt until it had gone from a pale lavender to a brown blotchy shade.*

*His slacks, once a bleached khaki color, now were tie-dyed with blood and yellow urine stains. Sometimes the material chafed him down around his crotch; a rash had spread out along his legs from his testicles down.*

*It made him feel more alive than he'd felt in years.*

*He scratched his balls just thinking about that warm, itchy feeling. He remembered the woman's face from last winter, after he had pulled her out of the hot tub, when she realized who he was.*

*I am the Juicer, bitch, and God has sent me to squeeze his harvest, the grapes of wrath, bitch, make wine out of human blood and turn flesh into bread, for this is your body and your blood which is given for me, eat, drink, and be merry, bitch, we gonna make juice of you, we gonna make the freshest fucking blood juice and then I'm gonna sit down and have a pitcher of fresh-squeezed bitch, yowzah!*

*The woman looked like she was about to scream, so he grabbed her by the lips and stretched them across her face. She still screamed, but it sounded funny. He even laughed when he tore her lower lip right off.*

*And then he juiced her.*

*He liked that part best.*

*He was damn strong. The strength of God pulsed through his veins. God was in him, and the Holy Ghost, too, and no man alive could stop him. Her eyes were the best part, the way they kept watching even after all the blood had been hosed out of her, her baby blues turning to pink when the end came. Juicy bitch, she was.*

*But then, after her, the last one, God had done what He always did: He left the Juicer to his own devices, to let the demons in him eat away at him from the inside.*

*That's just the way inspiration works, the Breath of God gets in you for a time and then blows out your ass like a Santa Ana wind. My daddy told me there'd be times when God would leave, but not to feel beat, oh, no, 'cause God abideth in the Soul of Man even when he sleeps, yowzah. When Daddy healed the sinners, he gave 'em God in a handslap, a squeeze on the shoulder, and they came from their wastelands to Daddy's tent for that squeeze. But even then, God could be cruel, leaving Daddy to die in a drunk tank. But Daddy's soul flew on, he got juiced by the Holy Ghost and got drunk by his Heavenly Maker. So the Piece of God that passeth understanding, that one Piece that gets in me and gives me the power to Juice, it comes and goes. When it goes, oh, Lordy, when it goes it don't leave nothing behind.*

*So he'd spent the rest of the winter and spring hibernating here in the desert canyons, eating jackrabbit and rattler. He didn't juice them, because it wasn't time. God had not come back into him. Even Jesus had his time without God in the wilderness, tempted by the devil, and the Juicer was beyond that, because he knew that God and the Devil were two sides of the same coin, the greater your torment and suffering, the finer the redemption, and The Juicer's demons helped send souls onto God, and now God lay sleeping. The Juicer accepted this, but prayed nightly for God to shoot back into his veins.*

*He was walking along the highway at four in the morning; the desert was even chilly in early June. The One Who Called Him Home, the Chosen Vessel of God, led him in this hour of darkness, called him back in these empty days. He hadn't seen the child since the first time it was sent into him, since the first day he'd truly accepted God in his life, the Dark God who willed him to juice.*

*And the woman. Her face would be different now.*

*She would be older.*

*But there was still a squeeze or two left in him, God willing, before he would return the gift she'd given him through that child.*

*The Holy Gift.*

*The Juicer could feel the Piece of God throbbing in his groin, and the need to Juice boiling*

*inside him. Oh, road, take me to a sinner's home
that I might juice the cunt, and send her soul to
the Lord Almighty who is above and below, that
she might be saved from eternal fucking damna-
tion, and that I might take on her sins, the Sins of
the World, that through her juice I might do the
Lord's work and turn her blood to wine and
break this her body and eat it, for this is the
bread of the covenant, yowzah!*

He glanced at the green sign at the highway's
edge.

Naranja Canyon had been crossed out with
spray paint.

Written in its place: Nitro

Beneath this, Palmetto ¾ mile.

And there was God, like cocaine up his nostrils until he could feel the blood trickling down
through his nose; he poked his tongue out his
mouth and slathered it on his upper lip to catch
God's blood as it dripped down.

*God said to him, Juicer, my man, you will find
a shitload of sinners in there, just waiting for
redemption. Send 'em to heaven, baby, and take
on their sins. Your God is a jealous God, Juicer,
and a thirsty one, too, so let's get the vineyard
pouring, 'cause this is the vineyard for fresh-
squeezed souls.*

A lonely wind blew across the desert landscape.

A musky sexual scent mixed with dust came to
him.

He glanced over in the direction of the scent—shadows of trailers out along a yellow mesa, backed by rocks formed from ancient volcanoes. The canyon was sketched in purple and red. Sharp dawn sunlight slashed an arrow between the trailers, and God illuminated his work for him.

The Juicer, feeling the word of God blocking his sinuses, turned off onto the gravel road toward the canyon.

He knew that this would be the last day of his life in the flesh.

Ah, he thought, the freedom of having no skin, no jail of bones, only the wind across the filth of life, and the sweet fire of darkness exploding across the desolation!

# Mommy

## Max Allan Collins

"Chilling!"—Lawrence Block, author of *Eight Million Ways to Die*

Meet Mommy. She's pretty, she's perfect. She's June Cleaver with a cleaver. And you don't want to deny her—or her daughter—anything. Because she only wants what's best for her little girl...and she's not about to let anyone get in her way. And if that means killing a few people, well isn't that what mommies are for?

"Mr Collins has an outwardly artless style that conceals a great deal of art."
—*The New York Times Book Review*

___4322-X                                    $4.99 US/$5.99 CAN

**Dorchester Publishing Co., Inc.**
**P.O. Box 6640**
**Wayne, PA 19087-8640**

Please add $1.75 for shipping and handling for the first book and $.50 for each book thereafter. NY, NYC, and PA residents, please add appropriate sales tax. No cash, stamps, or C.O.D.s. All orders shipped within 6 weeks via postal service book rate. Canadian orders require $2.00 extra postage and must be paid in U.S. dollars through a U.S. banking facility.

Name_____
Address_____
City_____State_____Zip_____
I have enclosed $_____ in payment for the checked book(s).
Payment <u>must</u> accompany all orders. ☐ Please send a free catalog.

# BRASS

# ROBERT J. CONLEY

The ancient Cherokees know him as *Untsaiyi*, or Brass, because of his metallic skin. He is one of the old ones, the original beings who lived long before man walked the earth. And he will live forever. He cares nothing for humans, though he can take their form—or virtually any form—at will. For untold centuries the world has been free of his deadly games, but now Brass is back among us and no one who sees him will ever be the same . . . if they survive at all.

\_\_\_4505-2                                  $5.50 US/$6.50 CAN

# SHADOW GAMES

# ED GORMAN

Cobey Daniels had it all. He was rich, he was young, and he was the hottest star in the country. Then there was that messy business with the teenage girl . . . and it all went to hell for Cobey. But that was a few years ago. Now Cobey's pulled his life together, they're letting him out of the hospital, and he's ready for his big comeback. But the past is still out there, waiting for him. Waiting to show Cobey a hell much more terrifying than he ever could have imagined.

___4515-X                                      $5.50 US/$6.50 CAN

# Elizabeth Massie
# Sineater

According to legend, the sineater is a dark and mysterious figure of the night, condemned to live alone in the woods, who devours food from the chests of the dead to absorb their sins into his own soul. To look upon the face of the sineater is to see the face of all the evil he has eaten. But in a small Virginia town, the order is broken. With the violated taboo comes a rash of horrifying events. But does the evil emanate from the sineater...or from an even darker force?

___4407-2                                    $5.99 US/$6.99 CAN

**Dorchester Publishing Co., Inc.**
**P.O. Box 6640**
**Wayne, PA 19087-8640**

Please add $1.75 for shipping and handling for the first book and $.50 for each book thereafter. NY, NYC, and PA residents, please add appropriate sales tax. No cash, stamps, or C.O.D.s. All orders shipped within 6 weeks via postal service book rate. Canadian orders require $2.00 extra postage and must be paid in U.S. dollars through a U.S. banking facility.

Name_____
Address_____
City_____State_____Zip_____
I have enclosed $_____ in payment for the checked book(s).
Payment <u>must</u> accompany all orders. ❏ Please send a free catalog.
   CHECK OUT OUR WEBSITE! www.dorchesterpub.com

# HUNGRY EYES

## BARRY HOFFMAN

The eyes are always watching. She can feel them as she huddles there, naked, vulnerable, in an iron cage in a twisted man's basement. Someday she will be the one with the power, the need to close the eyes. And she'll close them all.

___4449-8                                    $4.99 US/$5.99 CAN